E.M. Powell

The King's Justice

A STANTON AND BARLING MYSTERY

THOMAS & MERCER

Published by Thomas & Mercer, Seattle

www.apub.com

Amazon, the Amazon logo, and Thomas & Mercer are trademarks of Amazon.com, Inc., or its affiliates.

ISBN-13: 9781542046015
ISBN-10: 1542046017

Cover design by Ghost Design

Printed in the United States of America

Chapter One

The City of York, 12 June 1176

Pit or punishment: Hugo Stanton couldn't tell which excited the folk of these hot, crammed streets more.

Three men accused of vicious murder but who would not confess. Innocent, they'd claimed to King Henry's travelling justices, sitting in the court in the high keep of the city's castle.

The men's claims mattered not.

Today, under this cloudless early-summer sky, the water would judge them. Each would be lowered into the brimming pit in turn, as recounted by the very few who'd seen the ordeal before. Sinking would tell of a man's innocence. Floating would have him hauled out to the gallows to be strung up to die.

Every soul in the place wanted to witness the awesome power of the King's law for themselves. York's many inhabitants thronged every approach to the cathedral, where the ordeal pit had been dug next to its soaring height. People pushed, called out, their numbers swelled by the hundreds who'd arrived with the mighty royal court.

'Move aside there!' came a yell from Nesbitt, staggering beside Stanton. His fellow messenger of the court liked ale as much as Stanton did. 'Make way for the King's men.'

Stanton's chest tightened as Nesbitt's drink-edged, curt orders worked with only the mention of Henry's name. People shuffled aside on the waste-clogged cobbles to make space as best they could.

The King's men.

Scant words for the huge retinue, led by the justices, that had arrived here two weeks ago, of which Stanton was but one lowly member. Henry had sent them across the land to make sure all followed his law. Those who didn't were being punished, and punished hard. His justices were making sure of it.

'The King's men,' shouted Nesbitt again.

Though a mere messenger, Stanton was indeed one of them. And to the very depths of his soul, he wished it were not so. His gaze met lowered looks of respect, of fear, on sweating faces as he passed by, and he silently cursed those who wore them for fools.

Nesbitt clapped him hard on the back, sending him into a stagger. 'Step on, young Stanton. We'll be late for the ordeal.'

'Get off me.' Stanton steadied himself as much as he could with his ale legs. 'The accused men won't be going anywhere.'

'Course they won't. But we want to see it all, eh?'

'Don't care what I see today. All I care about is that I'm not sat in the court looking at the justices.' Stanton grimaced. 'Nor listening to them. Too much talk for me.'

And what talk. The cases about land had had his head nodding as the three justices droned on and on in the packed, stuffy keep.

Then had come a man, a grieving husband and father, to appeal the murders of his loved ones. With him, as Stanton had come to learn was needed by law, a jury of presentment: twelve men who swore before God that those suspected of the crimes were of wicked character. No one had seen the terrible deeds take place, but they could describe what had been found.

Stanton had tried, failed, to close his own ears.

A young girl. Her mother. Ripped clothing. Knives. Throats. A silver ring brooch taken. The man wept as he gave his account of his discovery of the worst of horrors, which, mercifully, few would ever have to face.

Yet Stanton had. Only three short months before, when he'd seen the woman he'd loved lying slaughtered before him, murdered because of the King, God rot him. Stanton's tears might have dried, but his loss still burned hot and fierce within him.

In York's court, the justices paid no heed to the men's protests that they were innocent. The King's law would be followed, they announced. The ordeal by water would bring the necessary final proof of guilt or innocence. Proof with God's judgement.

Now that day had arrived.

Nesbitt wheezed a laugh. 'There's a lot of talk with the law, Stanton. Not much else, if you ask me.' He shoved forward into the press of bodies again with another loud shout. 'King Henry's men. Make way, there.'

'Make way.' Stanton added his call, though he'd have cut his drunken tongue out rather than use it for Henry's name.

'Some flowers for you, good sir?'

Stanton halted at the young female voice beside him.

'Flowers?' She held out a few thin bunches of blooms.

The way she boldly met his eye told him she wasn't just offering wilting petals. He'd sampled a good number of the city's many whores, though he'd not seen her before. He shook his head and set off again with stumbling steps. 'Not now.'

'It wouldn't take long' – she fell in beside him with a sure tread, her sharp gaze still on him – 'for a fine young servant of the King such as yourself to buy what I have to offer.'

'I don't think so.'

'Sir. Please.'

He caught a note of desperation in her terse reply.

The drooping blooms she held told him she'd been out for many hours already without much success, despite the crowds. While she looked clean enough, the girl's weak jaw made her plain, and her mud-coloured wool dress hung on a skinny frame. Her one beauty was plaited brown hair that lay thick as a rope over one shoulder.

Stanton fumbled his belt pouch open and the girl stared in naked want as he sought out a coin. 'Here.' He placed it on her ready palm, and her bitten-nailed fingers closed around it. 'Now be off with you.'

'Thank you.' She flashed a smile that didn't reach her hard eyes. 'Sir.'

The bell from the looming cathedral boomed out a first solemn peal. A roar rose up in response.

'Stanton!'

He hardly heard the shout over the noise. He looked over.

Nesbitt beckoned over a sea of heads. 'Move your backside, man.'

Forget this girl. It was time.

Time for the pit.

Chapter Two

'Have they come out?' Stanton pushed into the gap created by Nesbitt's muscle in the heaving crush outside the cathedral.

'Not yet,' replied Nesbitt. 'The doors are still closed.'

People stood three or four deep in front, but now Stanton could see clean over the tonsured head of a squat monk.

'God's eyes.' He pulled in a sharp breath at the sight of the ordeal pit before him. Guards edged the open space where it sat, keeping the crowd at bay. 'That's something, isn't it?'

'It is.' Nesbitt grinned. 'Took many men many hours to dig and fill. And all for this one day.'

Stanton shook his head. 'It must be twenty feet wide.'

'Aye,' said Nesbitt. 'And it'll be twelve feet deep.'

A large wooden platform covered about one third of the huge pit, its planks fresh and pale and still smelling of sap. Despite the clear blue sky, the water beneath had no shine or sparkle. It sat muddy and dark and still.

'Long way down, then.'

'Aye,' said Nesbitt again. 'Better down than up, though.'

Sinking into that murk, unable to help yourself. Down and down as the water filled your mouth, your nose, your lungs. And that was the fate of the innocent? A shudder passed through Stanton. 'I suppose.'

Nesbitt stretched to his full height. 'The doors are open. They're coming out.'

Others took up his shout with yells, calls and whistles of their own.

Folk surged in an excited wave at Stanton's back, the hot, sweating bodies of strangers ramming his ribs against the protesting monk in front.

'Move back, curse you.' Nesbitt thrust out sharp elbows to loud swearing. 'You'll have us robbed of our life's breath.'

Stanton shoved back too, his pulse fast from the crush and what was about to happen.

York's Archbishop came into view and stepped slowly up on to the platform. Under his pointed mitre, his face shone scarlet from the heat of the day and the weight of his richly embroidered robes. Henry's three justices followed, familiar to Stanton from the court: the lofty Ranulf de Glanville, the shorter Robert de Vaux and the rounded Robert Pikenot. He'd hardly noticed their black robes in the gloom of the courtroom. Here, in the hot glare of the sun, they could be large crows looking for carrion.

Hands, fists, voices rose up with praise for them, for the King.

Then came the loudest shouts yet. The accused were here.

'By the name of the Virgin.' Stanton's mouth fell open. He'd seen these men in the court, standing before the justices. Tall men. Broad men. Hard-faced men all. Not poorly dressed but roughly dressed. The kind of men who it was easy to believe had robbed and killed an innocent woman and her daughter. But now? Now they filed on to the platform, heads down, one man sobbing in fear. And they were stripped naked, nothing except a loincloth keeping each man from shame.

'Yes!' Nesbitt thumped Stanton on the shoulder. 'I've got a wager on all three being guilty. They look like it to me.'

'Get off.' Stanton shoved his fist away. 'If you had fleas, you'd put money on which one jumped the highest.'

Nesbitt wheezed a laugh again, but cut it short as the Archbishop slowly raised his hands and held them wide apart.

All other voices dropped, the recent clamour a pounding echo in Stanton's ears in the sudden quiet. Only the prisoner's deep sobbing carried on.

The justices joined their hands and bowed their heads.

'Lord, our God,' said the Archbishop, eyes aloft. 'You, who are the most righteous judge. You judge what is just and your right judgement transcends all others. We beseech you to bring your holy blessings down on this water. That if the man placed in it is innocent, it will receive him in your holy name. That if he is guilty, it will reject his sin.' He dropped his gaze to the dark water and moved his right hand in a sweeping blessing. '*In nomine Patris et Filii et Spiritus Sancti.* Amen.'

'Amen,' chorused the justices and the crowd in a sombre rumble.

Stanton tried to join in and found his mouth had dried.

The Archbishop stepped back as de Glanville pointed to the first one. 'Bind him.'

A huge roar met his words and the press of people at Stanton's back grew stronger as the guards moved in on the accused man.

'First one going in.' Nesbitt's sight was locked on the platform. 'My luck's in, I can feel it.'

'Don't think you feel much, Nesbitt.' Stanton's hoarse reply got no reaction as around him people yelled and prayed in equal measure.

The man was now trussed tightly on the ground, bent double, his arms crossed and wrists secured to his opposite ankles. More rope tied his feet together, while a last sturdy loop circled his waist.

De Glanville raised a hand for silence. He got it in an eye-blink, his clear voice addressing the man. 'You have a last chance to confess, to cleanse your soul. God already knows your heart.'

The man said nothing, made no sound except the panting of his breath, his air cut short no doubt by the twisted position of his body, and, Stanton was sure, by his fear of what was to come. Stanton's own heart thudded hard, fast. This man's must be about to leave his chest.

'Very well.' De Glanville nodded to the guards.

In one swift movement, they dragged the bound prisoner to the edge of the platform.

De Glanville was saying something, but no silence this time, only a wall of noise as the guards did their work.

A long rope threaded through the waist rope, attached to a wooden cross-beam. Hard hauls on the rope. The man rose in the air, a bundle of bound limbs, swinging high over the surface of the water, his loincloth soaking in abrupt terror.

Then the rope ran loose. A low splash. And he was in. In.

Yet more people shoved to the front, frantic for a better view.

Stanton craned his neck to see through the heaving, clamouring throng before him. He didn't need to. The shouts, the screams told him.

'He floats!'

'God be praised!'

'Guilty!'

A shrieking woman lurched to one side and he could see. See the curved back of the bound man bobbing on the surface of the water, listing to one side, then to the other, whether caused by the man's struggle to breathe or attempts to sink, Stanton couldn't tell.

Another thump to his shoulder. Nesbitt again, jumping in glee.

Stanton didn't respond, couldn't take his gaze away from the hideous shape that still bobbed and span in the water.

De Glanville nodded to the guards. Swift, strong hauls on the rope again.

Accused no longer, the guilty murderer broke the surface, muddy water streaming from his upended body, his mouth, his eyes bulging in wordless terror as the water continued to choke him. The guards lowered him hard on to the platform. More water spewed from him as he gasped and wriggled for air.

'God's blessed water has rejected you.' De Glanville looked down at him from his imposing height. 'You are guilty of the two murders of which you are accused. You will hang today.'

A fresh outburst greeted his words.

'May you burn in hell!'

'Praise the Almighty, praise him!'

'Praise King Henry. God keep our holy King.'

'Hail the King! Hail his justice!'

'Hail him indeed.' Nesbitt gave Stanton a broad wink. 'His Grace's justice will be putting coin in my pocket.'

'You're going to hell too, Nesbitt.' It would freeze over before Stanton shouted for the King and his justice. He'd seen it fail, and fail badly. And yet. His eyes went to the bereaved widower, the man who'd lost his wife, his daughter. The widower's hands were clasped in silent, reverent prayer. Prayers of thanks, no doubt.

De Glanville pointed to the second, sobbing prisoner. 'Bind him.'

As the guards moved in as one, the man broke into screams. 'No! No! I beg you!'

Yells and shouts filled the air as hundreds of voices raised as one.

Now the man was fighting those who held him, his pale, naked limbs thrashing at the hands that grabbed him. 'Let go!'

Stanton shook his head as shouts and jeers spewed from those around him. Fighting was useless. The man was trying to fight the full might of the King's hand.

A heavy blow from one of the guards had the man subdued enough so they could bring him under control.

Stanton palmed the sweat from his own face, his pulse still fast, faster still as the stunned man was bound, hoisted for the ordeal. He could no longer hear individual words, just wave upon wave of frenzy.

Over the water. Still screaming. Screaming. Screams melting into those of the crowd in a piercing echo that made Stanton's head ring.

Then the man was down. Into the pit. Gone.

Now people surged harder than ever, desperate to see this new judgement of the water.

Stanton pushed back, fought for his own breath even as he knew that the man in the water would be fighting for his. The quiver of the rope told of that battle.

But. 'He's still down!' He grabbed at Nesbitt's sleeve. 'He must be innocent.'

His cry was echoed by others over and over.

Nesbitt spat in disgust. 'I know, curse him.'

Still down. No sign. Stanton put his hands to his head, wordless shouts now coming from his throat. Judgement again. But innocence this time.

A few huge bubbles broke the dirty surface. Nothing else. No sign of the man. The rope shuddered as if a heavy fish fought for its freedom.

Then all movement stopped. Nothing. It was utterly still.

'Bring him up.' De Glanville's order cut through the noise.

The guards hauled and hauled, and the motionless form of the man broke the surface, muddy water streaming from his body as it had from the first. But where the first man was still a coughing heap on the ground, the one now pulled from the water made no sound. His body landed on the soaked platform with a squelching thud, mouth wide, as it had been minutes before, yet silent now, eyes fixed and sightless.

Stanton's stomach dropped. The man was dead. An innocent man was dead.

A chorus of shocked gasps and a buzz of questions joined the clamour of those still shouting and praying.

Up on the platform, de Glanville exchanged a look with his fellow justices, then turned to murmur to both of them. As they did so, another dark-robed figure stepped up to join them.

Stanton recognised Aelred Barling, one of the senior clerks of the court.

'What could Barling want?' said Nesbitt.

Stanton shrugged. He didn't know and didn't care. The officious, fussy clerk couldn't give life back to the innocent man who'd just lost it.

After a terse exchange, Barling removed himself with a quick bow of his tonsured head.

All three justices exchanged nods, their faces sombre.

'Good people.' De Glanville faced the crowd again and gestured with an open palm to the dead prisoner. 'This man had three days in which to prepare himself for the ordeal. He heard Mass with the appropriate liturgy. Fasted. For that is how one should face the ordeal. Prepared. Calm. Putting one's absolute trust in Almighty God. With steadfast faith.' De Glanville shook his head. 'Not with disbelief. Nor fear. This man's lack of faith let him down. But his innocence has been proved. If he is without other sin, God will welcome his soul into heaven. Justice has been done.'

Huge cheers greeted his words.

Stanton didn't join in. Henry's justice. It hadn't changed. The blameless still perished. He clamped his jaw lest he shout his anger as the calls proclaiming Henry's greatness built once more.

Then in the din came a different shout. 'I'm guilty! Guilty!' It came from the third prisoner, much burlier than the other two, his naked muscles glistening in the sun.

The noise of the crowd fell away and the faces of those surrounding Stanton could be his own: eyes wide, mouths open in surprise.

Nesbitt gave Stanton a huge grin. 'That's more like it.'

Stanton nudged him. 'Listen.'

'Guilty, yes, I'm guilty.' The man tripped over his words in his haste to speak. 'Yes, my lord justices. But hear me, hear me, I beg you.'

De Glanville's face showed no emotion. Same with the other two justices. 'Go on.'

The man fell to his knees. 'I'm guilty, but guilty of being with him, nothing more.' He gestured at the live prisoner. 'He's a murderer, he is. Like the water says. The water's right. You're right, my lords. Me,

11

the dead man. We were both there. But we committed no crime. We're both innocent. I'm confessing, confessing, see? I . . . I don't need to go in. Not in there.'

Despite a few gasps and stifled cries, the quiet held. Nobody wanted to miss a word.

'You are admitting to being present at the murders?' asked de Glanville.

'Yes, my lord. Yes. I was there, at the house. When the woman and the girl . . .' The man shook his head. 'But that's all.'

'All?'

'Yes, my lord.'

'I see.'

Something in de Glanville's tone made Stanton's neck prickle.

The justice went on. 'Only a short while ago, before you were led out from the cathedral, you and your fellow accused were stripped of your clothing as part of your preparation for the ordeal. One of my clerks carried out a thorough examination of those garments. He found this sewed into your cloak.' De Glanville drew a small object from his own wide sleeve and held it up.

Stanton pulled in a sharp breath. Now he knew why Barling had appeared.

The man looked as if somebody had struck him as the widower gave a cry of anguish.

Confused questions filled the air.

Stanton didn't join in. He knew what de Glanville held, had heard of its theft in the court: a silver ring brooch.

'This,' said de Glanville, 'is what you stole in the most violent of robberies, which took the life of this man's wife and daughter.'

Howls of rage broke from those watching as the prisoner, bellowing, tried to lunge at the justice, while the guards grappled with him.

De Glanville stood like stone, raising his voice to echo over it all. 'You thought your false confession would spare you the water and so you would elude the King's justice. You have eluded nothing. Nothing. The punishment for your theft is the loss of that hand.' He pointed to the man's right hand. 'And that foot.' The left.

Stanton's stomach turned over as the rage became ugly, ugly cheers. He looked over at Nesbitt. 'Let's go. Time for more ale.'

Nesbitt shook his head, put his finger to his lips.

De Glanville still addressed the prisoner. 'The ordeal has established your guilt. You are guilty of robbery. And . . .' He looked at his fellow justices, who nodded. 'And guilty of murder. By the judgement of God, of King Henry, you will hang this day.'

The widower sank to the ground praising God, the justices, the King. His cries were taken up in a deafening roar.

'But first you will pay the price for your theft.' De Glanville gave a signal and a guard approached the platform, a heavy axe to one shoulder.

Stanton had to get out of there. 'Think I've had enough.'

'Not got the stomach for bloodshed, have you, young Stanton?' Nesbitt's wide grin mocked as much as his tone.

'My stomach's all right. I'm ready for more ale, that's all.' *And I know more about bloodshed than you ever will.* He went to push back through the press of people.

'See you later on, Iron Belly.' Nesbitt gave him a mocking salute.

A hand tugged at his sleeve. He looked down.

The girl from before with the thick brown hair stared right at him. 'I have some fresh flowers if sir would like to see them.' Her lip twitched with her arch look.

Stanton summoned up a wink for Nesbitt. 'Enjoy yourself, I'm sure you will.' He forced a smile at the girl. 'I'm off for my sort of pleasure.'

In return, she slipped an arm through his and led him off through the baying crowd.

Chapter Three

'Why does your friend call you Iron Belly?' The girl had to raise her voice as she threaded through the yelling throng with nimble speed, Stanton tight in her grip.

Truth be told, he was glad of her help. His legs felt as if he'd been running far and fast, all the ale he'd drunk mixing with the horror of the ordeal. From behind, piercing through every other noise, came a terrible thud and the shrillest scream.

He swallowed hard to bring spittle back to his dry throat. 'He's not my friend. We both serve the justices. As do the many men that have travelled with them. That's all.'

'Oh.' She ducked into a shaded narrow alleyway to the side of a shuttered shop, so narrow the sun must never reach it. 'I thought all important men like you were friends.'

He coughed at the reek of the urine of cats and men. But the walls and low roofs made a welcome shield against the dreadful happenings nearby. 'I'm not that important.' His boots squelched on the damp, mossy muck underfoot.

'Oh,' she said again. 'I think you are.' She pulled him into a broken-down rotting doorway, the better to shield them from any prying eyes.

Better for him as well – it gave him something to lean his drink-fuddled head against.

'You serve the King. And a man as fair as you must be important.' She reached one hand up to rake her fingers through his hair. 'Such golden hair. Such blue eyes. I thought you must be a young prince or a brave warrior when I saw you.'

Whores' flattery. He knew it well – yet her boldness made him smile. 'You could call me Prince Iron Belly. But I'm no warrior, no fighter.'

'No?'

'No. And the women I know like to call me Hugo.'

'You know many women, do you?' Her other hand dropped to below his belt.

'More women than warriors.' He slipped his hand under her coarse skirts, found warm, yielding flesh. 'Which I prefer.'

'I'm glad you do.' She opened the fastening of his braies with practised ease. 'Hugo.'

'And what shall I call you?'

She slid expert fingers around him. 'Daisy.'

He caught his breath at her touch. 'Daisy?'

'Like the flower.'

'Of course.' He gasped again. Saints be praised, this girl knew what to do. 'You're a flower seller.' He lowered his mouth to hers, and she parted her lips for him. He closed his eyes, tried to lose himself in his body's reaction to her hands on him, to how she felt under his touch. She wasn't his love, this wasn't love. His love, his Rosamund, was dead. But this girl, this plain whore who called herself Daisy, was here, was alive. Her skin was whole, soft against his. And there were no blades, no screams, no bloodshed, no gallows.

She stopped dead. Thrust herself from him.

He opened his eyes. 'What?'

15

'Hugo.' Daisy pointed a trembling finger down the alley. 'There. A robber.'

A ragged man lumbered towards them, club in one hand, his muscular bulk the width of the dank alley. 'Good day to you,' he said, showing broken teeth below a wide nose.

'A plague on it.' Stanton fumbled his breeches shut with one hand, grabbing Daisy's arm with the other. 'Down the other end of the alley. Quick.' They made it less than five steps when another armed man filled the exit.

'We're trapped,' came Daisy's anguished whisper.

Stanton stepped back to the doorway and pushed Daisy in behind him with a string of quiet oaths.

The first man reached them. 'Are you two fine folk deaf?' He gave his gap-toothed grin again. 'I said good day.'

'Good day to you.' Stanton made his reply as firm as he could, tried not to sway on his feet.

'And to you.' The second one was here now. He gave an exaggerated bow. 'Sir.'

'Yet a solemn day,' said Stanton. 'With the ordeal. Where a robber is paying the price for his crime. The very highest price.'

He had a slim hope that calling on the nearby judgement would help. It didn't.

'Solemn?' The man pointed his club at Stanton's belt. 'I'd say happy.' He raised the club level with Stanton's face. 'Happy for us that everyone is busy at the pit. While you hand over that full purse of yours.'

Stanton gave the slightest of nods. Any more and his nose would be on the knobbly wood. 'I willingly give it.' His hands sought out his purse tie, with a silent Daisy pressed behind him. He prayed she had the sense to stay that way. His purse contained her payment. But this was no time to protest. This was the time to stay in one piece. He placed the bag of coins in the robber's hand. 'There. Now I wish you a final good day.'

The man shoved the purse under his patched tunic. 'We'll have the girl too.'

A soft gasp from Daisy.

Damn it all. 'No.' Stanton squared his jaw and met the robber's gaze. 'She's with me for now.'

'Don't, Hugo.' She tried to push past him. 'Don't.'

But he had to. Had to try. He stayed her with a hand. He'd failed the woman he loved; he couldn't, wouldn't fail another. 'You're welcome to my full purse, my friend. But leave this girl be.'

The robber put his head to one side. And lowered his club.

Stanton swallowed hard. 'Now, on your way.' He gave the man a civil nod, his shoulders and legs locked to try to keep steady.

He didn't even see the man's fist, caught a blur of movement, and then he was down on the filthy, stinking ground, doubled over with a burst of pain in his stomach and the wind driven from him. Fighting for breath, any breath, he looked up to see the robber hold his hand out to Daisy.

She stepped over Stanton without even a glance down. 'You took your time,' she said to the man.

He patted her face with one huge palm. 'Never far away, don't you worry. And we could tell you'd have no trouble with this fool.'

Stanton rolled to one side, hands clawing at the sticky mud, coughing, chest heaving, his breath returned but every one a sharp stab, as were the man's words. A fool. He managed to rise on one elbow.

The robber smirked down at him and jerked his head at his companion and the girl. 'Come on. Before someone sees. I want to keep all my limbs.'

'Wait.' She dropped to her haunches and grasped Stanton's chin in her hand.

He tried to push her off, but he still had no strength.

'Prince Iron Belly, you're so sweet, trying to defend me. Sweet.' She gave him a little shake. 'But stupid. Either of this pair could snap you in two. You're right when you say you're not a warrior.' She kissed him hard on the mouth. 'So keep that pretty face for the girls.' She stood up. 'That's my advice.'

'As for paying the price,' said the leader of the robbers. 'A man's only guilty if he's caught.' He drew his boot back. 'We're not getting caught.'

Stanton ducked away. Not fast enough. And the boot hit the same spot as the fist. Then his face.

He would never get up again.

Chapter Four

Aelred Barling, clerk to the King's justices, checked the number of cases left to hear on this, the last day that the court would sit in York.

The hours of the evening and the night to come would see the many, many preparations needed for moving such a large assembly. Tomorrow the court would start its progress on to the next county. As ever, the numbers involved would mean it would not be swift. These visitations, these eyres, as demanded by the lord King, were an enormous undertaking. The court in which Barling now sat, headed by the justices de Glanville, de Vaux and Pikenot, covered the northern counties from Lancashire to Northumberland and beyond. The long hours of the fierce June sun would slow the pace even more. Barling did not look forward to the inevitable heat and discomfort.

But for now, around him in the keep of the castle, all was proceeding in the correct manner and order, despite the early hour. The court would finish its business here today as planned.

The justices sat above Barling on their raised dais immediately to the left of his desk, the pipe rolls and writs they would need arranged before them on the wide table. Many of the clerks had their heads down as they made careful notes on wax tablets. Others moved back and forth with quiet efficiency in their necessary, orderly tasks, with any discussions taking place in a low murmur. Those people appealing the next cases waited in awed silence, many clutching documents of their own. As their appeals were heard, they would be replaced by others.

The first case was under way, a straightforward land dispute where a tenant claimed he had been improperly ejected from his land. A jury of twelve lawful and free men were with the tenant to support his claim.

'The plaintiff has been unjustly dispossessed,' said de Glanville, commencing his judgement.

The familiar rhythm of the wording in the quiet of the court brought Barling a satisfying calm. He allowed himself a small nod as he wiped his hands on a piece of linen before picking up his stylus. A perspiring hand made for an unsatisfactory grip. He began his letters, one ear still open for anything that the justices might require.

While the demands of this court were very considerable and often without cease, Barling took on the burden of duty willingly, as he always did in his service of the King. Duty, however, did not always equate with enjoyment.

Here in the stifling summer heat of York, he found it difficult to recall the piercing cold of London in January, when he had first heard the news from Northampton as he sat in the peace of the King's writing office.

Yet he had no difficulty remembering his disturbance. He had not shared the excitement of the news that had spread through his fellow clerks of the scriptorium. King Henry had been meeting with his barons. The method for bringing royal government and order to the people would be greatly improved. While the King had had justices travel his realm for some ten years, henceforth there would be six travelling courts, each headed by three justices on circuit. They would make judgements on the possession and inheritance of land. Equally importantly, they would hear cases of serious felony, such as murder, robbery, theft and arson. Punishment would be ruthless and effective. The justices would make sure of it in the name of their lord King.

Barling had listened without comment as the clerks discussed at length the anticipation of many more opportunities to travel with the court, perhaps even the chance to serve as one of the King's itinerant justices. The idea had filled Barling with utter displeasure. He had no wish to venture from his desk and his books, which were his safety and his sanctuary. But his Grace had decreed that those responsible for his law should travel. And as his lord King demanded, so Barling would serve.

As so often with the brilliance of his Grace, the new system was breathtaking, not only in its ambition but also in its effectiveness. Not two days ago the ordeal had been a demonstration of the might of the King's power. No man or woman on this earth could have looked upon it and not quailed.

But as for becoming a justice, it held no attraction for Barling. He relished his reputation as a compiler and adviser, one who could devote his time and talents to detail. Just as he had at the ordeal on Saturday, when he'd checked the discarded clothing of the accused and found the hidden brooch. Yet he'd been perfectly content to leave the verdicts to the justices. He was not worthy of taking on the weight of final judgement.

The morning proceeded in a regular, steady order of case after case.

Barling completed his writing and laid his pen down once more. After applying a neat wax seal to each one, he collected the letters that needed to be dispatched and slipped out quietly as yet another jury gave their evidence to the court. There were several clerks who could deal with anything the judges might require, and he would not be long. His next task was to hand over these letters to the messengers to make sure of their timely delivery.

As the doors closed behind him, the building heat of the morning met him. He descended the steps of the motte, squinting in the harsh sunlight. The messengers were assembled in the busy, spacious yard below, as they should be, awaiting his orders. Their horses were saddled and tethered nearby, the animals smartly groomed, as he insisted upon.

A respectful chorus came from the men. 'Good morning, sir.'

'Good morrow.' Barling ran his eye over each man and rapped out orders as he handed out his letters. 'Richmond: by sundown. Nothing later. Rievaulx Abbey: await a response from the abbot. Lancaster: fix your hat on straight, man.' And so on until he reached the end. The end where he had no letters left. But no messengers, either.

'Who is missing?' he asked with a frown.

'Cobb is still laid up with the flux, sir,' replied one.

'I know that,' said Barling. 'I sent a query to his inn yesterday.' He took another look at the familiar faces before him and gave a sharp, short sigh. 'It is Hugo Stanton, is it not?'

'Looks like it, sir.'

'Look at the hour,' said Barling. 'Do any of you know where he might be?'

The shaking of heads met his question.

'No, sir. No idea.'

'No, sir.'

'Perhaps he's ill as well, sir.' This came from the one called Nesbitt.

Barling gave a short, sharp sigh. 'Well, I am not going to delay you any longer. You may go. Godspeed.'

As the messengers went to their animals, Barling caught a grin and a mutter from Nesbitt to another. 'I'll wager you that Stanton's still with that whore he left with on Saturday.'

'Nesbitt.' Barling's crisp order had the man pause and look around.

'Yes, sir?' His face fell at being overheard.

'I expect a truthful answer when I ask a question. And if you know where Stanton is, then make sure you send him to me. At once. Whore or no whore. Do you hear me?'

'Yes, sir. Sorry, sir.' No longer grinning, Nesbitt continued on to his animal.

Barling stood and watched as the messengers all rode out. If anything of importance arose in the court, he would be called for. In the meantime, he would wait for Stanton and make sure the man suffered repercussions for his distasteful tardiness.

Enough was enough. It was not simply a problem of lateness with Stanton. It was so much else.

For a start, the young man had only joined the travelling court a month ago. De Glanville had informed Barling with a terse explanation that Stanton had been a good messenger in the rebellion and so was now joining the ranks of the court messengers. Nothing more. Barling had been perfectly satisfied with that, though it was an unusual occurrence. Nevertheless, it should have sufficed.

Then young Stanton had arrived.

Oh, Stanton was a fast rider, no doubt about that. The fastest of all, should he choose to rouse himself. But he had a careless appearance that was never up to the standards of the court. A fondness for alehouses and, even worse, bawdy houses. An air about him that suggested he thought he was better than most men, though that suggestion had no evidence whatsoever to support it. That he could live his life as he pleased. Worst of all, a demeanour that showed no respect for authority.

The same demeanour that had Stanton, on this bright morn, sleeping in the arms of a whore when he should have been serving his King.

Barling folded his arms, uncaring of the eye of the sun on his tonsured head.

When Stanton arrived, he would have a suitable greeting ready for him.

It was time Hugo Stanton learned his true place in the world.

And Aelred Barling would be the one to teach him.

Chapter Five

Stanton ran, one hand to his aching ribs to hold them steady.

The bells of Terce sounded from churches and monasteries as he hurried along the uneven cobbles, cursing at every jar to his bones.

He swore quietly to himself. He was late. So late. The amount of ale he'd drunk on the day of the ordeal would have made him sleepy enough. The thumping he'd had from that robber made his head even thicker.

Yet he was lucky to still have a skull that was in one piece. Another whore had led a man into the alley, screamed at what she saw and ran off along with her customer. But God had smiled on him, he reckoned. His attackers fled as well, leaving him to stagger back to his small airless room at an inn. He'd not said anything. A *fool*. The robber's word for him. Yes, he was. And it was nothing new.

Yesterday, the Lord's Day, he'd spent mostly in restless, uncomfortable dreams. Now Monday had dawned, he should be in his place at the back of the court, awaiting orders, not dodging past slow-walking traders laden with full baskets and swaying, rumbling carts that took up half the street.

He spied Nesbitt riding towards him at a brisk trot, his fellow messenger's lively horse clearing a ready path. Nesbitt saw him too, raising a hand in greeting before pulling to a halt beside him.

'Barling's looking for you. And he's not happy.'

Stanton swore again.

Nesbitt grinned. 'Not seen you since the ordeal.' He pointed at Stanton's eye. 'Out scrapping, were you?'

'Yes. No. I'd best be off.'

'And me.' Nesbitt clicked to his horse. 'Good luck with Barling. You're going to need it.'

'Barling? Luck won't help me with that pain in the backside. Godspeed, Nesbitt.'

Stanton set off again, faster this time. Forget his ribs.

The small, slight Aelred Barling might only be about a dozen years older than Stanton, but the clerk's nature, duller and drier than the piles of manuscripts he surrounded himself with, made him seem even more. While the man was meek and mild to all the justices, he was the opposite to those under his charge if they made a mistake. And that included late messengers.

Stanton made it to the busy castle bailey faster than he had any morning before. It didn't matter.

He could see Barling waiting for him by the steps that led up to the motte, dressed in his usual black robes, arms folded, for all the world like an angry bat.

Stanton hurried up to him, trying to bring his breathing under control.

'Now here is Hugo Stanton.' Barling didn't raise his voice. He never did. 'The saints are smiling.' His smooth, pale face wasn't.

'I'm sorry, sir. Very sorry I'm late.'

'Yes, you are late, Stanton. Your apology does not cause the church bells to unring, nor the sun to unrise.'

'You're right, sir.'

'Of course I am right. As you are in the wrong.' Barling's slender nostrils pinched in his annoyance. 'Not only are you late, your appearance is a disgrace. Aside from your clothing looking like you plucked it from a washerwoman's basket, the injury to your eye would suggest that you have been brawling.'

'I had too much ale, sir. I fell over. That's all.' He hated his own lie. But the shame of being duped and robbed by the gang was worse than lying.

'That is all?' Barling drew out the *all*, eyebrows raised almost to his thin, dun hair.

'Yes, sir. I mean, no . . .'

'Stanton, I care not one whit about what you mean. What I care about is the efficient running of King Henry's court. The court that has been sitting while you lay abed on top of a whore in your ale-filled slumber. I have dispatched all the messengers already this morning. Had I others at my disposal, I would send you away until you are fit to be seen. However, I have no choice. I cannot risk disruption to the court because I have no messengers to hand.' Barling's thin lips pursed. 'Mark this: you are in the worst of trouble. I will deal with your unacceptable behaviour personally later. Is that clear?'

'Yes, sir.'

'Now get yourself up to the court,' said Barling. 'And ensure that you are placed where the justices cannot see you in your disgracefully dishevelled state.' He went to lead the climb up the steps.

'You two. Stop there.'

Stanton turned along with Barling to see who'd uttered the slurred command.

A richly dressed nobleman sat on a fine horse, his bulk swaying in his saddle. He was clearly very drunk, far more so than Stanton had been at the ordeal, and, Stanton guessed, used to being so. The man's deep red, meaty face told of many years of winebibbing.

'I have come,' the nobleman went on, 'for the law. Bring me there. At once.'

'Do you seek the King's justices, my lord?' Barling made his tone polite for this wealthy stranger.

'That's what I said, man. Are you deaf as well as disobedient?'

Barling's nostrils drew in again.

Stanton kept silent, not wanting to draw any ire.

'You address one of the senior clerks to the justices, my lord,' said Barling. 'I will need to know your name as well as your appeal.'

'I can tell the justices that. Not you.' The word ended on a stifled belch.

Stanton braced himself for a public scene. Barling was as irritated as the nobleman was drunk.

'I respectfully request your name, my lord,' came Barling's clipped reply. 'Without it, I cannot allow your entry to the court of the King.'

'If you must.' The man's glower matched his tone. 'My name is Sir Reginald Edgar. And I wish to appeal a brutal murder.'

Chapter Six

Stanton followed Barling and the stranger called Sir Reginald Edgar into the crowded castle keep, where the court was sitting.

As always, the warm, stuffy air smelled and felt musty: no breeze found its way in here. Neither did the light from the bright morning sun. Instead, scores of candles threw out yellowed light as well as heat and smoke. The many clerks had their tonsured heads bent to their scribbling, while the three dark-robed justices sat in their usual position on the raised dais.

A jury of twelve men was assembled before them, brought in to make some sort of declaration or other.

De Glanville was addressing them and another two men, who stood to one side.

'Sir Reginald,' whispered Barling, 'please remain here in silence until the justices have concluded this case. I will then inform them of your appeal.'

Edgar grunted but did as asked.

Barling's look went to Stanton. 'As for you,' he hissed, 'try and stay out of sight lest you attract displeasure.' He gave him a last warning nod, then made his way to his seat at the side of the dais, the very nearest to the judges, steps silent on the rush-covered stone floor.

Stanton let out a long breath, wincing as his ribs protested. He reckoned he'd attracted enough displeasure from Barling to last him a good while. He doubted de Glanville would care if he was missing an arm, let alone bother about a black eye. But if Henry's judge even glanced at him, let alone remarked on him, Barling would have Stanton pay for it for the rest of his days. He tried to melt into the stone wall at his back as de Glanville carried on with his judgement.

An inheritance case, guessed Stanton. Even he recognised many of the words by now. Plaintiff. Dispossession. Disseisin. What they meant, he still had little idea. Even less about what kind of men these justices were. To hang two men on a Saturday and drown another. Then to sit here again from the early morning on a Monday, calm, emotionless. Rested-looking. Despite the many hours he'd spent in bed, Stanton's own sleep had been fitful, broken, filled with throttled faces and dirty water and the thud of axe blade on limbs.

'Let it be therefore judged that the tenant is the party with the greater rights on the land sought.'

De Glanville's conclusion seemed to make one of the men happy. He bowed many times, a huge smile on his face, while Barling gestured at him to stop.

De Glanville didn't even seem to notice. His attention, along with that of the other justices, was back on one of the manuscripts in front of him, the justice looking at what Stanton assumed should be the next case.

As winner, loser and jury mingled and filed out in a buzz of quiet chatter, Barling got up and slipped to de Glanville's side, head bent to the justice's ear the better to murmur into it.

De Glanville looked up with a frown, seeking out Edgar with the help of Barling's discreet point. He said a few brief words to Barling, who retook his own seat.

'Sir Reginald Edgar.' De Glanville's call had the lord step forward with a grumpy 'Finally!' that the whole court must have heard in the newly settled quiet.

Stanton bit the inside of his own lip to hold in his grin at the look on Barling's face.

All three justices exchanged glances as Edgar shuffled forward with careful steps.

'My lords.' Though Edgar had stopped, he stood with the steadiness of a man aboard a ship at sea. 'I thank you for your generosity in hearing my case this morning. Your wisdom is excelled only by your efficiency. My lords.' He gestured at the startled-looking clerks. 'And you. All of you.'

'Sir Reginald,' said de Glanville, 'the King's court acknowledges your generous praise and thanks you in return. However, my fellow justices and I would be greatly assisted by your laying out what your appeal is in the briefest, simplest of terms.'

'Well then, my lord.' Edgar raised a finger, which seemed to unsteady him even more. 'I cannot put it more briefly. Or simply. An outlaw has murdered my village's smith.'

'Does your smith have a name?' asked de Glanville.

'He did when he was alive, my lord.' Edgar's words landed on the right side of insolent. Barely.

'And that was?' De Glanville's question had an edge that warned, same as the day of the ordeal.

If Edgar noticed, Stanton couldn't see it.

'Geoffrey Smith,' said Edgar. 'A well-respected member of the community. Murdered by Nicholas Lindley, an outlaw who most definitely is not.'

'How did he murder him?'

'Lindley broke into Smith's forge. Late one night. Ten days ago.' Edgar swallowed hard and lost much of his high colour. 'He . . . he took Smith's own branding iron. He beat Geoffrey to death with it. Broke his skull clean open. Smashed the iron into Smith's face too.'

A ripple of stifled disgust went through the room, matched by Stanton's own stomach turning over. His beloved uncle had worked the anvil, had had a forge.

Barling bent to his tablet to make a note.

'I see,' said de Glanville. 'You have brought your witnesses?'

'Witnesses?' Edgar shook his head. 'Only one witness. It was Smith's daughter, Agnes. But the woman's still back in Claresham.'

'Always problematic when a woman's accusation is involved.' De Vaux, the second, smaller judge, gave a sage nod.

'Indeed,' came from Pikenot, the third, round-bodied judge, who hardly ever spoke.

'Yet this Lindley did not harm her?' asked de Glanville.

'No, my lords,' said Edgar. 'Agnes Smith wasn't there when it happened. But she found her father's body.' His thick lips pursed down. 'A horrible business. Horrible.'

A shudder passed through Stanton. Not just a terrible end for Smith, but a terrible discovery for his daughter too.

De Glanville frowned. 'Then who did witness it?'

'No one exactly, my lords.' Edgar's ruddy face glowed in the flickering light once more. 'But it's clear as day who did it. This Lindley fellow was living in the woods for about a week before he murdered Smith. A beggar, or so we thought.' He swayed a bit harder. 'A couple of folk had seen him on the side roads as well. Some food had gone missing from stores. Lindley had been living amongst us as a rat lives unseen in the walls. Until . . .' He broke off, shaking his head.

'Terrible events, Sir Reginald, I have no doubt of that,' said de Glanville. 'But it would be of great help to the proceedings of this court if you were to ask your jury of presentment to come in so we can hear their full accusation.'

'A jury?' Edgar blinked hard. 'I have no such resources to call on at the moment. Many, many souls on my estate have perished this last terrible winter past. Many.'

De Glanville gave a sympathetic nod. 'As they have over the whole land.'

'If God is good, we will not see its like again,' said the second judge.

A murmur of agreement met his words, Stanton joining it. Impossible to imagine now, in the warmth of June, the ice and snow that had buried houses and barns as high as the roofs for many months, making every road near impassable. Yet one thing had been able to move: a fever and a liquid cough that claimed lives with ease.

'Amen, my lords,' said Edgar. 'But my fields need working with the greatest of urgency by the men I do have left. Bringing them here would have been a waste of time. A jury is not needed in this case.'

Barling's head rose from his tablet as the faces of all three justices went rigid too in their surprise at being told the law.

Edgar's clear drunkenness made him blind as he carried on. 'My lords, there has not been a murder in Claresham in living memory. It is a respectable, God-fearing place. The word of a nobleman is surely all that is needed in such an obvious case as this. I can go back and hang Lindley myself.'

De Glanville recovered first. 'The King's justice, sir, is what is needed. Not what you decide.'

Yet again Edgar spoke back. 'Lindley is an outlaw, my lords. I can hang him. All I need is your permission, as his Grace has decreed.' He grinned. 'I would not want to pay the fine imposed on me had I done so without such permission. Now I can—'

'Silence, sir!' De Glanville's anger was obvious now.

Stanton had to wonder if Edgar's drunkenness was accompanied by madness.

'What you have presented,' said de Glanville, 'is a secret homicide. You have no witnesses to the actual deed. Your only familial accuser is a daughter. Such crimes require proper consideration by the court of his Grace. Such as we have had in this past week, when we had three other men accused of murder. When we had them prepare for the ordeal. When they purged themselves by the ordeal.' He leaned forward. 'When we – *we* – judged that the guilty should be executed. Not you.'

Edgar opened his wide mouth.

'I ordered silence.'

He closed it again.

'Such consideration took a great deal of time, as is right and proper,' said de Glanville. 'Yet during said time, when you could have brought your case, you stayed on your estate, an accused man locked up in your gaol. And did nothing.'

Finally, Edgar looked embarrassed. A bit. 'My apologies, my lords. But a severe flux kept me abed for many days. I will return and find a jury and—'

'No, Sir Reginald,' said de Glanville, 'you will not. Tomorrow this court moves on to the next city. You are too late.'

'Then I can hang Lindley?' There was no mistaking the relish in his voice.

'No, sir, you may not.' De Glanville shook his head. 'This case does not seem straightforward. You said yourself that this man Lindley arrived in your village as a beggar, not an outlaw. Not straightforward at all. It requires the hand of the King's justice.'

His fellow justices nodded.

'This man here, Aelred Barling, is the court's most experienced clerk,' said de Glanville. 'He can oversee matters on our behalf. Barling, you will return to Claresham with Sir Reginald and administer that justice.'

Barling's look of surprise instantly became a tight, if fixed, smile. 'Of course, my lord de Glanville. It would be the highest of honours.'

Stanton held in a cheer at his own unexpected reprieve. It looked like he'd got away with his tardiness and his bruises. Barling would be gone for days. His aching head and ribs felt better already. He might even manage a visit to an alehouse tonight. A later one to a whore, one that he knew. Better, one he trusted not to have robbing friends in tow.

But de Glanville was speaking again. 'Sir Reginald, you will provide Barling his accommodation and every courtesy of your hospitality.'

'My lord.' Edgar nodded but had the look of one who'd been asked to clean out a privy.

'Barling,' continued de Glanville, 'you have admirable knowledge of the law. I am sure you will not need to consult with me and my fellow justices. But in case you do, take a messenger with you.'

A messenger? Oh no. Stanton fought the urge to make for the door.

Barling was looking straight at him.

Stanton glanced right, left, in the vain hope that another messenger had returned. But no. It was just him.

So Barling was off to Claresham to investigate the murder of one Geoffrey Smith under the order of the King's court.

And Stanton, God rot it, was going too.

Chapter Seven

God has committed to the King the care of all his subjects alike.

Aelred Barling repeated this refrain to himself many, many times on the hot ride to the village of Claresham. More specifically, he revisited it every time Sir Reginald Edgar irritated him afresh. Which was several times every hour.

Had it not been for this man, with his untimely appearance before the justices and his inebriated confusion about the law, Barling would not now be sat astride a sweating horse, his muscles cramped from many uncomfortable hours in the saddle. He would be in the shade and calm of the court, with its ordered rhythm of document, case, document, case, as soothing as a mother's heartbeat to an infant.

To add to Barling's annoyance, the thick-set Edgar, riding close beside him on an equally coarse-bodied horse while the messenger, Stanton, brought up the rear of their trio, was one of those individuals for whom the retelling of a tale was an equal pleasure to the first time. The man went over and round and back over the hideous murder of Geoffrey Smith and much besides: how it was a singular event in the whole time he had had control of his lands. How extensive his lands were. Yet even so, how he normally kept the best of order, with not even a turnip thief escaping retribution. How, in his experience, swift justice was the best justice. The man's rambling tongue was no doubt kept loose by the large leather bottle he drank from with great frequency.

'Swift, sure, strong, Barling,' Edgar wittered on. 'That's what you need with the law. Men like Lindley: dispatch them. Show no mercy, show them none. None whatsoever.' And on.

Fortunately, the man shared that other feature of lovers of incessant speech: he did not seem at all concerned with checking if the listener had heard or cared. Debate was certainly not required.

'Indeed.' Barling swatted at the flies that danced before his sweat-coated face, landing on his mouth and nose with a foul tickle. To no avail. They were back again the second he stopped. Under his neatly pinned cloak, his body perspired worse than his face. But he would not loosen any of his clothing to allow the benefit of the soft breeze. He was the representative of the King's rule of law. His appearance must reflect that at all times.

'Do you not enjoy a draught of the good grape, Barling?' Edgar held up his depleted leather drinking bottle.

'No, I have very simple tastes.' Barling's innards rebelled, not only at the trail of spittle attached to the neck of the vessel, but at the idea of what warm wine would do to his overheated body. 'I require water for my thirst. Nothing else.'

For once, his answer seemed to interest Edgar. 'I'll say that's simple.' Edgar took a sup from his own foul receptacle. 'And unusual. Men of the court like the best things that life has to offer.'

Barling had no wish to respond further. 'Speaking of water, I have very little left. If we have much farther to travel, I will need to collect some.'

'No need.' Edgar tipped his head back to take the last draughts, reminding Barling of a pig opening its mouth for an apple. 'We're almost at Claresham. You see that dip in the road up ahead? That's the start of my estate.'

'Did you hear that, Stanton?' Barling looked back and his hands tightened on his reins in impatience. As if God were not testing him enough by sending him out into the disordered, violent world, He was sending the young Hugo Stanton along with Barling as a further trial.

'Yes, sir.' Not only marked with his blackened eye, the young Hugo Stanton had flung his cloak back over his shoulders and undone the top of his undershirt. His hat rested on his saddle pommel and the wind had blown his hair about in a tangled mess.

'In the name of the Virgin,' said Barling, 'tidy yourself up. You are here as a servant of his Grace, not a peasant on his way to the fields.'

'Sorry, sir.' Stanton set about making himself look respectable with a visage that lacked even a hint of apology.

Edgar gave a sharp whistle. 'You.'

Barling looked to where a young boy collected kindling from under a stand of yews by the side of the road.

'Fetch my nephew at once,' said Edgar. 'Tell him to meet me at my hall.'

'Yes, my lord.' The boy darted off.

'My nephew, William Osmond, is the rector of Claresham,' said Edgar. 'You can see the roof of his church from here. His house is next to it. My hall is over there, in those trees.'

Barling followed his point to see where he meant, then gave another glance back. Stanton now looked as well presented as possible, which was not a great deal.

The village came into view, unremarkable in every way.

A fair size, but nothing to compare to the teeming, tightly packed London streets that had always been his home, or even the busy city of York.

The wattle and daub houses and cottages built along the main thoroughfare were mostly modest, with one or two large ones and a handful wretched. A high-walled well stood about halfway along, and a family of ducks feasted on the thick grass which grew near to it. Floods seemed unlikely from the high-banked small river, which kept the mill wheel turning in a steady, splashing trundle. Much of the place still bore the scars of the terrible winter and stormy spring. A mighty fallen oak had crushed a small barn. Many damaged roofs still needed tending to even after so many months, while others had fresh thatch repairs. Fields stretching into the distance had sheep grazing or were busy with men making the best of the last of the good day. Smoke rising from roofs and the smell of cooking told of women preparing supper.

But nothing out of the ordinary was to be seen. Nothing to suggest this was a place where a stranger had cracked open the skull of the village smith in a vicious attack.

The clatter of the three sets of hooves on the road that led down into the village had caused raised heads in the fields, had brought curious faces to front doors.

'My nephew will be surprised that you have come to join us for our meal,' said Edgar to Barling. 'I'm sure he'll be very interested in why you are here too.'

'Sir Reginald, our meal can wait,' replied Barling. 'Where is the gaol?'

'The gaol? It's down that way.' He pointed to a narrow track that led from the main street. 'But we have travelled for many hours, we—'

'Your prisoner is the reason for my travelling, Edgar. Not your repast,' said Barling. 'Do you have the keys?'

'Of course,' said Edgar. 'As I have told you, I keep the best of order here.'

Barling ignored the lord and nodded to Stanton instead. 'Stanton: the gaol. We need to be prompt.' Their arrival had already been noticed. It would not be long before the villagers gathered, he was certain of that.

'Yes, sir.' His messenger set off at a swift trot that Barling struggled to match. Edgar still protested but followed along. They dismounted outside the gaol and tethered their horses.

Barling's stiff, sore muscles felt like they belonged to another.

'You can see our murderer isn't going anywhere, Barling,' said Edgar.

'It certainly looks secure, sir,' said Stanton.

'It does.' Unlike many of the other village buildings, the low-roofed gaol appeared to be in the best of repair. Thick stone walls and roof, a stout wooden door, the metal lock large and new. Behind it, the man who had to answer for this crime. Barling stepped up to the door. 'So that means Lindley is available to answer my questions.'

'As he will be tomorrow,' said Edgar, 'when I have rested my backside from this journey.'

'Unlock it, Edgar.'

'Sir.' Stanton's brow creased in concern. 'Perhaps we should wait. The prisoner could be very dangerous.'

'The only danger is to him,' said Barling. 'We are the law, and there are three of us.'

'Uncle! You have returned.'

'Four.' Barling corrected himself with a satisfied nod as a man hurried towards them, clad in priest's robes. Edgar's family blood flowed in the veins of the approaching young rector, no doubt about that. Barling saw much of an old boar in Edgar, and while the nephew was softer and pinker, the blunt nose and the small, angry eyes were the same.

'I have, William,' replied Edgar. 'Though not with the news you hoped.'

'What news would that be?'

As Edgar launched into a tangled explanation, Barling met the gaze of an uneasy-looking Stanton. 'Pull yourself together, man,' he muttered. 'To show doubt is to show weakness.'

'Yes, sir.' Stanton nodded, but his expression did not alter.

'And that, William, is why we have the King's men in our midst.' Edgar finished with his hands flung up in disbelief.

The King's men. Barling opened his mouth to correct the preposterous idea that a messenger could be included in his own authority.

William Osmond interrupted him. 'You needn't have troubled yourselves, good sirs. My uncle could have overseen the man's hanging while I will pray for his soul.' His eyes rose to heaven. 'Though to no avail, I fear.' He crossed himself with great extravagance.

'It is not about need, sir priest,' said Barling. 'It is the law.' He could see that many of the villagers were hurrying along the street to the gaol. To be expected, but most undesirable. 'Edgar, no more delay. Please unlock the door.'

Edgar exchanged a frown with his nephew, then hammered on the robust planks with a meaty fist. 'Lindley! Move away from the door!' He unlocked it as he spoke, then flung it open.

Chapter Eight

A wave of foul, stale air met Barling. His stomach rebelled, but he refused to let his face change.

'Hell's teeth,' said Stanton with a grimace.

Edgar coughed and spat. 'Stinks like the animal he is.'

'You speak the truth, Uncle.' Osmond's mouth turned down in revulsion.

'Has the time come?' The call came from a sun-reddened young ploughman heading the approaching crowd of men and women of the village. 'Are we hanging the outlaw Lindley now?'

Raised fists and angry yells met his words.

Barling's ire grew in response. Edgar's people were as volatile as their lord. 'Sir priest,' he said, 'please remain out here and convey to the people that what is taking place is not of their concern.'

'Yes, yes, of course.' Osmond nodded with vigour in his clear desire to remain outside the hot reek of Lindley's prison, pudgy cheeks wobbling. 'I will appeal for order.'

'I would request that you keep it also. Edgar, Stanton: with me.' Barling squared his shoulders to carry out this latest grim duty and led the way inside, his shoes meeting filthy, damp straw as Osmond pulled the door to behind them.

A scuffling noise came from the shadows of the far corner. Barling was unable to make anything out as his eyes adjusted to the gloom.

'Oh, have mercy, have mercy,' came a young male voice, thick with sobs. 'I beg of you, have mercy.'

To Barling's surprise, the voice did not have the tones of the uncouth.

'Show yourself, Lindley,' said Edgar. 'If you move so much as a hair's breadth without my say-so, I'll throw you out the door and let the villagers deal with you. They'll tear you apart with their hands.'

'I won't, my lord. I swear to you.' The outlaw stood up into the shaft of evening light that came from the small, high window that was set with iron bars.

'You are Nicholas Lindley?' asked Barling, aware at the edge of his vision that Stanton's hands had clenched into ready fists. Good. Barling had questioned many wrongdoers in his time but never in such unpredictable circumstances.

Edgar scowled. 'Of course he is.'

'Yes, sir. That is my name.' The man shook in terror, tears flowing over the high cheekbones of his filth-caked face.

'My name is Aelred Barling.' Despite the threat this man might pose, this Lindley intrigued him. The outlaw's dark chestnut hair was matted and his clothes consisted of the most dreadful rags. His hair and beard straggled with sweat and dirt yet were not overlong, suggesting he had not always been so unkempt. And his boots also told an odd tale: horrible with mud and worse, but nevertheless appearing to be of the best leather. 'I am here from the court of King Henry.'

'Brought here by me.' Edgar jabbed a finger at the outlaw. 'So that I may hang you according to the law.'

A desperate whimper broke from Lindley. 'Please, my lords, no. Mercy, I beg of you, mercy.'

Barling raised a hand. 'Sir Reginald, pray silence.' He reinforced his request with a glare. The lord had muddled things yet again. Barling would happily throw him out, but that would only leave the feckless Stanton to protect him should Lindley turn violent. Edgar at least had bulk. 'You too, Lindley.' They both obeyed.

From outside, a chorus of angry voices filtered through. The villagers had arrived. Osmond's words sounded over them, his half-hearted demands for calm achieving little.

'Now, Lindley,' said Barling, 'I want you to take no heed of what is being said out there and to answer my questions. First, did you kill Geoffrey Smith?'

'No, sir. No. I swear to you, I did not.'

A snort of disgust came from Edgar.

Barling ignored him. 'Yet the good people of Claresham believe you did.'

'Sir, again, on my life, I swear to you that I did not. I have been living in the woods, that is all.'

'A weak response,' said Edgar.

'All?' asked Barling.

The outlaw's gaze flicked to the glowering Edgar. And back. 'Yes, sir.'

'Weak.' Edgar again.

'Sir Reginald, please.' Barling held up a hand again. 'Lindley, why are you living in the woods?'

'I have no home, sir.'

'You must have come from somewhere. Where is that?'

A sudden thud sounded against the wall.

Lindley started even as Barling kept his own reaction in check.

An angry yell. 'Bring the swine out!'

'If it was me, I'd let them take you,' said Edgar.

Lindley said nothing, his panicked gaze on the entrance, breath fast, as if expecting the villagers to break through.

Barling clicked his tongue in impatience. 'Stanton, go to the door. If anyone dares to try to enter, tell them they will have to face me too.'

'Yes, sir.' Stanton did as ordered, still with a close eye on Lindley.

Barling addressed Lindley once more. 'I ask again, where is your home?'

'Far from here. It is my home no more. It matters not. All that matters is that I did not kill Geoffrey Smith.'

'Liar.' Edgar ground out the word and took a step towards him, fist raised.

Lindley cowered from him with a cry.

Another thud on the wall. Another yell.

'Uncle!' Osmond cracked open the door and Edgar halted.

The ugly sounds spilled in of people baying for Lindley's hanging, filling the small gaol and sending the prisoner into spasms of wordless terror.

This was intolerable. Barling turned. 'Stanton.'

To his relief, the young messenger stood steady in the gap. 'Hold, sir priest. You can't come in.'

'What is it, William?' called Edgar.

'Uncle, I can't persuade people to stay back much longer,' came the rector's panicked reply. 'They may take the law into their own hands at any moment.'

'Sir.' Stanton looked over his shoulder at Barling. 'I fear that's the case.'

'They have no need to enter,' replied Barling. Edgar had blabbed on about the good order in which he kept this sorry place. Nothing could be further from the truth. 'For we are coming out. With Lindley. Tell them.'

As Stanton did so, Lindley cowered afresh, his cries buried under Edgar's roar and those which came from outside.

'About time!' He went to grab Lindley, a huge grin on his face.

'Stop, Edgar.' Barling addressed Stanton once more. 'You take him.'

Edgar swore loudly, shoving Lindley into Stanton's grasp.

Barling's gaze flicked over both younger men. He did not have much faith in Stanton's physical prowess. But he had no choice. He walked to the door and gestured for Edgar to step out before him. 'You first, Sir Reginald.' Then he turned to Stanton with his prisoner. 'Proceed when I tell you.'

Stanton nodded, knuckles white with his grip on Lindley's clothing.

The uproar into which Barling stepped had his lips clamp in displeasure.

Angry faces, pointing fingers, fists and sticks waving. All towards the gaol and the man still within it.

Edgar appeared to pay his people no heed as he watched for Lindley, his nephew Osmond in similar thrall.

'Silence!' Barling raised his own voice in a shout, a vulgar action for which he had the most intense dislike, though he could do it with skill. 'Silence!'

The response was immediate, as he knew it would be. Real authority had its own tone.

'My name is Aelred Barling. I am here on the orders of the court of the King, so thereby on the orders of the King. The outlaw Nicholas Lindley is in my custody.'

'God rot him!' came a peasant's curse.

Barling met the man's eye as his wife shushed him, then continued. 'Lindley is therefore in the custody of the King.'

'And the King can hang him just as well.' Edgar's mutter of delight to his nephew drew others.

'Stanton.' Barling used the fresh interruption to look in at his messenger. 'Bring Lindley out.'

The two men emerged to howls of rage.

'Hang him!'

'Now! We've waited long enough!'

And more. The clamour was not for the purity of justice. It was for the ugliness of vengeance.

Barling kept his counsel, kept his own countenance composed as he waited for silence again. He wanted all to hear what he had to say.

The yells died away under his gaze. 'As I have said, Lindley is in the custody of his Grace.'

Edgar nodding. Grinning.

'For now, that is all you need to know.' Barling was pleased to note that Edgar had stopped nodding. 'Now, Sir Reginald, I would request that you lead us and our charge to Geoffrey Smith's forge. With all haste, if you please.' Even better, the lord had stopped grinning too. Best of all, he was stunned into complete silence.

Barling preferred him that way.

Chapter Nine

Clouds of dust rose up from the dry road under the many pairs of boots and shoes, making Stanton cough and his eyes water. But he didn't dare use a hand to wipe them. He held Lindley tight in his grasp, his own pulse fast in readiness for action. He knew what the outlaw was capable of. Knew too that the man might break from him, leave him standing like a ninny on the roadway to the forge with a handful of clothing, while it fell to Edgar or one of the angry villagers to contain him. And contain him they would. Or worse.

'You'll burn in hell!' An older woman, grey hair escaping from her coif in her efforts to keep up with the crowd.

'Hang him, I say!' A squat man's eyes almost left his head in rage.

'Yes, hang him now.' The younger, wiry ploughman, who walked close alongside, but with half a wary eye on Barling ahead.

The clerk's pace matched Edgar's hard, quick steps, the lord's pace telling of his fury, as did the deep red of the back of his square neck. Osmond scurried along with them, casting many anxious looks back over his shoulder.

'Hell!' The old woman screamed right in Lindley's face, causing the man to stagger.

'Steady.' Stanton didn't know if he said it to himself or his prisoner as he shoved his own shoulder under the man's arm.

'God help me.' The outlaw's eyes glazed as he stumbled on in terror, Stanton taking much of his weight now. 'God help me.'

No wonder. Being mobbed by folk shouting for his neck in a noose. Stanton pushed that thought away. *Take a hold of yourself.* Geoffrey Smith's death had been horrific. It needed to be punished.

Yet what Barling was up to with this grim parade to the forge, he'd no idea and didn't want to know. Being sent to serve Barling here had been the worst luck. Stanton cursed himself for it, as he had many times on the long journey to this place. Had he reached the court just a few minutes earlier, Nesbitt would have been here and not him.

'Let me through!'

A high-pitched scream above the many voices. A woman's scream.

'Let me at him!'

A scuffle came from the crowd to Stanton's right.

'Agnes, no!' A man's ragged shout.

Barling and the others in front halted, turned round at the commotion.

The crowd parted and a dark-haired young woman burst through. 'You bastard! I'll kill you myself.' She leapt at Lindley, kicking, hitting, clawing at his face and eyes.

'Leave him.' Stanton let go of Lindley with one hand to try to fend her off as the outlaw ducked his head, his forearm raised against the attack.

'My love, stop.' A hugely fat man was with her now, breathless in his useless efforts to pull her back.

'Kill you!' Her nails rent Lindley's cheek.

'What is going on?' Edgar's roar echoed out, Barling's pale face set in fury at the edge of Stanton's vision as he tried to wrest his prisoner free in a new chorus of yells.

The girl threw a punch at Lindley's face, half on target, her fist glancing off and catching Stanton on the side of the head in a ringing blow.

'Agnes. No.' The ploughman put large, sinewy hands on her shoulders and hauled her off.

'Let go of me, Simon.' She twisted in his hold, but he held her firm.

'Agnes Smith! Desist!' Edgar stomped towards Stanton, Barling with him.

'Not till I see Lindley in his grave.' She tried without success to break free from the ploughman's strong grasp, even as the obese man wheezed an anguished plea at her again.

'My. Love. Stop.'

Stanton dragged Lindley back from her reach.

'What on earth is going on here?' Somehow Barling's sharp question cut through the melee and brought a bit of order.

'This . . . this malapert is Geoffrey Smith's daughter,' said Edgar.

'I see. Perhaps you would explain your conduct, miss.' Barling's look carried a cartload of disapproval. Stanton knew it well.

Yet Agnes Smith didn't flinch. 'No explanation, sir.' Still in the ploughman's hold, her breath fast, she tossed her head to get the long, dark curls of her loose, uncovered hair off her face. 'This outlaw killed my father.' Head high, she kept her light brown gaze fixed on Barling. 'He must pay. I'll do it if no one else will.'

Stanton didn't doubt she would. Her voice had a venom in it that could melt a rock. What was more, she was a strapping woman, almost as tall as him. His head still smarted from her punch, indirect as it had been.

'My love, please.' The fat man again.

'Theaker.' Edgar addressed him. 'Have you no control over your betrothed?'

'Of course, my lord.' The obese Theaker wrung his hands. 'She's just upset, that's all. Isn't that right, Agnes?'

She gave him a withering look. 'I'm not upset.' Her square jaw set. 'I want Nicholas Lindley to pay for what he did.'

Secure in Stanton's hold again, Lindley shook his head in silence, slow beads of blood seeping from his rent cheek.

'I would not in the usual circumstance repeat myself,' said Barling. 'But in acknowledgement of the death of your father, Agnes, I will do so this once. Lindley is in my custody and so therefore that of the King. If you do not agree to progress in peace, then you will be facing charges also. Do you understand?'

'Yes.'

The wiry young ploughman, who held her, muttered something into her ear.

'Sir,' she added through gritted teeth.

'Good,' said Barling.

'You can let go of me.' Agnes pried herself from the ploughman's hold.

'All will be well, my love.' Theaker, her betrothed, lunged to grab her in a clumsy embrace, yet she shook him off without a glance.

Barling went on. 'Now, there has been enough delay. I need to continue to the forge. Stanton, with me.' He set off, not bothering to ask anyone else to follow him, yet all present did, as if he'd issued an order.

'Come on.' Stanton urged the unsteady Lindley forward the best he could. No doubt the outlaw dreaded seeing again the place where he'd taken Geoffrey Smith's life.

Truth be told, Stanton was dreading it too.

Chapter Ten

For Stanton, entering his uncle's forge had meant many things.

Security, for one. His uncle, quiet like his late father, and with equally as kind a heart. Shoulders like a cross-beam and no time for fools or those who wanted to try their luck. Boredom, too. Put stoking the fire, Stanton as a small boy would whine that it was too hot. Put sweeping straw, he would sigh that it was too windy. Put standing and watching his uncle's sure strikes at the anvil, he would sway in long complaint that his legs were tired. Then one day: excitement. The day a horse came into the forge. Not just any horse. An animal utterly unlike the big, tired plough horses or placid rouncys. It was the finest palfrey, bursting with muscle, power and spirit. And speed. Oh, the speed. The rider who'd brought it in was a messenger, so impatient to be off and gone. And once the shoe was on, he took off at a gallop. Stanton had watched him go down the road and could only marvel that anything moved that fast. From that moment he knew he'd ride like that one day. He'd told his uncle, who'd simply nodded with his quiet smile in the warmth and orange light of the forge.

Now, entering a forge meant looking at death.

'Close the doors,' said Barling. 'I wish for privacy.'

Stanton stood with Lindley still firm in his grasp, as Edgar, the one other person Barling had allowed in here, swung the high doors shut.

Dead, cold ashes in the grate. The anvil, silent on its high mount, never to ring out from Geoffrey Smith's strike again. A stained floor splashed with what would have been an unspeakable red, now a terrible decaying brown, with bloated flies buzzing on, above and around it. The heavy stench could be that of a slaughterhouse, yet it was a man, not a beast, who'd died here.

Outside, the calls had started again for Lindley's hanging, headed by Agnes Smith, with the rector, Osmond, trying without much success to start a prayer.

Edgar jabbed a finger at Lindley. 'You see what this monster has done, Barling?'

Lindley gave a low moan, a sudden weight in Stanton's hands.

'I can see what has been left behind.' Barling's gaze moved over the scene as he took measured, slow steps.

Edgar snorted. 'Same thing.'

'Lindley's losing his sense, sir.' Stanton's arms strained to keep him on his feet, but the man was becoming a dead weight.

Barling looked over and tutted. 'Put him on the ground, then. At least for now. He will need to be revived.'

'Yes, sir.' As Stanton lowered Lindley, Edgar moved in with a booted kick to the man's stomach, so hard it sent him sprawling down on the hammered-earth floor.

Stanton recovered his own balance to Edgar's grin.

'That'll revive him,' said the lord.

'Edgar.' No 'Sir Reginald'; Barling was clearly livid. 'This' – he gestured to the coughing, retching Lindley, who was trying to claw his way out of the reach of Edgar's boot – 'is unhelpful and distracting. No more.' He nodded to Stanton, who moved to stand between Edgar and the cowering Lindley on the floor.

'I didn't do it.' Lindley's pleas came through more coughs. 'I swear, I swear. You must believe me.'

Stanton folded his arms, refused to look down as Edgar moved his shoulders inside his own cloak as if preparing for a fist fight.

Trouble was, Lindley's pleading sounded real. Just as three months ago Stanton had gone to visit an innocent man who faced the noose. The King had ordered it so. But Stanton had spoken up that day. Saved a life. He put the memory aside. *No.* He wouldn't become involved. The King's justice would do its own work. And yet. The pleas of the men in York who'd gone on to face the ordeal echoed in his head, along with Lindley's voice. And one of those had been innocent. He shook his head to himself. *No.*

'Listen to the scum.' Edgar flung a hand out in disgust, then bent with a grunt of effort to the floor. 'This is what he says he didn't do.' Edgar straightened up, holding a long-handled branding iron.

Stanton blinked in a vain attempt to banish the sight. The head of the thing was in the shape of a letter – he didn't know which. But caught in the sharp angles of the metal, angles which should have been clean and smooth the better to make a clear brand, was a foul oozing clump. A clump that held a tuft of dark hair.

Barling barely gave it a glance, now peering into the shadowed corners. 'It was indeed a vicious attack on Geoffrey Smith. It is still the case that no one saw what took place here.'

'No, no one saw the deed,' said Edgar. 'But think of his poor daughter. You should have heard her piteous cries when she found him.'

From outside came Agnes's continued shouts. 'String him from a tree. Now!'

'Hardly piteous.' Barling raised his eyebrows.

'But correct,' said Edgar. 'The sooner the better. Eh, Barling?'

Barling ignored the lord, moving instead to look at the tools hanging from the walls.

'Anybody with half an eye can see what has gone on here.' Edgar looked at Stanton, pointed at his bruised eye. 'Even you, man.' He laughed at his own weak joke, Barling still not responding.

Trouble was, Stanton could see. See that something wasn't right. Same as the day an innocent man, a knight called Sir Benedict Palmer, was about to be hanged. The day Stanton picked up on a detail. A small, small detail. He'd spoken up, even when the King believed the accused man's guilt looked complete; even when Stanton knew it could have terrible consequences for himself.

'I have seen all I need to here.' Barling moved to the door. 'Stanton, bring Lindley outside again. I need to address my remarks to everyone present.'

'Finally,' said Edgar, following him. 'We can leave this putrid place.'

But Stanton didn't budge, instead blurted out, 'Sir Reginald, how tall was Geoffrey Smith?'

Chapter Eleven

Stanton braced himself as Barling stopped dead and glared at him.

'I beg your pardon, Stanton?' The clerk's tone was one of utter disbelief.

No going back now. 'How tall was he, Sir Reginald?' repeated Stanton.

Edgar had a ready scowl. 'He was tall.' He waved a hand three inches above his head. 'Broad. What of it?'

He'd been right. The height of the anvil on its mount. Agnes, the smith's daughter, tall too. 'Then how could this man here overpower him?' Stanton winced inside at the thunderstruck look on Barling's face but ploughed on. 'Lindley here' – he gestured to where the outlaw cowered on the floor – 'is the height and build of regular men. Surely it wasn't possible for him to overpower Smith. Maybe Lindley speaks the truth.' He swallowed again as his heart hammered at the sight of the two faces before him.

Edgar had gone puce. 'Barling, have you no control over your man's tongue?'

'Of course I have.' Barling remained pale as ever, but his look worried Stanton far more than the blunt-nosed Edgar's.

'Good! Then we need to get on with this pressing matter.' Edgar marched to the doors and hauled them open.

Golden evening light flooded in, along with the sound of angry voices, scattering the cloud of feasting flies.

Barling went to go out too. 'Pick Lindley up,' he ordered Stanton. 'Bring him out.' He took a quick glance at Edgar, who was busy shouting to his nephew. 'And, Stanton?' Barling's eye fixed back on him.

'Yes, sir?'

'Mark my words: I will deal with you later. Do you hear me?'

'Yes, sir.' He doubted if Barling had even heard, as the clerk was now on his way out of the doors. 'Come on.' He hauled the quaking Lindley to his feet and marched him out, cursing himself for a fool. He'd only added to his troubles with Barling. He should've kept his mouth shut.

The glow of the setting sun fell on his face. A glorious evening, one for lying in the long grass with his lost, beautiful love. Not standing facing a circle of angry, shouting people, people who wanted to take a man's life. And wanted to take it now.

Barling raised a hand. 'Pray silence.'

An uneasy quiet fell.

Stanton kept his grip on Lindley. This lot looked on the verge of ripping the man from him, Barling or no Barling.

'Sir Reginald has appealed this man, Nicholas Lindley,' said Barling, 'of the murder of Geoffrey Smith.'

Cries broke out again.

'Then he's guilty!'

'Hang him, by God!'

Barling raised his hand once more. 'But Sir Reginald has not provided me with a detailed and supported accusation. I have not established guilt.'

'What?' Edgar's roar joined the shouts of those watching. He marched over to Stanton, his rage-filled face inches from the messenger's. 'This is your fault!'

Fine spittle dampened Stanton's face. He didn't dare wipe it. He had to keep hold of Lindley.

'And yours!' Edgar stomped back to Barling. 'It was plain to see what happened in that forge! You said so yourself, Barling. Then this . . . this man of yours starts asking questions and you change your mind.'

Fury met his words in voices, in faces. And now that fury was aimed at Stanton too.

'Me?' Stanton's gaze flew to Barling. 'No, I'm not—'

'Silence!' Barling's sharp order cut through the noise. 'I will remind you that my word is King Henry's word.' The King's name brought a tense silence. 'The King's.' His gaze moved over those present. Slow, precise. 'Would you consider shouting at his Grace?'

One or two dropped their gaze. Others stepped back in spite of themselves.

Barling nodded. 'I did not think so. Hugo Stanton and I are here as his representatives. You would be well placed to remember that.'

Stanton kept his face still at Barling's reference to him. He wasn't Henry's representative. He was a lowly message boy. But his gut told him now was not the time to say anything. At all.

Barling went on. 'I will be investigating the truth of the matter. I will be making various enquiries and interrogations, asking many questions, and Stanton will be assisting me in that endeavour.'

'Questions?' Edgar's mouth hung open.

Stanton kept his own clamped shut. Just. If being talked of as Henry's representative was startling, his asking questions alongside Barling was even more so.

'Is that all?' The agonised scream came from Agnes. 'What if there are no answers? How is that justice?' Her man Theaker tried to shush her, but she paid him no mind. 'How?'

'I will assume that your grief for your late father makes you unaware of your behaviour.' Barling's clipped tone told of his annoyance. 'But I warn you, my patience is growing thin. I strongly suggest you keep your counsel.' He looked at Edgar. 'That everyone does.'

This time Agnes allowed herself to be hushed, though her stare at Barling resembled that of a cat at a mouse hole.

Edgar's tiny eyes narrowed, almost lost in his fleshy face. But he said nothing.

'And question we will,' said Barling.

We. Again. Stanton sucked in a deep breath.

Barling went on. 'As many of you as we need to. And your answers will be truthful. Remember, God sees into the hearts and minds of all men and women, as well as their souls.' Barling looked over at Lindley.

'Oh God, help me.'

Stanton barely caught his whisper.

'Truth and truth only,' said Barling. 'That is what we seek on behalf of his Grace.'

A loud snort came from Edgar. 'And what if your questions don't find the truth?' He almost spat the final word. 'What then?'

'If,' said Barling, 'our every effort and enquiry fail to uncover the truth, then God has granted us a way to establish whether or not this outlaw is guilty.'

Stanton knew what was coming. He had witnessed it in York.

'For which I have been granted full authority.' Barling's gaze went to Edgar. 'Full.' He folded his hands. 'Nicholas Lindley will be made to purge himself by the ordeal.'

A low moan of despair came from Lindley as gasps and calls broke out and folk turned to each other in excited chatter.

'The water!'

'He'll face the water!'

'By God, what a thing to see!'

Stanton held tight to his trembling prisoner and stared straight ahead. He could not, would not look at him. He knew his own face would betray what the ordeal meant.

'However.' Barling's single word brought instant quiet. 'While the ordeal of water is the trial to which I would normally submit Lindley, in this case there is another which I believe to be far more fitting.'

Stanton's confusion was reflected in the many faces before him.

'Geoffrey Smith was brutally murdered in his own forge,' said Barling. 'The place where he earned his respectable livelihood and met his heinous end. Therefore Lindley will not, if it is necessary, ultimately face the ordeal of water.' He paused.

Every face craned forward, rapt.

Barling pointed at Lindley, shaking even harder now in Stanton's hold. 'It will be the ordeal of hot iron.'

A great shout greeted his words, fell away again as people strained to hear.

'This means, Nicholas Lindley,' said Barling, 'that an iron bar will be heated in a fire until it is red hot. Heated in Geoffrey Smith's own forge. You will take that iron in your hand.'

Screams of excited horror broke from every gaping mouth and filled the air.

Barling held up three fingers. 'Walk with the iron for three paces.'

More shouts as Stanton's guts turned over.

'Your flesh will cook,' said Barling. 'You will have a wound. Deep, deep in your palm.'

If he hadn't had such a tight hold of Lindley, Stanton knew the man would fall to the ground in terror.

'God be praised for the ordeal!' cried Osmond. 'The ordeal!'

Others took up the chant, their faces flushed in a baying chorus of vengeful joy, as Barling waited for silence. Got it.

'That wound will be bandaged,' he said. 'Left for three days.' Three fingers raised again. 'It will then be uncovered. God will then give His judgement. If your flesh is uncorrupted, then God will have told us of your innocence. If corrupted, then He will have shown us your guilt.' He dropped his hand. 'And you, Nicholas Lindley, will hang.'

Chapter Twelve

'I knew, Hugo Stanton, when I first saw you early this morn that you were not fit to serve his Grace.' The King's clerk hadn't raised his voice. He didn't need to.

For his part, Stanton already knew he was in the deepest of trouble. He had been expecting it ever since he and Barling had finally arrived at Edgar's spacious hall in the gathering dusk.

Though a fine building once, it was in a state of decay and chaos similar to that of the nobleman. Edgar had sent many servants scuttling across the soiled floor rushes.

'Food! And quickly! My belly is like an empty sack.' The lord was already guzzling from a dented goblet full of wine. 'And we have guests. Prepare rooms for the King's men.' More scuttling.

Stanton had been following a servant to his own accommodation when Barling's murmur came close to his ear. 'With me. Now.'

So here he stood, tired, hungry, thirsty, still in his sweaty, dusty clothes from the day's travel as the clerk's pale eyes bored into him.

'Not. Fit.' Barling bit the words off.

'No, sir. I'm not.' Stanton doubted his answer would do any good. It didn't.

'I should have listened to my own counsel. To have had no messenger to hand would have been problematic. But not nearly so problematic as one that decides to interject in matters that do not in any way concern him.' Barling shook his head. 'May I ask why?'

'Why – I mean, what, sir? I mean, I'm not sure—'

'May the Lord in His goodness grant me patience.' Barling rolled his eyes. 'Why you, a mere messenger, inserted yourself into my investigation. Why, at the forge, you suddenly took it upon yourself to enquire about the height of the late Geoffrey Smith.'

'I don't know, sir.' But he did.

And the clerk could tell. 'Yes, you do. Stanton, you are an appalling liar. Why did you ask about Smith?'

'Sir, not long since I've witnessed innocent people punished for crimes they did not commit. For one of those people, I spoke up. Spoke up because I noticed something wasn't quite right. Like today. My uncle was a farrier. The anvil height, you see. It made me think. And Lindley sounded like he was telling the truth to me.' He knew he made little or no sense. Barling's look had him getting his words all mixed up. 'Before when I said something, it was almost too late. But because I said something an innocent man lived. And because of that others did as well.'

'You are talking in utter riddles, man. Explain yourself. Properly.'

'I'm afraid I can't, sir.'

'Are you so boneheaded that you are unable to do so?'

'No, sir. I mean that I can't explain fully because it all happened before I became a messenger with the travelling court.'

'Stanton, you simply do not understand your place. I am a senior clerk of the court of King Henry. You will answer any question I ask of you.'

Stanton took a deep breath. He had to stop Barling from trying to dig any deeper – and stop him now. 'Then I shall answer you this, sir. I was a messenger elsewhere. I joined the travelling court with the approval of the lord justice de Glanville. That is all I am permitted to say. On my life.'

His answer worked.

'I see.' Barling sniffed in displeasure but no more. 'And is your black eye also from defending the innocent? Or will you direct me to de Glanville to answer that also?'

'No, sir. It was from unwise action.'

'Action you perhaps should not have taken?'

The girl at the ordeal, leading him down the alley, him not having a clue. 'Yes, sir,' he muttered.

'I thought so. Your behaviour is like that of so many young men.' Barling began to count out Stanton's flaws on the fingers of his raised hand. 'Rash, for one. Impetuous, two. Three: never stopping to consider the consequences of your actions.' He dropped his hands. 'Precisely as you acted in the forge, blabbing out your half-formed ideas. Not even half-formed! Lindley's height is of no consequence. The branding iron gives plenty of extra reach.' He sucked in a breath. 'And because you did so, you set Edgar off, with him challenging my competence before that outrageous assembly. You, Hugo Stanton, came dangerously close to making me look a fool.' He paused to draw breath.

Stanton didn't say a word. He didn't dare. Not with Barling like this.

'Tell me, Stanton, if I look a fool, who does too?'

'King Henry, sir.' *God rot his Grace.*

'Precisely. His name, his law. All of it.' Barling's colourless fists clenched. 'A disaster. That is what would have happened had I not had the presence of mind to tell the people of Claresham that you are assisting me.'

'I'm sorry, sir.'

Barling held up a hand. 'An apology is no substitute for considered action.'

'I know, sir. Thank you, sir, for thinking so quickly. I won't get in your way again, I swear to you.'

Barling stared at him. 'But you are in the way, Stanton. You are in the way because you have put yourself there.'

Put myself where? 'I'm sorry, sir, I don't quite understand.'

'Stanton, it is clear that you do not understand at all.' Barling slowed his speech as if he spoke to a dullard. 'Permit me to make it as clear as I can for you. I have announced publicly that I will be investigating the circumstances of Geoffrey Smith's murder. That is the truth. I have also stated publicly that you will be assisting me in that endeavour. That was not true, at least not up to an hour ago. But now it is. I cannot make such a statement and then not act on it. In short, Stanton, I cannot lie. Nor can I be seen to be lying. Now do you understand?'

Stanton did. Damn it all to hell, he did. 'That I am to be your assistant, sir?'

'At least in name, to make sure my authority stays intact.' He gave Stanton a pained look. 'I have every confidence that your questions, or the answers that you receive, will be of little use.'

Useless. A failure. Again. Stanton clamped his jaw.

Barling continued. 'I believe any such questioning to be futile because it is becoming abundantly clear that none of the villagers saw anything. Despite this, they have very much made up their minds about Lindley's guilt.' He sighed. 'What is of most use now is the power of the ordeal. You may find that the outlaw's lips are loosed by that power when you go to question him.'

'When *I* go, sir?'

Barling frowned. 'Yes, you, Stanton. Try not to look so appalled, man. I will of course be questioning Lindley too, and mine will be the one visit of any importance. But tomorrow I need to try and get sense out of Sir Reginald Edgar and write up a coherent account for the court of what he has done so far. I suspect it will take me a very long time.' He gestured to the solar. 'Not only is the man's home in disorder, his speech is as well. While he is occupied with me, you can go and speak to

Lindley privately. At least you will not have Edgar barging around like a bull waiting to be released into a herd of cows.'

Stanton cleared his throat. 'I'm not very good at fighting, sir.'

'Your eye tells the world that.' The corner of Barling's mouth twitched. 'Rest assured, I am not asking you to fight him, merely question him. I am also aware that Lindley potentially poses great risk, despite his supposedly meek appearance.' He shook his head. 'I have seen the mildest of men transformed into monsters when their wrath grows within them. You will of course need one of Edgar's men to come with you to unlock the gaol. Make sure he remains close by in case you need assistance.'

'Yes, sir.' Stanton relaxed, but not by much. The idea of being cooped up alone with Lindley filled him with some alarm.

'Once you are finished with Lindley, take yourself around the village and ask questions. Again, it matters little what those questions are. Make your presence obvious so people are reassured that the King's justice is being administered.'

'Yes, sir.' Stanton kept his face still, unwilling to let Barling see his anger at being viewed as of so little worth.

'In the meantime,' said Barling, 'my greatest hope for a confession is with the threat of the ordeal. Lindley is in dread of his hand being roasted. If he is guilty, he is likely to say so very soon. He knows his hand will suppurate from his foul crime. He will have no wish to add to his own agony.'

'Yet he may not confess even so.' Stanton tried to put the idea of carrying a red-hot iron from his head. The pit, the water, entered it instead. 'Like at York.'

Barling looked askance at him. 'I did not ask for your opinion, Stanton.'

'No. Sorry, sir.'

'But your point, surprisingly, is well made. Then justice is with God himself. Once Lindley has carried the iron, we wait to see what the Almighty decides. If the man is innocent, he has nothing to fear.'

Stanton flinched inside. Were he Nicholas Lindley, he'd be in absolute terror. But he said nothing. He'd already said enough.

'Now, leave me to wash before my meal.' Barling clicked his tongue. 'I would say that the linen has been used to wipe away the cobwebs. But the cobwebs are very much still in place.'

'Yes, sir.' Stanton gave a quick bow and made for the door. He couldn't wait to get out of there. He had not many hours left before he had to face Lindley and the villagers. Getting out from under Barling's eye for the first time on this longest of days would help. A few draughts of ale would as well.

'And, Stanton?'

Oh, what now? 'Yes, sir?'

'Make sure you do the same. Or at least try. You cannot come to Edgar's table in that filthy state.'

Stanton wasn't sure if he heard him right. 'Me at Edgar's table, sir?'

'Of course, man. I have presented you as my assistant. That must be maintained.'

So Stanton was still in the company of the ever-watchful, prickly clerk. The bad-tempered bully Edgar too. 'Yes, sir.' He left with a bow, closing the door behind him.

And let a string of silent curses loose in the empty passageway.

His step down from being a secret royal messenger to serving the travelling court had been a welcome one, the first step in a journey that would take him away from Henry's service altogether. Now he was being dragged back in, carrying out public duties in the name of the King. He hauled his hands through his hair and cursed once more.

One thing was sure: he would never, ever sleep late again.

Chapter Thirteen

Finally, peace. Even better, solitude.

Barling sat down at the scratched table he'd requested to be placed in his solar at Edgar's hall.

The spacious room should have had every comfort. Beeswax candles threw out a steady, pure light, for which he was grateful. But while a blessing for writing, the light had summoned several large brown moths through the tall window shutters, which stood open on this warm, airless night. The candlelight also served to show the state of the room and its sorry contents. Everything was in need of replacement or repair. The large bed's lumpy feather mattress smelled of damp. The linen and rich red wool coverings upon it would have been fine once but were eaten through in a multitude of tiny holes. The yellow curtains, thick with embroidered green leaves, that hung from the carved frame above it to keep light out and warmth in were in the same condition. No rushes covered the floor.

Yet Barling cared little. His rooms as a student in Paris, so many years before, had been worse. At least there were no rats to greet him. At least not yet.

And the table before him contained every treasure he needed. His selection of pipe rolls, brought with him here for consulting on points of law. Fresh paper, a seal, red wax for any letters he would need to write. Precious vellum for his permanent record. His capped ink holder, the carved horn yellowed and worn smooth from many hundreds of hours of handling. His wooden writing tablet, its wax overlay smooth and pristine and awaiting his first notes. His collection of fine styluses and his sharpening knife. Last, a sealed document from the Archbishop at York.

Barling picked up a stylus, stifling a yawn as he checked its point in the flickering light. Not quite sharp enough. He reached for his knife to bring it to the required standard. The hour was well past midnight and the bed summoned his tired bones. Yet he knew it did not do to delay in compiling one's notes. Especially not in this present situation, a situation brought about entirely by the intemperate, incompetent Sir Reginald Edgar.

Had Edgar been a man worthy of his title, the lord would have brought the case before de Glanville and the other justices in York in the correct manner. And it would have been heard there. In the confines of the court. The correct location. Barling's pressure on his stylus snapped the point. He reached for another, frowning at his own tension.

He should not allow himself to be so annoyed by being sent here to Claresham. No matter how uncomfortable the journey, no matter how difficult it was to deal with Edgar, no matter what chaos engulfed this place, Barling's mission on behalf of King Henry was clear in Barling's heart: uniform rule of law and administration of this great land.

The law that allowed for the ordeal. His eyes went to the Archbishop's letter again. The authority, should it be needed, for an ordained priest to carry out the necessary blessings for the ordeal.

That priest would be Edgar's nephew, the unpleasant William Osmond. The rector had joined them at their meal earlier, his small eyes glittering at the prospect of the ordeal of hot iron. Yet Osmond seemed less concerned with the blessing of the iron, more with the detail.

'Should it be red-hot, Barling? Or is it better that it is white-hot?'

Edgar, quite drunk once more and the horribly better-humoured for it, had roared with laughter at the question, chewed beef visible in his open maw as he pressed his knife blade flat on to his own palm.

Barling had tried to quell their unseemly eagerness. 'It may not even be needed, sir priest. Part of the ordeal's power lies in its anticipation. Remember, I also have much work to do before we move to the ordeal.'

'Still.' Edgar shoved his knife flat on his nephew's hand. 'Hisssssss, eh?'

The two men had laughed until they cried.

Opposite Barling, a silent Stanton had drunk a plentiful amount too, yet the wine did not draw any mirth from him. Sulking, no doubt, at being told a few truths about his disgraceful behaviour. As for his claims about being with the court with the approval of de Glanville, they were puzzling. De Glanville had indeed informed Barling of Stanton's arrival, but no more. Never mind. Barling would seek out a full explanation, but that was for another time. What he had was sufficient for now. There were far more pressing matters to address.

He placed the newly sharpened point of his stylus on to his tablet and began the first of his notes. *Geoffrey Smith: Murdered. On the fourth day of June in the Year of Our Lord 1176.*

The wine did not draw anything at all, in fact: the young messenger had remained quiet throughout.

In the village of Claresham, in the county of Yorkshire.

Messenger? If only that were so. His pen moved on.

Blacksmith. Secret Homicide.

Now Stanton was his assistant, in the most unfortunate turn of events. Better fortune was that neither Edgar nor Osmond showed the slightest disbelief in his position. Barling did not think they had any cause to. He'd cast his mind back: he and Stanton outside the court, inside it, the journey here. Barling's story that Stanton was his assistant would hold.

No thanks to Stanton. 'Sir Reginald, how tall was Geoffrey Smith?' The messenger's question asked not once but twice in the foul atmosphere of the forge.

Barling had wondered if his ears had deceived him as he'd stared at Stanton. His fingers tightened on his stylus in annoyance. He was in the middle – the middle – of examining the forge. That was the task in hand at that moment. To approach it with order. With method.

Murder took place in Smith's own forge. No witnesses.

The examination of the forge. That should have been the one task at that moment, nothing else. But Stanton, taken hold of by a personal memory, had opened his mouth and immediately disrupted that order.

Death was by fracture of the skull. Branding iron caused fracture. Face also fractured with branding iron.

As so many others had done before. Barling had witnessed passions take over in matters of law on far too many occasions over many years, when facts and distance were needed. The law was based on consistent, sound judgement. That was how it worked. Emotion made for neither. And emotions indeed ran high here.

Body was discovered by daughter, Agnes Smith.

The emotions of Agnes Smith in particular. Not only had she suffered the grievous loss of her father, she had made the terrible discovery of his body. Her strident boldness was another matter, however. He had not encountered very many young women who would be happy to hang a man.

Body is buried in the churchyard – I have not viewed it.

In the confusion of the assembly outside the forge, he had wondered – feared, even – that Agnes would tear Lindley from Stanton's grasp and do it there and then. It would not have been difficult. Stanton was not a natural guard. Barling shook his head.

Accused is Nicholas Lindley. An outlaw who had claimed to be a beggar.

Barling could also understand the villagers' naked thirst for vengeance. Feelings always drove the ignorant and uneducated. They could not be expected to consider the proper administration of justice. It fell to Barling to make sure they did. A heavy burden, but one he was happy to shoulder for his King.

Lindley swears he is innocent.

Stanton's question about Smith's height came back to him and he sighed. Naturally, Barling had had the same question. He'd had it the second he saw Lindley. But he'd kept his counsel, which Stanton should also have done. Once Edgar had presented the branding iron, Lindley's height was no longer an important point. A smaller person of lesser strength could wreak havoc with such a weapon. Thoughts needed to be organised to be effective, not scattered hither and yon. One needed the whole picture.

Lindley is of middling height and build. He is not an especially strong-looking man.

Barling's hand cramped and he stretched out his fingers, yawning again. He could do little more tonight. He had done what he always did: recorded line by line by line.

And then he also did as always. He read back through what he'd written.

After *No witnesses*, he inserted a question mark.

Then he underlined *looking*: *He is not a strong-looking man*, inserted *But branding iron was weapon.*

Finally, he wrote one more line:

Why would Nicholas Lindley want Geoffrey Smith dead?

Barling laid down his pen in satisfaction. Order. Method. That would bring justice. Barling knew it always did.

Line by line by line.

Chapter Fourteen

Hugo Stanton had thought that the previous morning in York was bad: sore and shamed from his beating, late to court, an angry Barling waiting for him.

But on this hot new day in Claresham, his first task was to be alone with a man accused of beating another to death in the most brutal way, and to ask him questions about that murder.

After that, questions to all the villagers.

And none of it mattered.

Barling had sent him out here for appearances only, nothing more.

He went at a measured pace, as if that could somehow mean he never reached Claresham's gaol. But reach it he had.

He turned to the burly servant Edgar had provided on Barling's orders. 'Open it up, please.'

The man didn't answer, a look on his face of barely hidden contempt. Stanton had no doubt that Edgar's claim about Stanton interfering had spread far and wide.

'Stand away from the door, Lindley.' The man pounded on it with his fist.

Stanton squared his shoulders. To have the rude servant in here with him would be better than no protection at all.

But when Stanton had been summoned by Barling earlier, before he left for the gaol, the clerk had been very definite. *'Make sure you speak to Lindley alone, Stanton. If Edgar's man is present, that means Edgar is as well. I do not want any further disorder of my enquiry. There was more than enough confusion yesterday. Do I make myself clear?'*

Stanton had nodded, not daring to ask for the extra presence of the servant. Barling's look as the clerk had sat behind a large table set out with documents and papers had told him it was useless. It also told him who Barling blamed for causing the muddle.

The servant swung the door wide. 'There you go. Sir.' He cast Stanton a sour glance.

Stanton pulled in a deep breath, both to steady his nerves and to get a last gulp of clean air before he faced the reek of the prison. His ribs hurt less this morning than they had yesterday. That was about the only thing better about this new day.

'Lindley?' His voice came out steadier than he felt as the door closed behind him. 'It's Hugo Stanton. The King's man.' He could bite his own tongue out for having to announce himself as such.

The early sun brought a bit of light to the wretched place.

Lindley stood at a safe distance away, hands clasped. 'Good morrow to you, sir.'

'And to you.' It felt strange that this man called him 'sir' and not the other way round. Despite his rags and dirt, Lindley spoke well. Stanton had noted it yesterday. Noted also that the outlaw's filthy boots were of far finer leather than his own as he'd marched him along the roadway. A riddle, this man. But he wasn't the one with the skills to solve it. Barling couldn't have made it any clearer last night.

Lindley watched him expectantly, his large dark eyes troubled, his lanky, red-brown hair hanging in filthy strands to his bowed shoulders. His left cheek showed the deep marks of Agnes Smith's attack.

The man seemed harmless, hadn't shown any great strength when Stanton had contained him yesterday. But Barling's comment from last night pounded in his head: *I have seen the mildest of men transformed into monsters when their wrath grows within them.* Stanton knew what he meant: physical strength was not always needed for pure evil. He swallowed hard. Questions – he knew he had to ask questions. A waste of time, as Barling had made clear. Worse, a wrong query could set this man off. 'How, em, how does this morning find you?'

The outlaw smiled sadly. 'As every other morn these past ten days. I am locked in this place, God help me.'

'I'm sure God will if you ask him.' Stanton hoped that sounded more truthful to Lindley than it did to his own ears.

'Oh, I think He has, sir,' said Lindley. 'When I heard Sir Reginald at the door yesterday, when you all came in, I thought that was it. That you had come for me.' A tight sob came through his words. 'To hang me.'

Stanton couldn't reply. He'd never been one to inspire terror. Never wanted to. And now he had.

Lindley went on. 'But God listened to me, listened to my prayers.' He raised his clasped hands. 'I am still alive. And it is thanks to your blessed intervention, good sir.'

Stanton shook his head, embarrassed. 'I didn't make any decisions, Lindley.'

'But you saw that I am not an especially strong man, sir. You guessed that Smith was a tall, broad man, and that guess was correct. I saw him a couple of times.' He gave a small laugh. 'When he was still alive, of course.'

Stanton fought the urge to call for Edgar's man. 'Always alive?'

'Yes, sir. Not, not like in that forge.' Lindley brought a hand to his forehead. 'That terrible place. I dreamed of it last night. That poor man. In life, I saw him around his cottage, his forge. Perfectly hale.' He bit his lip. 'When I was living in the woods as a beggar. I would try and see if there were any food scraps around the village.'

'You mean steal?'

'Is it theft to raid a bird's nest in the Smiths' thatch, sir?' Lindley shrugged. 'But I did hear him arguing once with his daughter.' His hand slid to his cheek. 'Agnes. I couldn't quite hear what it was about, but they were both very angry.'

Stanton shook his head at the man's clumsy attempt to push suspicion on to Agnes. The girl's grief at her loss was in no doubt. 'Many people argue, Lindley, especially in their own homes. It's their own business and it should stay there. Folk don't expect somebody to be hanging off the roof, listening.'

Lindley's look darkened. 'No.'

The sudden shift in his demeanour had Stanton quickly glance at the door. Three paces. That was all.

Yet when he looked back, Lindley's face was earnest again. 'I mean, no, sir. As I keep saying, I know nothing of the murder. Nothing whatsoever. I've been begging here. That's all.'

Earnest enough for Stanton to ask, 'Were you out looking for food the night Smith was killed? Is there anything you might have seen?'

'No, sir. It was a miserable night. Pouring with rain on and off. I was in my little shelter in the woods, though I was soaked through. My shelter wasn't really much of one. But it didn't matter. I was going to move on from Claresham anyway. The very next day. There was nothing for me here, you see.' His voice dropped. 'And then the villagers came for me, howling that I'd killed Smith. Seized me from my shelter. Set upon me. Dragged me before Edgar.' Dropped more. 'I kept saying I was innocent. Innocent. But everyone said I was guilty. Everyone. Then Edgar too. And he told me I'd hang.' A whisper. 'I've been waiting ever since for my fate.' Sobs broke from him.

Stanton shook his head. He couldn't imagine what that must be like.

'Then you came, sir.' To Stanton's mortification, Lindley fell to his knees. 'You were the first person to speak up for me.' He was sobbing harder now. 'The only one. You saw the truth, sir.' He raised clasped hands to Stanton. 'The truth, God bless you.'

'Stop, Lindley. Please.' Stanton didn't want this. The time when it had really counted, when it was right in front of him, he'd not seen the truth at all. 'My opinion doesn't count. Barling's does.' And the ordeal. But he wouldn't remind this wretch of that now. The day of searing metal, of agony, and then a wait of three days. That day would come soon enough.

'I'm sorry, sir. But you've given me hope.' Lindley sobbed on, his head bowed. 'Hope. God bless you.'

'I'll take my leave now, Lindley.' He doubted he'd get any more from the outlaw, who seemed lost in his own upset now. As he went to walk out, he saw that the small pail which held drinking water for the prisoner was almost empty. He paused to add to it from his own leather bottle. The man might not have long to live. Being plagued by thirst in this heat seemed an extra cruelty.

Stanton hadn't, as predicted by Barling, got any real answers from the man, who was in peril of being hanged; just more protesting from Lindley of his innocence.

Next, Stanton needed to try and find some from those who would do the hanging.

Chapter Fifteen

Stanton watched as the guard locked the prison door again, the sounds of Lindley's anguish now mercifully silenced by the thick walls.

The guard caught his eye. 'He's secure again. Sir.'

'My thanks,' said Stanton.

He got no reply save for a stiff nod from the guard, who set immediately off back to Edgar's service without a backward glance.

Stanton started after him along the track that led to the main street. He wouldn't catch the man up, not with his long, fast strides. He didn't want to, either. The guard's look at him had been as pitying as that of the robber who'd stood over him as he lay in the mud in York: *Fool.* Stanton pushed the memory away. Barling had ordered him to question Lindley, which he'd done. Next were the villagers.

As he turned on to the main thoroughfare, an empty street stretched out before him, front doors shut. He'd been a while with Lindley. People would already have set off for the fields and elsewhere – another sunny day like this one couldn't be wasted. Still, he had to try.

The first four cottages he went to sat shut and silent, despite him knocking more than once.

A dreadful tumbledown hovel came next. At least this door was ajar. Stanton went up to it, rapped with his knuckles. 'Hello?'

A quavering male voice answered. 'God ye keep.'

'I've come to ask you a few questions. May I come in?'

'God ye keep.'

Stanton peered round the door.

An ancient man, toothless and feeble, lay on a bed of dirty straw. 'God ye keep.'

'Good morning to you,' said Stanton. 'I'm the King's man. I have a few questions for you. About Geoffrey Smith.'

The man's eyes roamed, vacant and unknowing. 'God ye keep.'

No point in bothering this fellow. Stanton pulled his head back out. And started.

A high-pitched scream had rung out. A woman's. Not with an echo, like in the open air. But muffled, as if a woman cried out indoors. He looked left, right. Could see nothing.

Another scream.

'Hello?' His breath caught on the call as his heart jumped.

Silence answered him.

No. It couldn't be. Not again. He was too late, too late to help a woman in danger. 'Hello!'

Yet another scream. That went on and on.

'Where are you?' He broke into a run, looking left, right at the closed buildings.

Louder. It came from this one.

Stanton ran to the door. Pounded with his fist as hard as his heart banged in his chest. 'Open up, damn you! Open up!'

The door swung open.

A furious middle-aged woman, her sleeves rolled high on her arms, sweat coating her badly pockmarked face, glared at him. 'What is it?' She saw who it was and checked herself. Barely. 'Sir?'

Behind her, writhing on a straw bed, slumped a half-naked woman, huge belly quivering as she let out a scream as if from hell itself. 'Oh, God release me from this. Now!'

'Nothing.' Stanton backed away, his face hot. 'My mistake. Sorry.'

'Sir.' The midwife slammed the door in his face without waiting for an answer.

Stanton let out a long breath even as another shriek rose again from behind him. His foolishness would be all over the village by this evening, he'd no doubt of that. Another mistake to add to Barling's long list. He looked at the remaining cottages, tempted to turn his back on them and go and sit in Edgar's stables for the rest of the day with his beloved horse Morel. He might as well for all the good he was doing. At least Morel wouldn't laugh at him. But if Barling found him in there, it wouldn't be laughing he'd have to worry about.

Stanton squared his shoulders and went on to the next couple of doors. Still nothing.

Morel and the stables beckoned again.

He came to the last home, one set back from the road, with a separate sizeable, windowless building in its tidy grounds. As he walked up to the door, he heard clacking and soft thumping sounds from inside. They stopped at his sharp knock.

The door opened, to another woman of a similar age to the midwife. A drawn, sour face sat under a tight coif, from which not a single hair dared to escape. 'God save you.' Her voice matched her look.

'Good morrow, mistress.' He produced the smile he knew brought a flush to the cheeks of older women.

Not this woman.

'And you.' Her face didn't change.

Behind her, a man of her age sat behind a large loom, hunched over the half-woven cloth stretched before him. 'Who is it, Margaret?' His hands continued their steady work, the loom making a soft thump as it tightened the cloth.

Stanton raised his voice. 'It's Hugo Stanton. The King's man.'

'And what can we do for the King's man?' The man carried on with his work.

His wife folded her arms in a way that didn't suggest help, either.

'I wanted to ask you some questions,' said Stanton. 'About the murder of Geoffrey Smith.' He made his tone as firm as he could. 'And I'll need to have your name.'

The thump of the loom stopped. 'It's Peter Webb, sir.' The weaver rose from his loom with a stretch – as much as his stooped shoulders would allow – and exchanged a glance with his wife.

Her arms went tighter – her lips too.

Webb came to her side. His unsmiling look could be a mirror of hers. 'And this is my wife, Margaret.' No invitation to cross their threshold. 'You have questions, we'll answer them.'

'Did you see anything the night Geoffrey Smith was murdered?'

Both Webbs shook their heads as one.

'Sir Reginald asked the same question of us,' said Peter. 'Over and over. Our answer is the same to you, sir. We saw nothing.'

'Nothing at all?'

'It happened late at night,' said Webb. 'We'd been up working since the dawn, as we are every single day. First we knew was Agnes Smith's screams.'

'A different sort to usual, mind.' Margaret sniffed.

'Do you mean like when she was calling for Lindley to hang, mistress?' asked Stanton.

'No. I mean like when she's out with her latest man.' She shuddered. 'Worse than cats mating.'

'I see,' said Stanton. Though he didn't. That the obese thatcher Theaker could bring his betrothed to screaming ecstasy came as a surprise.

Webb gave a dour nod. 'A brazen, lustful girl. One that refused to contain her appetites. Geoffrey Smith would despair of her to me.'

Stanton didn't comment. Lindley had said he'd heard an argument between Agnes and her father. The outlaw must have spoken the truth about that.

'May God keep poor Geoffrey's soul,' said Margaret.

Another nod from Peter. 'I ran to help when the hue and cry was raised. It was a terrible sight in that forge, I can tell you.' His grey eyes met Stanton's. 'If you'd seen what I'd seen, you wouldn't think twice about stringing Lindley up. Believe you me.'

Stanton couldn't imagine and didn't want to. Without Smith's ruined body, the scene was bad enough. With it, it would've been horrific.

'Margaret!' A call came from up the street.

Stanton looked around. It was the midwife from earlier, looking worried.

She went on. 'I fear that the baby's turned. Can you come and help?'

'May I, Peter?' Margaret asked her husband.

'Have you finished with us, sir?' said Webb to Stanton.

'Yes, thank you,' said Stanton.

'Then you must do your duty to our neighbours, Margaret,' said Webb. 'Go and help Midwife Folkes.'

'Give me a few moments, Hilda,' called Margaret.

The midwife waved and hurried back to her charge as Margaret set about grabbing a shawl and putting clean linen into a basket.

'But I need to speak to others,' said Stanton. 'It's very quiet here in the village. Has everyone gone to the fields?'

'Yes,' replied Webb. 'They're all about their work, as all honest folk are. You'll have to go to the quarry too.' He pointed past Stanton's shoulder. 'It's over yon.'

'Excuse me.' Margaret stepped out past Stanton, then paused. 'Remember this: when you do find Agnes Smith, your questions won't get good answers. Like all whores, lies trip from her sinful tongue.' She didn't wait for a reply but started up the street.

'If you'll excuse me as well, sir.' Webb gestured to his loom. 'I'm behind in my work as it is.'

'Of course,' said Stanton. 'Good day to you.'

'And you, sir.' Webb shut the door as he spoke.

Above the lintel, a bird flew from the damaged thatch, startled by the noise.

Stanton wondered if Lindley had secretly climbed this thatch, as he had the Smiths', in his search for nests with eggs. If Lindley had, Stanton suspected he wouldn't have heard arguments.

Along the street, Margaret Webb had almost reached the cottage where the birth was taking place, her spotless white coif gleaming in the sun above her rigid shoulders, small clouds of dust puffing up from every one of her steps as she marched along. From inside came the regular clack and thump of Webb at his loom.

Both Webbs were united in their hard work and their hard virtue.

Just as they were united in their desire to hang Nicholas Lindley.

Chapter Sixteen

Stanton made his way along a deserted track that led back to the village from the farthest fields, the high bushes catching the heat of the afternoon sun but allowing little of the breeze to find its way down here. He shook his leather water bottle. Almost empty, curse it. He should have used Morel today, not done it all on foot. He'd had no idea that Sir Reginald Edgar's lands stretched so far.

True, the lord had boasted about them to Barling on the slow, dull ride to Claresham, but Stanton hadn't believed a word by then. Edgar's long, long list of his own achievements had overtaken even the King's, and still the lord had yammered on.

Had Stanton been a gambler like his fellow court messenger Nesbitt, he would have put money down that the bumbling bully Edgar's land claims were false.

Just as well Stanton didn't like a bet. Well, not much. He palmed the sweat from his face.

So many miles he'd walked today, for so many hours, asking the same questions over and over. Barling had said his, Stanton's, questions wouldn't matter. The clerk had been right.

Do you know anything about the murder of Geoffrey Smith? Did you see Nicholas Lindley that night? Did you see anything?

Asked first of the lone man working in the small quarry.

'No.' The stone hewer, a man who went by the name of Thomas Dene, with heavy muscles and sharp, handsome features that looked carved from stone too. 'No.' His answers were matched with a powerful strike of hammer on chisel, splitting a stone more easily than Stanton could split wood. 'No.'

Dust and powder filled the air, making Stanton's eyes sting and his lips and mouth dry. 'You're sure?'

'Sure.' Another hard strike.

'Did you hear anything that night?' The Webbs might have been long tucked up in bed. Maybe this man had still been awake.

'No.'

'Not even Agnes's screams?' Stanton frowned. 'Other folk in the village say she woke them up.'

'Don't live in the village.' Dene straightened up from his work, his full height a head and a half above Stanton. He raised a forearm to wipe his face, smearing the stone powder coating it. 'Not from here. I'm from the town of Hartleton, over thirty miles away. This is where I lay my head for now.' He nodded to a neat hut nearby made from rough-hewn planks. A circle of rocks next to it held the smoking remains of a fire, above which a metal pot swung from a tripod. 'I'm only here for a few weeks. The rector wants new stone for his church floor and that's almost finished. Wants a new mantel carved in his hall as well. Once that's done I'm off.' He bent to his work again. 'Shame what happened to that man Smith.' A blow that opened the stone as if it were pages of a Bible. 'But I didn't know him.'

Nothing from the quarry. Then nothing from the fields, either.

The many, many fields. Many faces and voices: young, old, men, women. A number, like the young ploughman driving the pair of plodding oxen, he recognised from the angry crowds in the village. Almost all, to his huge relief, were polite, even friendly. He got a couple of unexpected smiles.

The one exception was the ploughman Simon Caldbeck, the one who'd contained Agnes as she railed in the street. The man didn't even halt as he followed his lumbering ox across the fallow field, his wiry strength making the guiding of his animal and the control of the heavy plough look easy. His pointed features reminded Stanton of a watchful weasel as he gave his surly replies.

'No, I don't know what's going on here. And I don't care. I'm working to buy my release from this place.' He spat hard into the furrow next to him. 'The life of a poor villein is no life. Spending my life and my strength working Edgar's fields and putting food in the barn of that nephew of his. Soon as I get my chance, I'm off to a town. Have a real life.'

Stanton didn't respond. Though he wasn't here to hear Caldbeck's resentments, he could at least understand them. Stanton too was in the service of a man he despised. Instead, he asked about Geoffrey Smith. 'Did you hear or see anything the night he was killed?'

'Nothing at all. It was a pity about Geoffrey Smith all right. But I was no friend of his. And we all have to leave this life sometime, don't we?'

Yes, Caldbeck's remarks had been unusual but still boiled down to the same thing. No matter how it was said or who said it, the answers were still the same: *No. No. No.*

Stanton opened his water bottle, tipped his head back to get the last warm mouthful.

'Thirsty work, asking questions, is it?'

He looked round at the sound of the loud voice. Agnes Smith's voice.

She walked behind him on the sheltered path, long skirt moving with her strong stride. He didn't know how long she'd been there: the grassy path made her boots as silent as it did his.

'You could say that,' he said.

'I just did. Hugo.'

No 'sir' from her. He didn't expect it. 'You did.' He waited for her to catch him up.

'And did you get your answers? The ones that told you Nicholas Lindley was pure as snow?' Her face was flushed from the sun, and her linen shift hung open at the neck, showing smooth, white skin that he knew would taste sweet and warm.

Same as the skin on his beloved Rosamund's throat had the last time they'd lain together.

Stanton pushed the memory aside. And he wouldn't respond to Agnes's goad. 'I got answers.'

She walked beside him on the path now but didn't slow down, so he had to match her long stride. Her long hair fell without its usual springy curls and he could see that it was soaking wet. 'But not the ones you wanted. Good. I'll be right in front of Lindley when he's in the noose, watching until he takes his last cursed breath.'

As she turned to him with a humourless smile of triumph, her shift gaped more, and he glimpsed the swell of a breast. She saw his glance but made no move to close her clothing.

'Like what you see, do you?' she said.

His body did, his flesh surging hard and unbidden. He held her gaze now. He had to. 'You're promised to another, Agnes.'

'Promised with all my heart to another.' She gave an odd little sigh as she pulled her clothing to again. 'The man who killed my father is going to hang, isn't he? You can tell me.'

'I can tell you nothing. My enquiries are for mine and Barling's ears. Nobody else.'

'That fussy little clerk?' Agnes rolled her eyes. 'All robes and rolls and show. His mouth reminds me of my cat's rear end.'

Stanton tried to hold in his laugh. Couldn't. Her picture of Barling was too good. 'You can't say that about the King's clerk.' He shook his head. 'I've heard you were brazen. That's one correct answer I got.'

'Oh?' Her dark brows arched and her full lips pursed. 'Who says that about me, Hugo?'

'Never you mind.' She'd already wormed something out of him. He couldn't let her do it again.

'It was Margaret Webb, wasn't it?'

'No.' A relief to give this girl a truthful answer, though she'd come very close. Peter Webb had been the one to claim she was brazen.

'I know it was.' Agnes tossed her damp hair. 'The sour-faced old witch. She called me brazen the other day for wearing my hair loose. Calls me a whore too. All the time. She hates me for being young and not a dried-up husk like her. Suits me. I despise her and her nasty tongue.'

Stanton opened his water bottle again. Nothing left. He stuck it back in his belt.

'Looks like you're a dry one now as well, Hugo.'

He wouldn't bite. 'Have you got any water? I'm plagued with thirst.'

She shook her head. 'No. But there's the reed pond down this way. You can't drink from it, but you could use the water to cool off.'

'I should get back. Barling will be waiting for me.'

'Oh, not him again. Come on, Hugo. It'll only take a few minutes.' She ran her hand through her hair. 'I've been bathing. You'll feel much better if you can wet your face, if nothing else.'

'Show me, then.'

He followed her down the side path, even more overgrown than the one they'd been on.

Under his feet the path got boggier, despite the heat, and buzzing, whining flies thickened the air.

Ahead, he glimpsed the dull gleam of the still pond through thick leaves. A wide area to the right of the path had been cleared, with cut reeds tied in tight bundles and neatly stacked to dry out in the sun until they were ready for thatching.

'There you are.' Agnes held a hand out as she reached the edge of the pond. 'It's muddy. But it's cool and wet.'

Stanton didn't need telling twice. He knelt down at the pond edge, scooped water over his face and head. 'That's better.' He straightened up.

'Hugo.' Agnes's voice dropped. Not brazen now. At all. 'What's that?'

He stood up, following the pointing of her shaking finger. At the next curve of the pond, half-buried in the tall weeds, was what looked like a large man. Lying down. But face down. Arms and hands down. In the water.

'God's eyes.' Stanton set off at a run, Agnes behind him, a stupid idea in his head that he could save this fellow. But he knew, he already knew, from the stillness, the position, that this man was dead. Still, he had to try.

He dropped next to the body, breathing hard. The huge body. The obese body. He knew who it was. He looked up at Agnes.

She knew too. She stood there, eyes fixed on the corpse of her betrothed. Her hands went to her mouth.

'Bartholomew,' she whispered. 'No.'

'Wait, Agnes, wait.' A miracle, maybe a miracle. Stanton put his hands to the clothing that strained against the fat shoulders of Bartholomew Theaker and hauled. No good. He couldn't budge him. Not only was Theaker huge but his limbs had stiffened. He tugged at one shoulder instead, pulled, pushed, to turn the man's head over, to get his face out of the water.

Agnes hunkered down beside him. 'Get him out. For God's sake, get him out.'

Together they tugged, pulled.

And Theaker's body rolled, his face and one of his rigid arms out to the air.

'Saints protect us.' Stanton staggered back to his feet as Agnes sat down hard on the boggy ground.

Theaker's face might be out. But it was the face of one dead many hours, hours in which the blood had pooled into it as he lay head first in the water, his flabby rolls of skin now an obscene dark purple in colour.

'Oh, Bartholomew.' Agnes's lips had turned white in shock. 'To drown alone like this? If only you'd had somebody with you.'

Stanton steadied his breathing and bent to put a hand to her shoulder. 'Agnes, I'm so sorry. We can't help Theaker now, but we need to move him.' Stanton helped her to her feet. 'And we can't do it by ourselves. We need to fetch others.'

'You go. I'll stay with him.' Her voice was calm and her eyes held no tears.

Her reaction disturbed him. A short while ago, she had been proclaiming such love for the man she was promised to. 'I don't think that's wise.'

'You can think what you like.' She folded her arms. 'I'm staying. There's nothing for me to fear here.'

Stanton glanced down, looked away again, ashamed of his own revulsion. 'Then I'll be as quick as I can.'

He set off, forcing his tired legs to move as quickly as possible.

Before he turned the corner, he took a last glance back.

Agnes stood, her back to the body of her betrothed, staring silently out over the pond.

Stanton shook his head. A horrible tragedy for her so soon after her father's murder.

At least Stanton had been with her. Otherwise, she'd have found the body on her own. Maybe his day hadn't been such a waste after all.

He needed to alert Barling. At once.

Chapter Seventeen

Barling had known that asking questions of Sir Reginald Edgar was going to be problematic. What he had not appreciated was precisely how problematic.

First, the lord had not appeared out of bed for the entire morning. Nor the early afternoon.

Barling's earliest enquiry of the servants as to what time their lord might arise had been met with the response 'Well past Terce,' a time Barling believed to be disgracefully late as it was.

Their reaction had been one of surprise – surprise that Barling would even consider seeing Sir Reginald at such an hour.

For, it would seem, Edgar loved his bed almost as much as he loved his wine. His love of wine being, quite literally, beyond measure meant that Edgar's attachment to his bed approximated that of a limpet to a rock.

The servants did not neglect Barling. Not in the least. But his irritation with them grew as the sun rose to its height in yet another cloudless sky. Grew still further as it began its long, slow descent once more and still Edgar had not appeared. He did not require bread, nor ale, nor cheese.

What he required was Sir Reginald Edgar.

He was sorely tempted to ask the servants why, if they had so much spare time, the hall was in such disarray. Daylight had brought an even more unforgiving eye on the contents of the hall. Dirty rushes were scattered with bits of food and discarded bones. A torn tapestry hung off one wall. Knife marks scarred the tabletop. While the padded chair he sat in was reasonably comfortable, its tapestry cover was full of holes and shiny with grease.

With his papers spread before him, Barling whiled away the time by reading one of his law tracts. Under normal circumstances, this would have given him the greatest of pleasure. But in these circumstances it was not even tolerable. For the joy of reading the law was to lose oneself in it, to apply one's full concentration to its complexity, its detail. Thinking that every footstep, every door opening might be Edgar, breaking off to check and then find yet again it was not, meant Barling ended up rereading through the same few pages in frustrating repetition.

When one of the finer points of inheritance claims was quite spoiled by an enquiry about an apple, Barling rose to his feet, about to go and sit in the lord's solar if need be.

Then Edgar walked in, wearing a loose, grubby tunic over his linens. 'Barling,' he said. 'Sit, sit. No need to get up.' The lord already had a goblet in his hand.

Barling sat back down. He should be pleased, or at least relieved, that Edgar had finally appeared. Not so. As well as the goblet, Edgar still wore the swollen face and high colour of last night's excess at the table. 'I trust you have slept well.'

Edgar placed the goblet on the table and flung himself into a chair opposite Barling. 'As well as can be expected.' He stretched, grimaced. 'I swear that long journey yesterday made me ill.' He brought a hand to the top of his head. Grimaced again. 'The sun on my head all day. It beats like a drum. You know how it can be.'

'Indeed I do.' Barling did, though he did not mean the sun. He'd not touched wine, the real source of Edgar's bad head, for many years, but he recalled full well how it could leave one pleading for dark and quiet. And more. 'Yet I hope that you are sufficiently well to answer my questions.'

A couple of servants hurried in, slovenly as their lord, bearing trays of bread, fruit and meats. Another bore a large chipped jug of wine.

'Questions about what?' Edgar rubbed his forehead with a meaty hand.

The servants set about laying their items in front of Edgar.

'The murder of Geoffrey Smith. As I said I would do.'

Edgar rolled his bloodshot eyes, ignoring the servants as they finished with quick bows and left. 'I already answered your friends in York, Barling.'

Barling's mouth tightened at the casual description of the King's esteemed justices. He would not respond lest he get deflected. 'I fully appreciate that, Edgar. But' – he gestured to his papers – 'I need to have the full record. For completeness.'

Edgar grunted, stabbing at a large piece of venison with his eating knife. 'Go on, then.'

'Firstly, I have already written up everything you said to the justices in York.'

'When?' Edgar stared at him, chewing. 'On the back of the horse yesterday?'

'No, last night. In my solar.'

'That was a jest, Barling.' Edgar reached for his goblet.

'Ah, of course it was.' Barling decided not to trouble himself with a laugh as Edgar drained his wine. 'So I have a record of what you said before de Glanville and his fellow justices.'

'Good.' Edgar reached for the jug and poured a fresh cup.

'Do you have any idea why Lindley would want Geoffrey Smith dead?'

'No.' He drank deep.

'What kind of a man was Geoffrey Smith?'

'What do you think?' He filled another cup as he spoke. 'He worked the forge, shoed my horses. Made and mended my ploughshares and my tools and knives. Did the same for other people, rich and poor. We all need iron.' He belched. 'Even you. Like for your ordeal.'

Barling itched to berate the lord for his rude, unhelpful reply. But it would not help matters. 'I mean more, what manner of a man was he?'

'A freeman.' Edgar shrugged. 'Always paid his rent on time.' Drank again.

'I mean rather his temperament. Was he a man who favoured strife? Or was he one that lived in harmony with his fellow man?'

'He seemed pleasant enough. Not a troublemaker, at least not to me. I never heard that he was.' Edgar shrugged. 'Beyond that, who knows?'

'Would Lindley have had any reason to attack him?'

'How should I know what's in Timothy Lindley's head?'

'Nicholas.'

'Eh?'

'The outlaw's name is Nicholas. Nicholas Lindley. Not Timothy.'

Edgar rolled his eyes. 'Timothy, Nicholas. Whatever the man's name is.'

Barling tried to get him back on track. 'Can you think of any reason why Lindley would murder your smith? And in so brutal a manner?'

'It was brutal, you know.' Edgar sucked down another deep draught, then gave a sage nod.

Barling's knuckles tightened. 'Yes, you said.'

The man rapidly was getting drunk again. If he ever truly sobered. Barling was beginning to understand only too clearly why the hall was in such poor order. Edgar had given himself over completely to the sin of gluttony, caring for wine and food and nothing else.

'Brutal!' said Edgar. 'That's why we need to get rid of him soon as we can.' He reached for the jug again, much cheerier in his look. 'Like I said in York. Justice should be swift. Strong as well. I even think—'

A commotion came from the door.

'What in God's blood is that?' said Edgar.

'Barling, where's Barling?' came Stanton's voice, raised in his agitation. 'I need to find the King's clerk. Now.'

He appeared at the door, breathless, dishevelled.

Barling frowned. 'Stanton, what on earth—?'

'Sir, there's been a horrible accident. Bartholomew Theaker has drowned.'

Chapter Eighteen

The progress to the reed bed was slower than Barling would have liked. He was only too aware that his own pace was nowhere as swift as Stanton's. And as always with those of younger years, Stanton seemed less bothered by the searing summer heat. Barling's entire body was coated with sweat, and he had to wipe at his face repeatedly with his kerchief.

At least his complete humiliation was saved by two things.

First, a couple of servants accompanied them as well, leading a placid horse that drew a cart for transporting Theaker's body. The bumpy track limited their speed.

Second, Sir Reginald Edgar had climbed into the cart, loudly proclaiming he had to do so because of the heat.

Barling doubted anyone would notice his own lack of pace in such circumstances. He had tried to leave the nuisance behind at the hall, but Edgar had insisted.

'It's just here, sir.' Stanton pointed ahead.

They rounded the corner and the whole sorry tableau came into view, lit by the setting sun.

Theaker, on the ground, his large limbs in the contortions of death.

Agnes stood near the body. But not with it.

'You have come for my betrothed,' said Agnes. 'Thank you.'

Dry-eyed, noted Barling. The girl would naturally be very shocked. Upset. Yet while her appearance would suggest the former, it did not convey the latter.

The servants with the cart stopped at a respectful distance, crossing themselves at the sight as Edgar clambered out in clumsy movements.

'God's eyes.' Edgar stared at the corpse but made no move towards it. He clicked his fingers to the servants. 'Get Theaker on the cart.'

'Wait.' Barling raised a hand, halting them. 'I wish to examine the body first.' He matched his steps with his actions, ignoring Edgar's stream of enquiries. He knelt down on the coarse, boggy grass. The flies had already found Theaker, and Barling swatted at them to no avail as he examined the blood-suffused face of the dead man.

He looked up to where Stanton stood nearby. 'You say he was face down in the water, Stanton?'

'He was, yes. Right next to where he lies. Agnes and I moved him to see if we might have saved him, turned him over.' Stanton glanced over to the girl for confirmation, but she didn't respond. 'But it was far too late.'

'I see.' Barling's gaze went to the pond's edge, then moved along the dead man, finishing at his feet. He beckoned to Stanton and the servants. 'Help me turn him over again.'

They did as ordered, though with expressions of surprise.

Edgar hung back. 'Have you lost your mind, Barling?'

Barling ignored him, concentrating on easing Theaker's hooded jerkin away from the back of his neck. And there he found what he suspected. So much for Edgar's prating on about how murder was the rarest occurrence in this place. 'Theaker's drowning has been no accident. He has been murdered.'

'What?' Edgar's roar drowned out the other exclamations of shock. The lord marched over. 'What are you talking about? This is nonsense, utter nonsense.'

'I offer you my sympathies, Agnes, on this terrible loss,' said Barling. She had her hand to her mouth, staring. Still she had no tears.

'Barling,' began Edgar, 'I suggest you explain your wild imaginings—'

'Look.' Barling indicated the row of bruises on the back of Theaker's neck. 'Finger marks. Somebody held him down in the water.'

'Could those not be from before?' came Stanton's question. A considered one from the young man, surprising Barling.

'A remote possibility,' replied Barling. 'But look at the ground around his feet. It is kicked up in new clods. If Theaker had simply fallen or collapsed, the ground would not be churned up so. Theaker was engaged in a mighty struggle with the hand that held him under the water.'

Stanton nodded, his gaze still travelling over the scene as described by Barling.

Barling stood up, brushing off his hands from the unpleasant but necessary task.

Interesting. Stanton was paying very close attention.

Edgar was not. 'So who did this wicked act?' Questions, nonsense poured forth from the lord. 'Did anybody see it? God's eyes, this is an abomination! Was anybody here at the time? Theaker, imagine. Agnes, you'll be faint, won't you?'

Barling did not think for one moment that Agnes looked faint. She was far calmer than Edgar, who was still going. 'Who would think to do such a thing? Unless it was an accident. Might easily have been—'

'Edgar, Bartholomew Theaker was the thatcher of this village, was he not?' asked Barling.

'Why?' Edgar glowered at Barling. 'What's that got to do with anything?'

'It has to do with order. I want to record that I have the correct name and the correct person.'

'It's Theaker!' Edgar flung his hands up. 'My thatcher!'

'But his murder is now under my area of authority,' said Barling. 'I want to make sure I have his details recorded properly.'

'But you're here about Lindley, Barling. That's all!'

Barling had to hold his tongue. At least for now. Edgar's knowledge and administration of matters of the law were an astonishingly incompetent tangle. If the man was representative of how the law was applied across the country, no wonder the King had decided to impose uniformity and order. 'Agnes, you need to stay with Sir Reginald's servants while they move the body and go back to the lord's hall with them.'

She opened her mouth to protest, but Barling cut across her. 'No arguments. It is not safe to stay out here on your own. Stanton, I need you with me.'

'Yes, sir,' said Stanton.

'Where are you going, Barling?' said Edgar.

'I want to go to the gaol and speak to Nicholas Lindley.'

'Lindley?' Edgar scowled anew. 'Why?'

'Because he is already under suspicion for one murder. Now that there has been a second, a mere eleven days later, after none in living memory, there is the strongest possibility that the two are linked somehow.'

'I have rarely heard such bilge water. We need to hunt for this new killer. Immediately!'

'It is not bilge water.' He could not resist a small barb. 'It is how one investigates such matters, Edgar. Properly. Yet you are quite right about the hue and cry. Can I leave that in your capable hands?' A second barb.

The barbs landed. Edgar gave a snort of disgust. 'I still know more about this place than you, Barling. I am coming with you. I can spread the hue and cry as we go. Then lead me to my own gaol, why don't you?'

Barling did not respond as he set off. The lord was a complete oaf. He would make it his business to instruct him in matters of law for as long as he remained here, though it would likely be a thankless and ultimately futile task. 'Now come, Stanton.'

As they walked through the village to the gaol, the cries and laments for the murdered Theaker filled the cooling evening air as Edgar spread the news. People hurried from door to door with the shocking tidings, some appealing to Edgar, who did not hesitate to confirm it over and over, giving his answers with apparent relish as his pace slackened.

To one man: 'It's true. Theaker's dead. Murdered! A terrible act.'

To another: 'No, I cannot stop. But yes, Theaker's been murdered.'

To a knot of gossiping women at the well: 'The King's man has important work to do. No, not at the reed pond. Theaker was murdered there. But I have to go to the gaol. On the orders of the King's man, you understand.'

Barling would not slow a single step. 'Keep up, Stanton.'

'Sir.' Stanton hurried alongside him.

Barling would not respond to Edgar's crude public jibes, either. For they pleased him, showing him that Edgar was acknowledging his authority. Showing him also how annoyed the boorish Edgar was by that. Barling allowed himself a little smile. It was down to Edgar's lack of competence that he, Barling, had had to leave the court for the churn and chaos of Edgar's lands. Bringing Edgar to heel with order gave him a deep satisfaction.

They had reached the gaol.

'The key please, Edgar,' said Barling. 'I pray your sun-sore head has not had you forget it.'

'I haven't forgotten what a waste of time this is,' said Edgar, producing the key on a belt loop.

'I hope you will see in due course, my lord, that an ordered approach is never a waste of time.' Barling nodded to Stanton. 'Be ready to escort Lindley elsewhere if need be.'

'Yes, sir.'

Edgar banged on the door. 'Back, Lindley! Stay away from the door.'

Barling folded his hands, his first questions for the outlaw ready in his mind.

Edgar unlocked the door and wrenched it open.

Stanton gasped.

And every single question deserted Barling.

For the gaol sat empty. Deserted.

Nicholas Lindley was gone.

Chapter Nineteen

It can't be. It simply can't be.

Stanton willed the sight to change. The small window gaped, bare of its iron bars, the stone surround hacked in the fresh cuts that had freed them. But it didn't change. Broken stone, scattered metal. An empty gaol. And the bellow of rage from Edgar told him it wasn't going to.

'What?' The lord's voice echoed in the small, stale room. 'What in the name of Christendom has happened?'

'It would appear' – Barling moved to the window, his tone calm but clipped – 'that Lindley has escaped.' He leaned out through the window.

'I can see that!' Another roar. 'God's blood, I can see it!'

Blood. Like the blood of Bartholomew Theaker, pooling in his dead face to give it a hideous, darkened hue. The heat of shame prickled every inch of Stanton's body. He'd been shocked when Barling had established that the luckless Theaker had been murdered. Yet relieved too. Relief that he, Stanton, had spoken up for a wrongly accused man, just as he had before. Lindley's pleas had been the truth. But now? Dread close to sickness gathered in his guts.

Barling drew his head back from the damaged window and looked at him. 'Push that door open as wide as you can.'

Stanton went to comply, but Edgar shoved past him and booted the door so hard it bounced on its hinges. 'There! Is that open enough for you? Would you also like me to remove the roof?'

Barling ignored him and hunkered down to peer at the floor beneath the window in the better light, sifting through the debris on the ground with his fingers.

'I'll give you your link between the murders, Barling.' Edgar snorted in disgust. 'Lindley's done them both. He'll be miles away by now.' He eyeballed Stanton. 'Thanks to your foolishness, warbling on about Smith's height.'

'I'm so sorry, Sir Reginald,' said Stanton. 'I swear to you I never—'

'Edgar, you need to guard your tongue.' Barling's reply came brittle as ice. 'Now. I remind you to whom you speak.' He rose to his feet, dusting off his hands. 'I believe Lindley had help from outside. Most likely somebody from within your village.'

'My village?' The veins stood out on Edgar's meaty face. 'You're saying Lindley had help from the folk who live here?'

'Yes,' said Barling. 'Judging from the way that the stone and dust have fallen, it would appear that Lindley used a hammer or similar to work his way out. Somebody has passed such an implement in through the bars.'

Stanton expected Edgar to share his own surprise. But the man just laughed. Laughed. Then his smile dropped.

'And what about the forge?' said Edgar.

'What of the forge, Edgar?' said Barling.

'Lindley ended up on the floor. This man here' – he jabbed a finger at Stanton – 'your man, was gazing around him. Thinking about things that didn't matter. At all.' He raised a clenched fist.

Stanton stepped back in spite of himself.

Edgar went on. 'Who's to say what Lindley did? That forge was full of tools scattered around after Geoffrey Smith's struggle. It would have been the work of a second for that evil man to conceal one in his clothing, then use it later.'

Stanton's chest tightened. *No.* 'No, my lord, I watched him, I swear.' His appeal was as much to himself as to the other two men. He'd missed something. Missed it. And an innocent life was lost. *It has happened again.*

Barling's mouth became a thin line. 'Yours is a ridiculous assertion, Edgar.'

'Oh, is it now?' said Edgar. 'Then explain to me how Nicholas Lindley was locked up in here for eleven days, completely secure. No *friend* – he sneered the word – 'appeared at his window to give him a tool that would allow him to break his way out.' His glower fixed on Stanton. 'Unless you, Stanton, were such a friend. You came to see him this morning. Alone! My servant told me, told me that he waited outside. Did you give Lindley the means to get out?'

'My lord, I can only swear—'

Barling cut him off with a raised hand.

Stanton tensed, expecting the clerk's anger. But no. Barling rounded instead on the lord.

'Edgar, that is enough,' said the clerk. 'I should not need to remind you that accusing Stanton, the King's man, of such an act is dangerous – dangerous for you.'

Barling's defence of him surprised Stanton as much as it infuriated Edgar.

'Then I bow to Hugo Stanton's greatness.' Edgar matched his mocking words with a rude bob of a bow. 'But I am in no danger by stating this: until you two set foot here, all was well. I was dealing with everything. Everything.'

'I am not yet in a position to explain anything, Edgar,' said Barling. 'Stanton and I have many more enquiries to make, especially now that Lindley has escaped. I suggest that your priority is to hunt Lindley down.'

Outside, the church bell began to toll.

'I suggest that the priority for me and my people is to bury the unfortunate Bartholomew Theaker and pray for his soul. Lindley was in that gaol alone since early this morning. He'll be miles away by now. You make all the enquiries you want.' He marched to the door. 'You have released a monster. May it be forever on your conscience. Both of yours.' He kicked the door again on his way past.

For once even Barling was silenced.

As for Stanton, he couldn't trust speech, not at this moment.

You have released a monster.

Chapter Twenty

Barling entered his solar, a very subdued-looking Stanton following him.

The quiet came as a merciful release after the commotion at the gaol, on the street, where Lindley's escape, Theaker's murder and Edgar's wild accusations against the King's men had all received loud, public airings. It was intolerable. One could not think in such circumstances. A clear mind was necessary to consider such a grave turn of events. Not that Barling would get much quiet until Stanton left.

'On my life, sir.' Stanton didn't wait for Barling to give him permission to speak as he closed the door behind them, ensuring privacy. 'I don't know how Lindley got out. I didn't do anything. He was in there when I left. I swear to you.'

'Calm yourself, Stanton.' Barling walked to his desk and sat down. 'You are beginning to sound like Edgar.'

'Sorry, sir.' Stanton steadied his breath.

'As I said in the gaol, it is clear Lindley had help. As I also said, I know full well that you had nothing to do with it. Now sit down and tell me what you have found so far in your enquiries. You and I have not yet had the chance to speak.' He picked up a stylus. 'Now is the time to start.'

'I thought that my questions were useless, sir. For appearances only.'

Though Stanton's was a sharp response, Barling almost smiled. He'd been correct in his recent observations of the messenger. The young man did have something between his ears, after all.

'That is indeed what I said, Stanton. But it is clear from your remarks that you have more wits than you have ever bothered to use.' He pointed at the chair. 'Now sit. The facts that you have found, Stanton, please, and nothing more. Emotions add little and can cloud a proper examination.'

Stanton lowered himself into the chair, obviously glad to be off his feet, but he gave Barling a deeply wary look. 'When I found Theaker—' he began.

'Stop.'

'I don't understand, sir. You told me to tell you what I've found.'

'Start at the start of your account, Stanton. Always the start. To start in the middle means things get forgotten.' He tapped the stylus on his tablet. 'Overlooked. So, the start.'

'From when I left you this morning, sir?'

'That would be a good place, would it not?'

'Well, I started with Lindley.' Stanton went through what he had asked Lindley and the man's answers, Barling asking him to be clearer at first, but Stanton quickly improving as he went on. 'And Lindley still said he was innocent, sir, crying, thanking me for believing him.' Stanton shook his head. 'He fooled me, sir. Completely fooled me.'

'You could look at it a different way: that an accomplished liar practised his arts on you. Many men are skilled in it.'

'And women, sir. Women too.' Stanton's abrupt, forceful reply took him by surprise. 'I'm sorry, sir.' Stanton rubbed at his eyes. 'I'm angry at myself. He . . . he seemed so genuine.' He gave a short, bitter laugh. 'I actually felt sorry for him. Not any more. Not after seeing Theaker.'

'We shall come to Theaker in a moment. Where did you go after speaking to Lindley?'

'Most cottages were deserted by then. People were at the fields. I found an old man without sense, a woman closed away in a birth. She had a midwife with her, name of Hilda Folkes.' He went red and would not meet Barling's eye for a second. 'I called there by mistake, but it wasn't really the time to ask questions.'

'No.'

'But then I went to the Webbs', sir.'

'The Webbs?'

'Yes, sir. Peter Webb's a weaver and his wife does spinning. They're both very respectable. Very stern. But it was just like Edgar told you. Both of the Webbs said they knew nothing about Geoffrey Smith's murder.'

'So you gleaned nothing from them.'

'No.'

'You sound unsure.'

'Nothing except that they don't like Agnes Smith. Especially Margaret. And, if you'll pardon me for going out of order, Agnes despises Margaret. She told me so herself. Right before we found Theaker's body.'

'In what way do they not like each other?'

'Peter Webb said Agnes was brazen. Margaret thinks Agnes is a whore. Agnes says Margaret is a dried-up old witch with a nasty tongue.'

'Goodness.' Barling made another note.

'Peter did help with one thing, though. He mentioned a quarry. I didn't know about it. I was only going to go to the fields to find people. There's a stonecutter, Thomas Dene, living and working there at the moment. He's not from the village. He usually lives in a town called Hartleton. About thirty miles away, he says. He's been here in Claresham doing work for the rector Osmond's church and hall.'

'I know of Hartleton, though I have not personally visited it. A town of modest size and of good repute, I believe.' Barling made a note. 'And as Dene hails from there, it makes him another outsider. Does he have any passionate opinions about the Webbs or Agnes Smith, or they of him?'

Stanton shook his head. 'Not at all, sir. He was a man of very few words. But he was clear that he heard nothing of Geoffrey Smith's murder.'

'Where did you go next?'

'The fields. Nothing different from anybody there either. Except from Simon Caldbeck, the young ploughman. The man that brought Agnes under control in the street.'

'Yes, I recall him.'

'Well, he doesn't like Edgar or the rector Osmond. He's trying to get released from here.'

'Hardly the picture Edgar painted of a harmonious Claresham.'

'No. I was on my way back from the fields when I met Agnes.'

'Had she not been out working in them?'

'No, sir. She'd been off bathing somewhere. I was out of water in my bottle. She showed me where the reed pond was, where I could cool off.'

'Did you discuss anything of importance?'

'Um, no, sir.' Stanton's gaze flicked to Barling's mouth and away again in an instant. 'Not of any importance. A lot more from her about how Lindley should hang, same as she was saying when we brought Lindley to the forge. And then we got to the pond.' He swallowed. 'Found Theaker's body. Face down in the water. It was bad enough finding him like that, but at least I thought it was an accident. Then your finding out it was murder. God's eyes. And the worst part, I still feel it's my fault.' He looked sheepish. 'No, the worst part was I was relieved. A bit. I thought that it meant Lindley was innocent, after all. I was wrong. I thought about riding out tonight, trying to find him. But what good would that do? I wouldn't even know which direction to set off in.'

'Precisely. Rushing around without a fixed plan helps nobody, Stanton. Again, you need to use your wits. But Lindley must be brought to justice, and it is my – indeed, our – responsibility to do so. That is what you must give your attention to. Lindley may have run from here. But everybody leaves a path. And exactly as with looking at events, it is the same with a path. We find its beginning and we follow it.'

'We?' Stanton's appalled question matched his expression.

'Yes, we. I have no intention of travelling in these woods alone, especially with the likes of Lindley potentially on the loose. Our path may have many turns and false lanes, but it will lead us to where we want to be. We will start our own search tomorrow. Start with Lindley's shelter in the woods. I want to view the reed pond again too. Now, go and get some sleep, Stanton. Remember to pray for Theaker's soul tonight.'

'Yes, sir.' Stanton rose and went to the door. 'And if I may suggest it, we should do the search on horseback, as Edgar's lands stretch out a long way in every direction.'

Horseback again. Barling sighed inside but nodded. 'Very well.'

'Goodnight, sir.'

'Goodnight.'

As the door closed behind Stanton, Barling stretched his arms and eased out his shoulders. A long day, but only one. So much had happened that it felt much longer.

He looked through the items he'd recorded, both from tonight as well as previously.

To *Lindley swears he is innocent*, Barling had added, *Lindley also still swears he is innocent to H.S. Lindley – no proof of innocence – ordeal?* He sighed as he added, *Lindley has escaped.* He was not Sir Reginald Edgar, so he did not write that a monster had been released by him, Barling, and Hugo Stanton.

Instead he wrote, *No witnesses. Again.* At least, none that could be found.

His earlier note stared up at him.

Why would Nicholas Lindley want Geoffrey Smith dead?

Under it he wrote:

Why would Nicholas Lindley want Bartholomew Theaker dead?

Barling shook his head. He did not think for one moment that he or Stanton was responsible for Lindley's escape. Lindley was: he was the one who had found a way out of the gaol. However, Edgar, as well as many people in Claresham, clearly believed the King's men were blameworthy. Were angry, upset and more.

Emotion. Always emotion. He sighed again.

Truth be told, he had been very surprised by the discovery of the empty gaol. Shocked to the core, in fact. But justice could not be done by having hysterics. Dispassionate enquiry always served the truth best. He poured himself a cup of water, warm as his own blood in the heat of the night. The burden of justice had become much heavier today. Like so much in his life, he would shoulder it without complaint.

He had no other path.

Chapter Twenty-One

Though the day promised to again be very hot, the morning held a slight freshness, much to Barling's relief.

But as his horse broke into a fast trot to match Stanton's, he rapidly became overheated once again as he fought to keep his balance. 'I would like. To view the reed pond again, Stanton.' By the Virgin, his speech bounced as much as he did.

'Of course, sir.'

The younger man might as well be sat on one of Edgar's padded chairs. He seemed so at home on a horse, unlike Barling. Given any say in the matter, Barling would prefer to walk, or ride in a litter, or take a barge, as he liked to do in his beloved London. All were steadier, more pleasing ways of getting about. Horses needed constant watching, were given to sudden fits of unpredictable behaviour. Yet sat astride a horse he was yet again.

'The reed pond it is, sir.' Stanton pointed to a track that branched from the main street. 'It's down that way.'

'Stanton, I am giving you permission to call me by my name.' Barling had thought about this for a good while after Stanton left last night. 'If you always call me "sir", then you will be viewed in less regard. I do not want people to view you as some sort of servant.'

Dismay would probably sum up Stanton's reaction. He nodded, looking as if he would rather never utter another word.

'While we are making our way there,' said Barling, 'show me every place within Claresham that you now know of, or any of which you have heard.'

'May I ask why, si— Barling?'

'You heard me mention connections to Edgar, how the murders may be linked. When looking into a murder, into any crime, it is not only the people who are linked. Places often are too. One should look at all different elements together, separately and in combination. You have already been out and about more than me, so you can pass that knowledge on.'

'I see.' Stanton raised a hand and began indicating the different homes and buildings and which patches of land were worked by whom.

Barling nodded in approval at Stanton's sharp memory.

The younger man's pace slowed as they approached the reed pond, and his gaze darted everywhere.

'Is there something amiss?' asked Barling.

'I'm a bit bothered that Lindley might still be around. And I can't believe I left Agnes alone here yesterday. Anything could have happened to her.'

'You did not know at the time that it was murder. There are two of us here, Stanton. We have fast horses at our disposal. Even if Lindley were here, those would be foolish odds. We shall remain vigilant. If there is any cause for concern, we ride away and raise the alarm.'

They dismounted, Stanton with ease and Barling taking great care not to end up in an undignified heap on the ground. He looked over the still pond, then led the way to where the body had lain.

A few crushed plants. Patches of churned-up grass. Water lapping against a bit of the bank that had crumbled in. Nothing more to suggest this was where a man met his violent, untimely death.

'Looking at it now,' said Stanton, 'I find it hard to believe it happened.' He shuddered. 'But it did.'

'A peaceful place indeed. Or rather should be.' Barling's gaze swept around the pond.

'But also a quiet place.' Stanton still appeared on edge. 'Maybe Lindley was hiding out here and Theaker disturbed him.'

'Perhaps.'

The reeds that Theaker had cut over many weeks sat stacked a few yards away, drying in the sun.

'We need to check over there, Stanton.' Barling led the way to them, his horse's reins firm in one hand. He did not expect to find anything. The stacks were low and tightly packed. Reeds did not have the softness, warmth or concealing qualities of hay.

'All down to Theaker's hard work,' said Stanton. 'And now he'll know none of it. A shame.'

'As he will never have his betrothed, Agnes, as his wife.'

'I wonder how she is,' said Stanton. 'She seemed to go into a sort of walking faint yesterday.'

'She did. Time to move on from here.' Barling put a foot in one stirrup, prepared to mount.

'Her heart must be broken, mustn't it?' Stanton was already back in the saddle. 'First her father, now Theaker. Poor Agnes.'

'You make a good point about Agnes Smith.' Barling was up too, though with a struggle that had him huffing with effort.

'That she must be heartbroken?' replied Stanton. 'I think most folk would guess that.'

'No, your good point is a link. Lindley may have some sort of a grudge against Agnes's family.'

They set off once more.

'But Theaker wasn't Agnes's family,' said Stanton. 'At least, not yet.'

'Links are not always the full answer. But they may lead to it. Now we must proceed to examine Lindley's shelter in the woods, the one he told you about.'

'I'm not entirely sure where it is.'

'Then once we find it,' said Barling, 'we will be.'

Stanton merely nodded.

'And, in answer to the question that I know is on your lips,' said Barling, 'no, I do not believe for one moment that Lindley will still be there.'

Chapter Twenty-Two

'That must be the shelter.' Stanton kept his murmur low. 'There. Through the trees.'

'There is no need to whisper, Stanton.' Barling rode past him in an unstable trot. 'Follow me.'

'Yes, sir,' mouthed Stanton at his back. Barling's remarks about him, Stanton, having quick wits had been unexpected and pleased him to a depth that surprised him. But, God in heaven, why had Barling decided that Stanton should call him by his name? It was bad enough to have to do it, but the way Barling's face stiffened every time Stanton did so suggested the clerk disliked it as much as it made Stanton uneasy.

Stanton dismounted and secured Morel to a tree, with a quick pat to her sweating neck and a swipe at the worst flies that buzzed into her patient face.

Ahead, Barling climbed from his horse much as a man would climb down a flight of steep, icy stone steps: stiff, cautious movements and then a final awkward slide.

Stanton would bet Agnes would find it funny. He checked himself. She wouldn't be finding much amusing for a long time. It had been bad enough for him seeing Theaker's body. But he barely knew the man. For Agnes, Bartholomew Theaker was the man she'd been going to marry. Before the outlaw who'd lived in that shelter up ahead decided otherwise.

He joined Barling and they walked up to the shelter together, a sense that they were being watched tugging at him.

'Lindley was telling the truth when he described his shelter,' said Stanton, voice low. 'He said it was poor.'

'Poor does not even properly capture it,' replied Barling quietly. 'It is only a few green branches heaped together.'

Keeping at a safe distance lest its murderous owner had returned, Stanton crouched down to look inside. 'There's a pile of dry leaves in there. A few rags. Eggshells.' He straightened up. 'It's wretched.'

'Wretched indeed.' Barling's face changed. 'Did you hear that, Stanton?'

He did. His heart leapt into a fast beat.

A rustle in the bushes. Steady, definite. Something was moving through them.

Or someone.

Barling gave a silent point, his pale face even paler. A nod. A gesture.

Stanton returned it, showed he understood that Barling wanted them to close in on it. He wished he didn't.

He fell in alongside Barling, sweat trickling down his back. Lindley had taken down the tall Smith, the obese Theaker. Barling might be able to scare at will, but he was a small man.

The movement in the bushes was closer now.

Stanton prayed for a deer, a fox. Even a wild boar. Just not Nicholas Lindley armed with an axe or a knife.

Then came a sound. Short. Almost a bark. But human.

Stanton swapped a wordless, startled look with Barling.

Then the sound again and again, and a creature burst forth from the bushes, the noise coming from an open mouth.

'God's eyes!' Stanton recoiled, yanking Barling back with him.

But what a mouth. The lips were flabby, wet, and a large tongue lolled from it. The creature itself wasn't as tall as Barling, but heavily muscled, with a shock of dark hair. Yet it was no creature.

'Saints preserve us, it's a wild man!'

Stanton saw it even as Barling said it. Yes, it was a man. Barefooted. Muddied face. Dressed in a worn, dirty jerkin. One dark eye was half turned in on itself, the other was big, half bulging from its socket.

The man made a sort of gargle. Peered at them as he swayed from foot to foot, his hands raised and tugging at his own hair.

'I think he's going to attack.' Stanton gave a sharp whisper. 'We need to rush him first.' He wished so hard at that second that he was a competent fighting man.

A horrified whisper back. 'Both?'

'Yes.'

'Now?' Still horrified.

'Now.' Stanton raced towards the wild man, yelling as he left his feet and crashed into the man's chest.

The man staggered back with a bellow and a swipe.

Barling grabbed at his arm but was sent sprawling with a cry.

Stanton slammed into the man again, locking his double-handed grip on one powerful wrist and twisting it up behind the man's back to loud roars. The man landed a kick on Stanton's knee.

Pain shot through it and Stanton staggered, but he got one foot behind the wild man's legs, sending him to the ground. The man flailed and yelled, but Stanton was on his chest, pinning him down.

A shaken Barling was back on his feet. 'My belt, here.' Barling had it looped at one end.

The man hollered still more as Stanton got his hands secure.

Stanton stood up and dragged him upright, the man's yells sending a spray of spit in his face from that loose, huge tongue.

'Where to now, Barling?'

116

If Lindley had smelled bad from the gaol, their captive was much, much worse.

'Back to Edgar's hall.' The King's clerk gave a tight nod. The sweat pebbling his face showed how unused he was to this. But Barling would never admit weakness of any kind. 'I want to hear Sir Reginald Edgar's excuse for not having this dangerous man in his gaol.' Barling paused to drag in a steadying breath. 'A man who may well have killed Geoffrey Smith and Bartholomew Theaker.'

Chapter Twenty-Three

'Not long to go now, Stanton.'

They'd cut through the woods to get to Edgar's hall, as it would get them there faster. They needed speed; the man wouldn't be contained much longer.

'Just as well.' Shoulders straining, Stanton looked down from his horse.

The wild man stumbled and yelled alongside, secured to the saddle with a length of rope. Keeping Morel steady was a challenge. The noise and movement beside her made her nervous. If she bolted, the man would be dragged and trampled.

'With me, Stanton.' Barling climbed from his horse, and Stanton did the same.

He released their prisoner from the saddle, leaving the man's hands bound, even as he twisted and fought in Stanton's grasp. The man's strange shouts could now be a bull locked in a barn.

Stanton cursed silently as he got another kick. He could do with Barling's help, but the clerk stayed well out of reach.

As they entered the hall, Edgar glanced up from his place at the head of his messy, laden midday table, his face a red mask even at this hour from plenty of wine. His mouth fell open.

'What the devil's going on, Barling?'

'What is going on, Edgar' – Barling had to raise his voice over the prisoner's noises as Stanton grappled with him – 'is that I have spent a few short hours properly investigating matters. And in that time I have already managed to find and secure this unholy and dangerous creature.'

Edgar bit at the large lump of meat on his eating knife, looked at the man, looked back at Barling. And smirked. 'What you and your assistant have managed to find, Barling, is John Webb.'

'John Webb?' the clerk repeated.

Stanton felt sorry for Barling. Well, almost. Although Barling had started to grudgingly acknowledge that Stanton might have sharp wits, the clerk had made him feel boneheaded enough times. To see Barling in the same position was quite a sight.

'The very one.' Edgar spat out a piece of gristle to join others strewn across the floor. 'Only son of Peter and Margaret Webb. He is likely possessed by the devil. I don't know what he's doing out. They usually keep him in. He's an imbecile, but he can work in their fulling shed, doing the wool treading. A fine job for him, if you ask me. Nobody in their senses wants to stand knee-deep in stale piss all day.' He drained his wine and got to his feet. 'You need to take him back.' He staggered from the table, headed for the door. 'I'm for my bed in this heat this afternoon.' He paused in front of them, Stanton now trying to untie a wriggling, groaning John as Barling glared at the lord, stock-still. 'What a find for the King's men, eh? What a find.' He got as far as the hall before his huge laugh broke out and carried on. And on.

Now free, John Webb took off into a corner, crouching low on his bare feet as he kept his unmatched eyes on them, his moans quieter but constant.

Barling turned to Stanton. 'An unfortunate error.' His face gave little away. But his pinched nostrils told Stanton that he was crosser than fifty sticks. 'Most unfortunate.' He brushed at the dirt and twigs stuck to his cloak from the struggles in the bushes with John. 'I did mention false alleys, did I not, Stanton?'

Stanton nodded, sure that any word from his mouth right now would be the wrong one.

'And with false alleys, one simply turns around and comes back out.' Barling gestured at John. 'Please return the Webbs' son to them, Stanton. With all haste.' He brushed at his cloak again. 'I am going to my solar to remove the dirt of this morning. And, of course, to update my records.' He marched out without waiting for any reply.

Stanton let out a long breath. Easier said than done getting John Webb to his home. He moved a few steps towards him. 'John.' He made his tone as firm as he could. 'Come with me. Now.'

John responded by slapping the side of his own head, then shuffled sideways, still crouching, away from Stanton.

'Now. Or there'll be trouble.'

Nothing. The man wouldn't budge.

This wasn't going to work. The picture of Edgar, of Barling, returning to the hall later on and finding John still here came clear as the day outside in Stanton's mind. His life wouldn't be worth living.

If orders didn't work, he'd try a different approach. Even the best guard dogs could be tempted with meat.

Stanton went over to the table to see what Edgar had left. There should be something. While Edgar's home was a dirty jumble, his food and wine were always the best. Especially the wine. Stanton filled a goblet and downed it as he took a look. He needed it.

Bones picked clean didn't look very promising. Pottage, however tasty it looked, wouldn't work either. Then he saw what would: a plate of gingerbread. He picked up one of the small triangles, rich with honey as well as the delicious warmth of the spice. He broke it in two, threw one piece on the floor in front of John.

The wild man reached out a hand, pawed at it. Then he grabbed it, lifting it before his bulging eye, and sniffed hard at it. But he didn't eat. Instead, he shoved it into the folds of his own filthy clothing. But he'd calmed.

Stanton threw another piece.

Same.

He repeated the action as John repeated his own, Stanton moving a bit closer each time.

Then with a yell from John, Stanton had hold of a handful of his clothing. He pulled the flailing, shouting John to his feet.

This was going to be hard work.

And it was. By the time Stanton got to the door of the Webbs' cottage, he was sweating.

Sweating as much from wrestling a loudly struggling John along the hot road as he was at the reaction he feared he was going to get from the Webbs. His luck was in, in that the street had been deserted. Otherwise, he'd have had a crowd with him by now.

The door flew open before he had a chance to knock. John's noise would have alerted them.

Margaret stood there. 'God save us.' Her stunned expression puckered in a heartbeat into fury. 'What are you doing with John?'

'I'm sorry, mistress—'

'John?' Webb's call from within. 'What do you mean?'

'The King's man has him, Peter!'

Webb was at the door now too. 'What has John done now?'

'Nothing, nothing at all,' said Stanton. 'There's been a mistake.'

'I'll say there has.' Margaret yanked John from Stanton's hold to her own, where he instantly quietened.

'Do you mind telling us what sort of mistake?' asked Webb, his voice low and his grey eyes fixed on Stanton like stone.

'I . . . I mean, we – the King's men that is – were out looking into the recent murders. We found John wandering in the woods earlier. Didn't know, of course, that he was your son. Sir Reginald Edgar told us when we brought John to the hall.'

'He shouldn't be in any hall,' said Margaret. 'Shouldn't be anywhere except here.'

'Here with us,' repeated Webb.

'You should have left him be.' Margaret led a docile John over to the large shed Stanton had noticed before, which he now knew was the fulling shed. 'Like you should leave us all be.' She had the door to the shed open. 'All of us: leave us alone!' She slammed the door of the shed shut on her and John.

'My apologies for my wife, sir. Like all women, she forgets her place when she's riled.'

'No need, Webb. I'm the one who should be apologising. We didn't hurt your son. Not in any way. I think we alarmed him, that's all. But I'm very sorry that we did that too.'

'That's very good of you to reassure me, sir. I hope to God he didn't hurt you or the King's clerk.'

'No, a few bumps in the struggles, that's all.'

'That's a relief to hear, sir. John, see, he can . . . lash out. We never know when. Or why.'

He is likely possessed by the devil. Edgar's view of John.

Webb's stooped shoulders seemed to suddenly sag more under an unseen weight. 'It's hard, you know. With the boy. Hard.' Webb caught his breath. 'Thank you for bothering about him.' He glanced back at his loom.

'I won't keep you any more, Webb. Good day to you.'

'And you, sir.' Webb closed the door, and Stanton heard the steady rhythm of the loom start up again.

A hard life indeed for the Webbs to have a son like that. He started on the road back to Edgar's.

Like Barling, he also needed to get cleaned up.

He had the wake of Bartholomew Theaker to attend.

Chapter Twenty-Four

The sun had left the sky, but the dusk kept the heat in a suffocating blanket of still air.

Stanton walked with Barling up to the late Bartholomew Theaker's cottage for the thatcher's laying out. He'd enjoyed his thorough wash only a short while ago, but the clean linen he'd put on was already soaked in sweat.

'Like a baker's oven this evening,' he said to Barling.

The clerk didn't reply. Clad as always in his black robes, the man never seemed warm or had much colour in his smooth face.

People were gathered outside, their numbers suggesting that all the village was here. The steady murmur of prayer for the dead man came on the air, led by the rector, Osmond, who spoke from the doorway, the better to include those inside the cottage as well as out. Some folk raised their eyes briefly, nudged those alongside.

Stanton and Barling paused to allow the prayer to finish.

'Our arrival is noted, Stanton,' said Barling in a low tone. 'I did not expect otherwise.'

'Me neither,' replied Stanton in the same way. 'I see Peter and Margaret Webb are here. That's them, over to my right. The stooped man and the woman with the tight coif. I'm sure everyone knows about what happened with John.' Stanton had filled Barling in on the way over here about the reception he'd had from the Webbs.

'No doubt. But we must not let it concern us. To dwell on an error is never of benefit.'

Stanton shot him a glance. Barling's tone had changed abruptly, dropping with his last sentence. The clerk looked lost in his own thoughts, which was not at all like him.

'Are you all right, Barling?'

His usual sharp gaze snapped back. 'Of course. Now tell me: who else is here whom you have spoken to?'

'That man over there, the tall one. That's the stonecutter, Thomas Dene.'

'I see him. A handsome fellow, as you described. And that wiry man is Caldbeck the ploughman, is he not?'

Stanton nodded.

The prayer finished with a full-voiced chorus of 'Amen,' and the large assembly of villagers broke up into smaller groups in a muted buzz of chatter. Over to one side, under a scented white-blossomed tree, a full ale barrel had been opened, and many made their way there to slake their thirst in the heat.

'Ah! Good Aelred Barling, you have come to pay your respects.' Osmond hurried over with a loud greeting, his face blotchy in the heat. 'And Hugo Stanton too.'

'We have, sir priest,' said Barling.

Stanton gave a brief bow to the rector.

Osmond's echoing words had made sure that every ear in the place heard that the King's men were here. 'Good, good. Then would you like to do so now?'

'Thank you, sir priest,' said Barling, Stanton also muttering his thanks.

As Osmond led them through to the door, Stanton caught bits of conversation. He didn't need to hear any more. He knew what everyone was talking about.

That devil Lindley.

The law. Always the excuse.

A dreadful end, God rest him.

Hanging. The one answer to all this.

The stuffy heat in the cottage was even worse than outside. A low whisper of women weeping filled it.

'Please.' Osmond stepped to one side, gesturing for Stanton to move in to where Barling stood at the feet of the huge mound of Theaker's shrouded body. Candles burned brightly at the head and feet.

Stanton crossed himself and joined his hands in silent prayer, as Barling was doing. To his right, lined up on a settle facing the body, sat four women. Two he didn't recognise. Two he did. One was Hilda Folkes, the scarred midwife he'd disturbed in her work. The other was Agnes Smith.

But where the other three women wept and sobbed, their white coifs and veils moving with their grief, the bare-headed Agnes did neither.

She sat bolt upright, long dark hair curling past her shoulders, fists in her lap, staring straight in front of her.

'You can see that he is at peace now.' Osmond's loud whisper filled the room as he moved to the head of the body. 'Come and see.'

Agnes gave a wordless exclamation and shot to her feet.

'Agnes.' Hilda put a hand on her arm. 'Don't.'

'Leave me be, Hilda.' Agnes brushed her off and walked out.

'Very. Upset.' Osmond mouthed the words to Stanton and Barling.

Barling held a hand up to Osmond and nodded to Stanton to leave too.

The other women carried on their mourning for the corpse, despite the interruption, as Stanton filed out with the two men.

The rector flapped his hand in front of his face. 'I would wager that Theaker's shroud is the only dry linen tonight. And what spotless linen it is.' He gave a long sigh. 'Hilda always does such excellent work with the laying out.'

'It was indeed warm, Osmond,' said Barling. 'Now, if you will excuse us, Stanton and I have much to attend to back at your uncle's hall.' He shot Stanton a look.

'That's right, sir priest,' said Stanton, taking the hint. 'Much.'

'Then at least have a sup before you go on your way.'

War waged within Stanton. He'd love to get away from the accusing glances and half-heard words. But a long drink of ale would be a wonder in his dry throat.

'I insist.' Osmond was already waving to someone by the barrel. 'A small token for the work of the King's men.'

'Thank you, sir priest.' Barling hid his annoyance at the pointed remark. But Stanton could tell it a mile off by now.

'Here we are.' Osmond accepted a foaming cup from the alewife as she handed over the other two.

'To Theaker.' He raised his drink.

'Theaker,' said Stanton and Barling.

He'd been right about the ale. He drained half the cup as Barling clutched his.

'A good man,' said Osmond. 'Who liked a life where there was a good seat and a milk pudding and not too much thatch to mend. That priests and clerks could take such a relaxed approach to life, eh, Barling?'

'Indeed.' Barling nodded politely.

'Liked his betrothed as well.' Osmond gave a broad wink. 'Some say he liked Agnes even more than milk pudding.'

Stanton drained the other half of his ale lest he say something rude to the priest. Barling, he saw, kept his face still as always.

'And where has Agnes gone, Osmond?' asked Barling. 'She left the cottage quite suddenly.'

The gossipy Osmond seized on the new topic fed to him by the clerk. 'Oh, she's very upset. Very.' He warbled on to Barling.

Stanton's cup was empty. Neither Osmond nor Barling were paying him any attention. He might as well have another cup of that good ale. He went over to the beer barrel to get it.

He arrived at the same time as Simon Caldbeck.

'You first, sir.' The ploughman's angular face lifted in a smile that had no warmth. 'The King's man shouldn't have to wait, should he?'

'It doesn't bother me, Caldbeck.'

'You have to.' The smile was gone and the surly look was back. 'It's the way of things.'

The alewife served Stanton first, and he waited until Caldbeck had his. 'We should drink to Theaker, eh?'

'Whatever you say.' Caldbeck downed his ale in one swift draught. 'There. Done.' He handed the empty cup back to the alewife and walked off without another word.

Stanton ignored the slight. Taking his full drink, he went and sat on the far side of the blossom tree, where he made himself comfortable on one of the big roots. The thickets that lined the edge of the dead thatcher's property were full of birds singing the hot day to sleep. The man should be here to enjoy this place, as he surely must have done on many an evening. *Good rest to you, Theaker.* He took another drink.

Then paused. From the thickets, he heard fast, jagged breathing.

Not the wild John Webb again. He shot to his feet, spilling his drink, all peace gone.

He looked around. Everyone stood a good couple of yards away.

More long, laboured breaths. Moving leaves and branches.

He frowned. It didn't sound like John. At all.

But somebody was definitely in there. Watching from a distance. Hidden. Watching mourners at a laying out. The laying out of a murdered man. Despite the heat, the hairs rose on Stanton's neck. Somebody was watching the results of their handiwork. *Lindley.* He'd not gone anywhere.

He filled his lungs to call out. Then caught his shout back.

Out of the thicket came Thomas Dene, fastening up his braies. He stopped dead. 'What are you looking at?'

Stanton raised a hand. 'Sorry, my friend—'

'What did you say, Thomas?' A voice came from behind the stone-cutter. A female voice. 'I can't hear you.' A flush-faced Agnes emerged from the thicket too. Her smile dropped. 'You.'

Stanton bent to pick up his cup. 'I was just going.' He matched his words with his actions.

'I'll say you were going.' The powerful stonecutter marched up to Stanton, fell into step beside him. 'Were you following Agnes, is that it? I've met plenty men like you in my time.' His big fists clenched. 'Dealt with them and all.'

'I was sat having a drink.' Stanton held up a hand. 'That's all.' *Damn it to hell.* He could see curious faces turning towards the fuss.

'Thomas. Stop.' Agnes grasped at the stonecutter's arm, her voice also raised. 'I can fight my own battles.'

The stonecutter ignored her but halted his steps. 'Get off this property, Stanton. Do you hear me?'

Now came pointing, calls to others from those who had seen to those who hadn't.

Stanton saw Barling thrust his ale into Osmond's hand. 'Good evening to you, sir priest.' The clerk moved quickly alongside Stanton as they walked away, back to Edgar's hall.

The chorus of gossip and loud comments could be arrows at Stanton's back.

'Another public altercation blamed upon the King's men.' Barling's words came clipped, furious. 'Stanton, what were you thinking?'

'Listen, Barling.' Stanton had had enough of being publicly humiliated for his mistakes. 'You're the one who says I have quick wits, so just listen. I could be wrong – no, I'm not wrong. Agnes and Thomas Dene were together. A few minutes ago. Either they were pretending to be dogs in the thickets, or they were lying together. Which is the more likely?'

Barling's eyebrows went up. 'I see. Now, that is interesting. I did ask Osmond the question about where she had gone, a question to which you have provided the answer.'

'Because I notice things. Me.' Stanton pushed his point. 'Even small things.'

'What is small and what is important are not necessarily the same thing, Stanton.' He held a hand up as Stanton opened his mouth to argue. 'But yes, you do notice things. As for Agnes?' He frowned. 'Such fornication was not only a sinful act but one that is quite astonishing, given the circumstances. The girl's betrothed is not even in the ground.'

They were approaching Edgar's hall, the dusk moving into dark.

Barling continued. 'It is behaviour that requires much closer scrutiny. I shall speak to both of them tomorrow. But separately. Go and fetch Dene from the quarry first thing. I will speak to Agnes alone after that. Also, am I correct in that Hilda Folkes, the woman with the scarred face, is the midwife you met?'

'She is.'

'Then I shall see her while you are fetching Dene. If, as Osmond says, she lays out all the bodies, she may have useful information for our enquiries.'

Stanton couldn't believe the clerk's next words as they walked in the door of the hall.

'And well done, Stanton: a good evening's work.'

But he could believe the next.

'Good,' continued Barling, 'for one who is so new to learning how to exercise their wits.' The clerk carried on to his solar.

Stanton mouthed a favourite swear word at Barling's retreating back.

And for one who was supposedly limited in his wits, it was a fine, fine choice.

Chapter Twenty-Five

'I'll answer anything you want to ask me, sir,' said Hilda Folkes to Barling.

Sat across from him at the table in Edgar's hall, the midwife looked at him with all necessary respect, respect which was matched with her humble tone.

'Answer it truthfully too, I swear,' she went on. 'Though I'm not sure how the likes of me could be of any help to a man who is of the court of the lord King.'

With her clear eyes of a delicate blue, her good bearing and her neat coif and clothes, she should be a woman who carried her age well. But nothing could take from the ruin of her scarred face, the low morning sun casting a cruel light on her skin that picked out every one of the hollows in her flesh.

'I can assure you that your assistance is important, Mistress Folkes,' said Barling. 'As I am sure your answers will be. Please be assured also that anything you tell me will not be for common gossip within the village.'

She sat up a little straighter. 'I have nothing to hide, sir. Nothing.'

Barling gave a polite smile, as if he agreed, though he did not respond directly. His experience over the years was that those who made such claims very often did indeed have something they wished to conceal. 'Now, you are the midwife here in Claresham, are you not?'

'Yes, sir. I delivered my latest not two days ago, was doing so when your man, Stanton, came knocking. I hope I wasn't rude to him, sir. But that birth was a real struggle. I had to call Margaret Webb. She wouldn't have been my first choice to help. Many people say she's cursed, because of her son, John. Yet I had no choice, with everyone out in the fields. Without a second pair of hands, I'd have lost both of them. And Margaret is deft and strong. Both mother and her baby son are hale. Another safe delivery to praise in the Virgin's name. Always a relief for me, even after so many years.'

'I have no doubt,' said Barling. 'How many years have you carried out your services for the mothers and babies of this village?'

'For the last twenty-three, sir. I learned many of my skills from my mother, who was the midwife before me. But she died of a sudden fever when I was not much over twenty, and then it was just me. I wasn't anything like as experienced as her, but over the years I've managed to become so.'

'God chooses our path for us,' said Barling. 'Even though it is not always a path we would choose for ourselves.' He knew that well himself, as he could see did she.

A shadow of sadness passed over her damaged features. 'No.'

'Although you have birthed many who live here,' he said, 'you also carry out the washing of the dead before burial and dress them in their shroud. Is that correct?'

'Yes, sir. Not only me, you understand. Usually the deceased's womenfolk as well. But as often happens, there may not be any if the person who has died is very old, or in times of a sickness or plague.' Her clear gaze met Barling's. 'I want them to be buried with dignity, sir.'

'It is a laudable task you perform, mistress, and a holy one.' He consulted one of his notes before he asked his next question. 'May I ask if you washed Geoffrey Smith?'

'Geoffrey? Of course.'

'I appreciate that this may be a difficult question for you to answer, but can you describe his wounds?'

'It's not difficult at all, sir.' Her gaze stayed steady. 'His head had been opened. I was able to make that right with a bandage. But his face? His face was smashed open. His jaw was broken. Teeth missing. His mouth ripped. I did what I could to make him presentable. It was hopeless.' Her voice wavered. 'He'd been a good-looking man.' She sucked in a deep breath. 'Such a terrible end at the hands of that devil Lindley.'

'And if I may ask another delicate question, did you see any other wounds or marks on Smith's body?'

Hilda frowned. 'Other wounds, sir? May God keep him, do you not think he had enough?'

'The body of one who has been murdered should be examined,' said Barling, 'especially if it is a secret homicide. Other wounds may help to give an indication of what has happened. I examined Bartholomew Theaker's body, for instance. But I have no means of examining that of Geoffrey Smith.'

Her frown cleared. 'I see. Forgive my sharp response, sir. No, poor Geoffrey had no other wounds. Save those that killed him.'

'There is no need to ask my forgiveness, mistress. Yours was a truly sad task.' Barling nodded in sympathy, though he wondered at the deep emotion that entered her voice whenever she said Smith's name. 'It must have been even more so for Agnes to carry out.'

'Agnes?' Hilda shook her head. 'No, Agnes did not help.'

'But I thought you said the womenfolk of the dead would help to prepare the body.'

Hilda shook her head again. 'Agnes didn't help. I asked her if she wanted to, but she said she couldn't bear it. It was she who had found Geoffrey's body, and the shock was terrible for her.'

'With regard to the discovery of the body,' said Barling, 'did you witness anything on the night of the murder?'

'No, sir. I was asleep in bed. I was roused by the hue and cry.'

'And was your husband roused also, Mistress Folkes?'

'My husband, sir?' She looked startled by his question. 'I have never been married.' She brought her fingers to her ruined face. 'I think you can see why.'

'Not every man gives weight to looks. There are other qualities in a woman.'

'There are.' She gave a rueful smile as she dropped her hands and folded them on the tabletop once more. 'But no, nobody ever asked for my hand. I live alone.'

'Very well.' Barling made a note. Another dweller of this place with nothing to report about the night of the murder. Nothing seen, nothing heard. 'So you prepared Smith's body for his grave.'

'Yes, and I did the work alone.' A flush rose in her pitted cheeks. 'I was happy to do so. Geoffrey and I were almost the same age. We'd grown up together, him and me and Isabel. We had been close friends all of our lives.'

'Isabel?'

'Isabel Smith, his late wife. Agnes's mother.'

'I knew he was a widower, but I did not know his wife's name.' Barling made another note on his tablet. 'When did he lose her?'

'As many years ago as Agnes has been alive.' Hilda's hands tightened. 'Isabel Smith died in childbirth, sir.'

'Were you present at that birth?'

'Yes, sir.' Now her knuckles were white. 'It was the very first birth I attended after my own mother had died. As I've told you, I was young myself and didn't have my mother's knowledge. You can see with your own eyes that Agnes is a strapping girl. She takes after Geoffrey, while her mother was very small-boned. I know it doesn't always follow with childbirth. The smallest women can bring them out as easy as a cat having kittens. But with poor Isabel?' She shook her head. 'Agnes got stuck. Nothing I tried worked. Her mother was dying in front of my eyes, which meant the babe was dying too. I got my knife out and did what was necessary.'

Barling pulled in a long breath. 'A difficult task,' he said, aware of how inadequate his words were for the actions Hilda would have had to take.

'Oh, I can see your face, sir. But birth, just like death, can be a messy, bloody business. Like I say, I got Agnes out. Thought she was gone as well. I slapped her hard. Then she filled her lungs with the loudest yells I'd ever heard from a newborn.' A smile flickered, went out. 'Poor Geoffrey. He had the deepest love for his wife. Like I said, we'd all grown up together. Isabel's pregnancy had been easy. She blossomed day to day, with Geoffrey the happiest man in Claresham.' Her look changed again. 'It's like that, you know. The carrying of a baby never tells what awaits the woman at the birth. When I told him the news, he was devastated. Because I lost her, Geoffrey lost her. It was so hard. I thought – everyone thought – he'd take another wife. He was still a young man, a fine-looking man, with a good living. But no.' She bit her lip. 'He never did, never looked at another woman. He raised Agnes on his own.' The regret was clear in her voice.

'Not something many men would choose to do,' said Barling.

'No. And Geoffrey should have had time to mourn, but he had a baby to attend to. Agnes was wet-nursed by a woman in the village who's long dead. That was the only thing Geoffrey would allow. He did everything else himself. Saints preserve us.' Hilda rolled her eyes. 'A baby crawling around in a forge, then as a little one toddling around. It's a wonder she didn't burn to death or get hit by the hammer.'

'Then I suppose one could say that her father did a good job in raising Agnes.'

Hilda gave a sharp sigh. 'Geoffrey Smith, as much as I cared for him, was a fool with that girl. She could do as she pleased. He never chastised her. Ever.' Her mouth tightened. 'A must with any child. They need a firm hand. And if that doesn't work, they need the stick. They have to learn. But Agnes never did. She always got her own way, always got whatever she wanted. That's why she's as wild and brazen as she is.'

'Some say even worse about her.' Barling did not wish to repeat the Webbs' label of Agnes as a whore.

'I know, sir.' Hilda raised her eyes to the heavens again. 'And they wouldn't be entirely wrong. She came to me just a few months ago, worried about her belly.'

'Her belly?'

'She asked me if I could feel if she was with child, sir.'

'Ah,' said Barling as if he understood, though such an occurrence was a complete mystery to him. 'And was she?'

Hilda shook her head. 'No. But I told her if she was worried she was, then she should stop what she was doing. If you see what I mean, sir.'

'I do.' Barling paused a moment. Thomas Dene had been here in Claresham for a few weeks, nothing more. 'But you say she came to you a few months ago about this?'

'Yes, sir.'

'Then it would have been her betrothed, the late Bartholomew Theaker, that she had been lying with.'

'Theaker? No.' Hilda shook her head. 'She told me it was Simon Caldbeck, the ploughman.'

Barling felt his own brows raise. Perhaps the names flung at Agnes were not so ill-suited.

Hilda went on. 'As Agnes wouldn't listen to me, I took him aside and told him to have more sense. Told him Geoffrey would take a horsewhip to him as well.'

'Did Caldbeck listen?'

'I don't know, sir. Only he or Agnes could tell you for certain. All I know is that she hasn't come to me about anything since.' She glanced to the window, then looked back at Barling. 'Will that be all, sir? I've many tasks to see to today and the sun has already climbed.'

'I think that will be all for now, mistress. You have been extremely helpful. My thanks for your time.'

'I hope I have been of some help, sir. All I want is justice for Geoffrey. I hope you can get it for him. And Bartholomew too, of course.'

'Of course. I can assure you I am doing everything I can, Mistress Folkes. Good day to you.'

'Good day, sir.' Hilda rose to her feet and walked to the door, where she paused. 'One more thing, sir.'

'Yes, mistress?'

'When you find Lindley and string him up, I'll not wash his corpse. I can tell you that now. Send him straight to hell. Please.'

With that, she was gone.

As Barling went over his notes, parts of Hilda's account touched his heart again, just as they had as he listened to her. The woman had clearly had a deep love for Geoffrey Smith, a love that had never been returned, at least not in the way she wanted. Barling knew that torment only too well, and it was a wound that could reopen at any time. He pushed the memory down at once, as he had trained himself to do. He needed to concentrate on the business at hand.

Stanton had been going to walk to the quarry to fetch Thomas Dene but decided to ride instead. He reckoned the big stonecutter might be a bit less intimidating from the back of a horse. Four hooves would also get Stanton out of there a lot faster if the man refused to come with him, a refusal Stanton guessed might be emphasised with the man's big fists.

He'd been pleased when Barling had given him his instructions last night. The idea of Dene having to come back to the hall with him to face the clerk's enquiries had appealed to him.

But it had appealed to him after a decent bellyful of ale.

This morning, with the rising sun already a broiling disc in the sky, he wasn't so sure. He shifted in his saddle and patted Morel's neck. She'd get him out of there. No question.

The road down to the quarry was steep and the loose stones weren't good for iron-clad hooves.

Stanton dismounted and led Morel down. The quarry still lay in shadow, though it wouldn't be for long. Down below, he could see the thin plume of smoke that would be Dene's fire rise in a straight line in the windless air. Good. If the man had broken his fast, it might put him in better humour.

He half slid on a stone, Morel's reins saving him this time.

Finally, they were down. 'And in one piece, eh?' He patted her dark brown neck, and she nuzzled his hand with her soft nose.

Stanton left her free to search the ground for the odd tuft of grass that had forced its way through the stones. She wouldn't run off from here.

Now that the noise of hooves and feet scrabbling on stones had stopped, he realised he could hear no other sound. No ring of hammer on stone like there had been when he first came here. An efficient hammer as well. A row of fresh, raw slabs leaned against a big boulder.

'Dene?' His voice sounded odd down here. Flat. Not much of an echo. 'It's Hugo Stanton.' He licked the stone dust that already coated his lips, so fine it was invisible to the eye but must fill the air.

No reply.

'Aelred Barling, the King's clerk, requests your presence.'

Nothing.

The stonecutter must be in his wooden hut, next to which the fire burned. There was no other sign of him.

As Stanton made his way over to it, a rattle came from the side of the quarry. He paused and looked around. 'Dene?'

No. Only a loose rock that had lost its grip on the steep quarry side, rolling and bouncing down in little puffs of dust before it came to a rest.

He carried on to the hut, past the fire. To the doorway. The open doorway.

'Dene?'

After, he couldn't remember what he screamed. How loud. How long.

All he could remember was running, running for Morel, her back, her long legs that would take him, get him out of there.

Remember too the sight in the shed, which would never leave him.

The body of Thomas Dene. On the floor. No sign of his head.

Just one of his slabs where it should be as a mass of red, red, red oozed out from underneath it.

Chapter Twenty-Six

'You need to go out there, Barling.' Edgar jerked his thumb at the tightly shuttered window of the hall. 'Otherwise, people will either climb in here or burn my manor to the ground. Their fury at Nicholas Lindley is matched by that at Thomas Dene. The two outsiders, that's what they're saying. Dene, a man skilled with a hammer and possessing many of them, helping Lindley to break the stone wall of my gaol to escape. Lindley rewarding him with a crushed skull. And they're right, God's eyes, they're right!'

'I will be going out to your courtyard, Edgar,' replied Barling. 'I am only too well aware of the current mood, given what we now know about Dene. But I have not finished questioning Stanton.'

The young messenger sat on a chair, leaning forward, elbows on his knees. 'I think I've told you all I can, Barling.'

'May God protect us, it's enough.' The rector Osmond was pale as the linen kerchief knotted at his neck to catch his sweat in the stifling heat of the closed room.

'But it might not be,' said Barling. 'Stanton has been met with the most terrible of sights this morning with his discovery of Dene's body. In such circumstances, it is easy to miss out something of importance. We will go out when I am ready.'

A lone scream rose above the cacophony. The loudest yet. By far. A woman.

'Who in God's name is that?' Osmond clutched his hands together.

Edgar peered through the slats in the shutter again. 'It's Agnes Smith. And she's swinging a staff around.' He marched to the door. 'I'm going out there before she kills somebody with it.'

'Come on, Barling.' Stanton got to his feet. 'We have to.'

Barling followed Edgar, Stanton at his side.

Osmond hung back, dithering in panic.

'I will make the address short, Stanton,' murmured Barling. 'I can assure you of that.'

'Do what has to be done, Barling. I'll be all right.'

They went to the front door, where Edgar was already standing, yelling at his servants and grooms. 'Grab that thing off her! Now! She's only a girl! If you won't, I will!'

Barling emerged into a wall of noise and waving arms. It was no cooler outside. Heavy black clouds had rolled in to fill the sky, and the air quivered with the promise of a storm.

In the midst of the melee, Agnes had a long, stout stick in both hands, swiping it at anybody who tried to come near her, clearing a space around her.

'Saints preserve us.' Osmond had found the courage to come out.

One of Edgar's grooms got a hand to her arm. She kneed him neatly in the groin and he doubled and dropped to roars and whistles.

Barling collected himself. Took a deep, deep breath. And though he utterly despised doing so, let out his loudest, loudest shout. 'Enough!'

It worked. The sheer volume startled people into a few seconds' curious quiet. Even Edgar.

Agnes broke it first. Her gaze lit on Stanton. 'Is it true, Hugo?'

He nodded. 'Yes, it is, Agnes. I'm sorry.'

'No!' She brought the stick down on the cobbles with both hands. 'No!' Again. It shattered and she flung it away. 'No!'

Before Barling's eyes, in the sight of everyone there, she lost her reason as the news of Thomas Dene's death was confirmed to her. Her grief poured from her in a screaming, shrieking torrent as she beat her head with her fists. 'It can't, he can't. It can't be true! It can't!' Those present stared in open incomprehension at her. As far as they knew, Dene had taken it upon himself to help Lindley escape. But Barling understood only too well, thanks to Stanton.

And then she screamed it, screamed it to the world. 'Thomas Dene was my lover! He was going to be my husband.' She sank to her knees, keening like a wounded animal, hands buried in her hair.

Appalled roars, scandalised cries broke out.

'Bartholomew Theaker's dead because of you!'

'Dene let Lindley out!'

'You whore, you whore, you whore!'

'Let me through.' Hilda Folkes pushed out of the crowd and bent to Agnes, an arm across her shoulders. 'Up you get, my love. Come on.' She managed to get Agnes to rise.

'I need you all to take note of what I have to say,' said Barling. 'As most of you already know, Thomas Dene, the stonecutter, has been found murdered this morning. My assistant, Hugo Stanton, made the discovery.'

'It's that bastard Lindley!' A furious scream tore from a fat woman.

'He'll slay us all in our beds!'

'All of us!'

Barling put his hand up for silence. Edgar, he noted, who wore a brooding look, was not joining in. For now.

'Until Lindley is caught, it is important that you all take sensible precautions. All the men who have died at his hand have been alone. So stay in company, especially when you travel. Secure your doors at night. Make sure you have the means to defend yourselves.'

'You mean like Geoffrey Smith would have had?' Edgar. Of course. 'Or Thomas Dene, another powerful man? Even Theaker. He may not have been a fighter, but he was huge.'

A roar met his words.

But the lord hadn't finished. 'And I have grown tired of all this lack of action. Anyone who delivers Lindley's carcass to me will suffer no repercussions – I will reward them from my own purse!'

A louder roar and many cheers met his words.

A plague on the lord and his incontinent mouth. Barling summoned his shout again. 'Enough!' He brought his glare to as many watching eyes and angry faces as he could. 'Nicholas Lindley must be brought to justice, and it is my responsibility to do so. Lindley is to be held for trial by the King's justice. Mark my words: anyone who tries to administer their own will face trial too.' He finished on a look to Edgar. 'Anyone. The search for Lindley must be planned and orderly.' The lord glowered but stayed silent.

'And now,' said Barling, 'I will be withdrawing with my assistant, and Sir Reginald and sir priest as well. We are doing so because we are taking action.' He beckoned. 'Agnes, please come inside with us. Alone.'

Hilda released her hold on Agnes and stood back.

A loud rumble of thunder brought all eyes aloft. The first big raindrops plopped down, warm as blood.

Barling took advantage of the distraction to get back inside, and the others followed him.

Once they were assembled, he began.

'Agnes, you knew Thomas Dene the most intimately of anybody in Claresham. Does he have family in his home town of Hartleton?'

'Yes, sir. A mother.' She swallowed hard. 'Widowed.'

'Then we will arrange for her to be told as soon as possible,' said Barling. 'It is only right.'

'I'll go, Barling,' said Stanton.

'We can send another, Stanton. You are needed here.'

'I want to go.'

'You will also have to tell her that Dene was involved with helping an outlaw to escape.'

Stanton's jaw set and he began to reply, but Osmond cut him off.

'Is that really necessary, Barling? The man's dead thanks to his own sin. I'll make sure he is buried properly in the churchyard with all the proper rites. That would be fitting, as he was doing God's work. The man has done wonderful stonework in my church.'

'Sounds reasonable to me,' said Edgar.

'No, Osmond.' Barling struggled to give a polite response to such a ridiculous opinion. 'Dene's mother should know the truth. What if she comes here to Claresham to visit his grave and hears it that way? Far worse. The truth is always better, no matter how painful it is.' A lesson he himself had learned though wished he could forget.

'I suppose.' Osmond did not look at all convinced.

'May I wash him?' Agnes broke in, her anguished eyes on Barling's.

'Agnes,' said Stanton. 'No.'

'Please.' She would not drop her gaze. 'I have heard how Lindley killed him. I don't care what he looks like. It will be the last thing I can do for him.'

'If you insist,' said Barling.

'I do.'

'Very well.' The girl's attachment to the dead man knew no bounds. She had refused to wash her slain father's body but would do so for a lover whose skull had been completely crushed.

Stanton got to his feet. 'I need to make plans to go to Dene's home. I reckon it will take me about three days to complete the journey there and back. Where will I find Dene's mother, Agnes?'

'Oh.' Her hand went to her mouth. 'I don't know. How can it be that I don't know that?'

'Ask at the abbey, Stanton,' said Osmond. 'They'll know. They know all the widows in a place.'

Barling stood up too. 'I shall help you prepare.' He wanted to check, with no other listening ears, that Stanton had told him everything.

143

'How remiss,' said Edgar. 'I thought you'd got up to travel with him. Travel in company, like you told everyone else to do.' He reached for a wine jug and gave Barling an unpleasant grin. 'And as you've just shown me, Barling, you don't even believe it yourself. That's what—'

Lightning lit the room for a second and thunder crashed so hard that Barling feared the roof had come off.

'God save us!' shrieked Osmond.

After a pause like an indrawn breath, the abrupt rattle of a torrential downpour began.

Shouts and cries from the courtyard told of people fleeing for their homes.

Barling hesitated. 'Stanton, should you travel in this?'

'Frightened of a bit of weather, are you?' sneered Edgar.

Stanton shrugged. 'I'll be fine.'

The unmistakable drip, drip, drip of leaking water sounded from the corner.

'Not again. A festering plague on it.' Edgar slammed out, yelling for his servants.

'I need to go, Barling,' said Stanton.

'Let me help you prepare.' Barling gave a last glance back at the bereft Agnes as they walked out. Sinful she might be, but her heart was broken. He knew the same pain and he uttered a silent prayer for her, though he feared it would help little.

Overhead, the thunder crashed again.

And the rattling of the rain outside became a dull, unceasing roar.

Chapter Twenty-Seven

Barling had hoped that the storm would bring relief from the heat. Instead, it had made it worse. He wiped his face yet again as he sat at the table in Edgar's hall, papers spread before him.

The thunder and lightning had stopped, but the rain continued to pour, bringing unpleasant moisture to every breath. Last night, he'd lain on his bed instead of in it as the sweat pooled on his body under his linens. He could only imagine what it must have been like for Stanton, riding through the storm.

The one consolation was that the torrential rainfall was keeping everyone indoors, including Edgar. All the lord's shouting about a search had ceased as the man's hall leaked like an old bucket and his privies overflowed.

'This won't take long, will it?'

Barling looked up at the sound of the young female voice from the door.

By all the saints, Agnes Smith had such an abrupt manner at times. But Barling refused to let his irritation show. It would not help matters. 'It is to be hoped it will not, Agnes. Thank you for responding to my request to come here this morning.' He indicated the chair opposite from him at the long table. 'Please, come and sit down.'

'I can just as easily stand,' she said. 'I'm not tired.'

The pallor of her face and her sunken, red-rimmed eyes belied her words. Again, he would not challenge her, not when he needed to get her to speak to him. If he were to do so, in her current emotional state she might very well walk out. 'I am sure you are as resilient as ever, which is to your great credit. But a rest will help you to conserve your strength for . . . later.'

'Later?' She marched to the chair and lowered herself into it. 'You mean the funeral? My Thomas's funeral? You can say it. I am able to hear the words, you know.'

Her openly rude glare upon him had him wonder for a moment if he would have been better off riding out with Stanton to deliver the sad news to the mother of Thomas Dene. But no. Edgar could not be left alone with responsibility for the law in Claresham in its present state. 'I appreciate that you can be so open, Agnes. And I shall try not to take up too much of your time.' He consulted his notes. 'I know much of what I need to ask you about will be painful for you, and I apologise for that.'

'More painful than death?'

Barling accepted the barb without comment. 'Can you describe, Agnes, your relationship with your late father, Geoffrey Smith?'

'With Pa?' She looked perplexed. 'I loved him. Loved him very, very much.'

'Did you ever argue with him?'

'Of course.' She shrugged. 'I argue with everyone,' she added, as if that somehow explained things.

'Were these arguments with your father serious?' asked Barling.

'I loved my father. He loved me.' She gave a firm nod. The suspicion of tears glittered in her eyes, though none fell. 'But he made me very angry by insisting that I marry Bartholomew. I wanted to marry Thomas. Nobody else.'

'Not Simon Caldbeck?'

'How did you . . . ?' Her glare was back. 'No. Not Simon.'

'But you had an earlier closeness with Simon.'

'A fondness.' She shrugged again but would not meet his eye. 'Nothing more. Tongues been wagging about me, have they?'

Barling did not respond but instead made a note. Either she was lying or Hilda Folkes had told an untruth. 'Then to return to your relationship with your father, and his denial of permission for you to marry Thomas Dene, did he ever deny you your wishes prior to that?'

Her perplexed look returned. 'Why would he? My father and I wanted the same things.'

Now it was Barling's turn to be confused. 'In what way?'

'My mam died when I was born. I was used to being the one who shared Pa's life. The only one. And I loved it. I preferred the life a man led. Women always have to do what they're told. Cover their hair. Lower their gaze. Keep quiet. Not me, though it wasn't for want of other women and girls telling me I should. Pa didn't seem to mind. He was always proud of me. He showed me how to do tasks at the forge. I loved it in there.'

Her features softened at the memory as the rain drummed down outside.

Barling said nothing, not wanting to remind her of the current state of the forge, with its dreadful stains and the stench.

'Loved it,' she repeated. 'It was more of a home to us than our cottage was. When I think back, it always seemed to be winter. No matter how cold outside, no matter how thick the ice or deep the snow, it was always warm and cosy in there. I'd sit on my special carved stool, well back from where he worked. Watch Pa take the plain grey iron, heat it to red-hot. It was like it would come alive in his hands. With his strength, he'd hammer it into something new. Something useful. Something beautiful. I wanted to be able to do that too. I couldn't think of anything better.' She pulled in a long, deep breath.

'A life of such work is indeed a virtuous one.'

147

'If you're allowed,' snapped Agnes, her look soft no more. 'When I was little, Pa would always play along. Showed me how to work the hammer, how to do little bits and pieces. Never told me I wouldn't be able to do it for a living. Deceived me, really. I suppose to him it was childish games.' Her jaw set. 'But I was deadly serious.'

'I am sure of it.'

'There was one time when he said I wouldn't be allowed to work the forge but that my husband would, which would be just as good. I raged for hours when he said that, couldn't be quietened. Pa was beside himself.'

Barling summoned up a tight smile, privately agreeing with Hilda Folkes's judgement that Geoffrey Smith had spoiled his daughter. His own parents would not have hesitated to fetch the stick should he ever have behaved so. Not that he ever had.

'But my fuss wasn't about being a smith,' she said. 'It was about the idea of taking a husband. In my young heart, I had Pa and he had me, and we would never need anybody else.' She sighed. 'Things really changed when I started to grow into womanhood. Pa stopped me working there one day. No warning. Nothing.' She scowled. 'He said I had to think about my future. I created an even bigger fuss. But this time Pa didn't try to bring me round. All I got was no, no, no. I couldn't work in the forge. I had to do what was expected of me. Expected of me as a woman.' Her scowl deepened. 'Such as agree to a husband.'

'Yet you bowed to your father's wishes, did you not? You were promised to Theaker, God rest his soul.' Barling crossed himself in respect.

Her glare fixed on him again. 'The idea of lying with Bartholomew Theaker made me want to throw up.' She passed a hand across her face with a sharp sigh. 'I'm sorry, that was wrong of me. Poor Bartholomew. He didn't deserve the end he got. But I didn't want him as my husband.' Her mouth tightened. 'He should never have asked.'

'But you said yes.'

She slapped her hand on the table. 'I said no.' She leaned forward. 'I didn't want him, but Pa wouldn't listen. A good match, he'd say. Him and that old pig Edgar. Edgar was the one to give permission. He had to. Theaker was a villein, you see. Not a freeman. But he had plenty of money. And that makes him a good match – they kept saying it.' She sat back again. 'But that match was never going to happen. No matter what anyone said.'

'Never?'

'For I had given my love to another. Given it to my Thomas.' For the first time, her voice shook. 'Forever.'

'What did your father say?'

'I never told him about Thomas.' Her gaze slid away. 'Pa heard gossip and got very angry with me. But I denied it, denied it all. I could tell Pa didn't believe me, but I didn't care.' She looked at Barling again, leaned forward once more in her earnestness. 'Thomas and I had a deep love that was more powerful than any obstacles. We were going to be together always. You couldn't possibly understand our passion. Nobody could.'

Yet Barling could. He understood passion in its full, glorious, heart-breaking destruction. But he had put such feelings away. Forever. 'Yet you were still betrothed to Theaker, Agnes. How were you going to be with Dene?'

'Yes, my betrothal prevented Thomas and I naming our love. He even said to me one day, "How much happier our lives could have been without the hand of Sir Reginald Edgar." But we were going to be happy in spite of everything. You see, Thomas had it all planned. He told me that when he finished his work here in Claresham, he'd go to his home town and get everything set up for me and for our lives together. Then he would come back here and talk to my father, persuade him to allow us to be together. Thomas knew he'd be able to do so. Not only was he a freeman, he had plenty of money put aside.'

Barling drew breath to comment, but she cut across him.

'But do you know what?' Her face lit with her smile. 'I had a surprise for Thomas.'

'Oh?'

She nodded hard. 'A delicious surprise. I had my things packed. I was ready to leave Claresham the moment he did. We would run away together, marry before anybody knew about it. My name would be ruined, but I didn't care. No matter who objected, it would be too late.' Her smile dropped. 'And now it is. Too late for everything. Lindley has taken it all from me.'

'You have indeed suffered greatly,' said Barling as gently as he could. 'Do you have any idea why Nicholas Lindley would have wanted those close to you dead?'

'No.'

'Again, I know this must be very painful for you, Agnes. But you discovered your father's body, did you not?'

'Yes.'

'Thinking back to that night, did you see anything? Anything that might be important? Anything that might help us catch Lindley?'

Agnes looked at her hands, suddenly quiet. Different.

'Agnes?'

'Something . . .' Her hands balled into fists. 'Something happened to me on the night Pa was killed.' She raised her eyes to Barling.

To his surprise, he saw a deep unease within them.

'I haven't told a soul,' she said.

'Then it's time that you did,' said Barling.

She hesitated.

'Agnes?'

'I haven't lied. About finding Pa. But I haven't told the whole truth.'

'Go on.'

'I wasn't at home in our cottage. I was out in the woods. Late. In the dark. Out meeting Thomas. We had a special place there. Not far from the stone quarry there's a little glade that has the prettiest waterfall, with a pool under it.' She wouldn't meet Barling's eye now. 'It's very private.'

He nodded his understanding.

She went on. 'We had parted for the night. Thomas had gone back to his hut in the quarry, and I was making my way back through the woods to my home. It started to rain, not like now, but still bad, which made everything even darker. I had to take my time, to take care. We had that terrible storm at Eastertide, where so many trees had come down. I went to climb over a big trunk when I heard a couple of twigs snapping.'

'Thomas?'

She shook her head. 'Lindley. I thought it was my Thomas playing a joke. I called out to Tom. When I got no answer, I went to climb over the trunk. And a hand grabbed my leg. Grabbed it, yanked me down hard. I grabbed a branch to stop my fall and cracked my nose and chin.' She gave the sort of crooked smile that holds back tears. 'God help me, I still thought it was Tom, though I don't know why. I yelled at him to stop, that he was hurting me. Looked down.' A couple of tears broke through and her breath came faster. 'But it wasn't my love. It was a figure in a black cloak, face hidden in a dark wrap. I didn't know at the time it was Lindley. All I knew was that I had to get away. He grabbed hold of my other ankle. Pulling, pulling, pulling. But I got one foot free, kicked him as hard as I could.'

The ferocity with which she said it echoed in the room.

'And then I was over the tree trunk,' she said. 'And I ran. Fell once in the mud. Thought he was on me. But then he fell as well. So I picked myself up and ran again. I'd lost one shoe, and stones and thorns tore my flesh. But I didn't care. I was headed for home. Quick as I could. Home. I had to get home. Home to Pa.'

Now her tears fell in a steady, silent stream. But she made no attempt to wipe them away.

'I broke from the trees on to the road. Saw the orange light of the forge. Where Pa was working late. I ran to the door, got in. Slammed it behind me. And there was my pa.' A deep sob broke from her. 'Flat on his back on the ground in a puddle of blood. I knew he was dead. His eyes were staring. And he had no mouth left. Not much nose. Just a gaping hole in his face. And then the door opened behind me.'

'Lindley?' asked Barling with a frown.

'No.' Agnes let out a long breath and uncurled her white-knuckled fists, laid her palms flat on the table. 'I thought it was him coming for me through the door.' She smiled sadly. 'It was Bartholomew. He'd come to see Pa, to talk about our marriage. What he got was me screaming. And Pa. I couldn't stop.'

'You are indeed fortunate to have escaped his clutches, Agnes. Not only fortunate but courageous too. But why have you remained silent about this terrible attack?'

'I did tell Thomas.' She scrubbed at her eyes, to little avail. 'But he said I couldn't tell anybody. Because if I did, then people would want to know why I was out in the woods. And then our love would come out, and Edgar would stop it. Everyone.'

'Then why tell me today?'

'Because now I see that Thomas somehow knew Lindley. He was trying to protect him, just like he did when he broke him out of the gaol.' Now she sobbed without cease. 'And because he didn't let me say anything, my Thomas, the love of my heart, is dead at the hand of Nicholas Lindley, the man he helped.'

'And that is the whole truth of what happened to you in the woods?'

Agnes held up one hand with three fingers extended. 'My pa. My betrothed. My love. All dead. All at Lindley's hand. Is that not enough?' She dropped her hand. 'I swear to you, I can take no more. No more.'

Chapter Twenty-Eight

Normally, the busyness of a market town would have Stanton more on alert. Who might be a pickpocket? Who might want to overcharge him for an inn? Who, after what happened to him in York, might want to rob him?

But now the world stood on its head. He welcomed the bustle and noise of these crowded streets as he rode along them, Morel tired but still strong beneath him. She'd been steady as a rock as they battled through the storm in the first hours of the ride, but he'd sensed her relief when they finally left it behind.

He felt far safer here than he did in the quiet of the small village of Claresham.

Not that there was any quiet in that cursed place. Three men had been murdered brutally. And two of the murders were his fault, even if one man had helped to bring the fate on himself. He wanted to push his own blame away, banish it from his mind so he could close an eye at night.

But he couldn't. After his long ride of the best part of two days, with Dene's tools in a bag slung across his chest and every mile adding to his dread, he had to tell the stonecutter's mother that her son was dead.

Following the rector Osmond's advice, he pulled up outside the abbey walls and went to the gatehouse. As Osmond had said, the monk there knew of the widow Dene.

'You have brought sad news, my son?' said the monk, reading Stanton's look in a second.

'The worst,' was the terse reply Stanton could manage, a sudden lump of sadness in his throat taking him by surprise.

His own mother, the still-beautiful Alys, was also a widow. *'I have everything I need from God,'* he'd heard her say a hundred times. *'Everything my heart could want. I have my Hugo. My sweet Hugo. My angel of a boy, with his eyes like the summer sky and his golden locks.'*

That he was an angel and not a dunderpate who couldn't keep his mouth shut.

What if God were to rob his mother of her heart's love, as Dene's had been robbed of hers? Stanton knew the pain would feel like death to Alys Stanton, yet in the most cruel way it would not kill her, but instead she would feel its agony every day she had left on this earth.

The ride to the widow Dene's house was too quick.

Now here it was, a neat, ordered dwelling and shop set on a narrow street of many others.

Barrels in the swept, tidy yard. A yellow rose in flower growing across the door lintel. From the open shutters came the rich, malty smell of brewing ale.

Stanton dismounted and threw a coin to a tall boy who'd seen him arrive.

'Watch my horse.' He thrust Morel's reins into his hand. 'There's another coin for you if you can get her fed and watered.'

'Sir.' The boy led his horse to a nearby trough as Stanton went to the half-open door.

He knocked on it with a call. 'I have a message for the widow Dene.'

'I am she.' An answering call from inside, along with the high-pitched bark of a small dog.

The woman stepped out, wiping her hands on her apron, one foot holding the jumping brindle dog back. He definitely had the right house. He could see the handsome murdered Thomas in this woman's face, her bearing. 'What can I do for you, sir? A drink on this hot morn?'

'No. Thank you.' Stanton's stomach tightened. Her world would never be the same again. And he was the one to make it so. 'My name is Hugo Stanton. I've come from the village of Claresham with a message from its lord, Sir Reginald Edgar. May I come in, Mistress Dene? I have some private news for you.'

Then she knew. He saw it in her eyes even as he saw her not wanting to. 'It's about my son, isn't it? What's happened?' Her hands locked on her apron. 'What's happened to Thomas?' Her voice rose.

So he told her. Wanted to tell her as gently as he could. But there were no gentle words for what had happened. *Murder. Skull. Slab.* Useless ones too. *Sorry. Very, very sorry.*

Mistress Dene gave a long, terrible wail, her knees buckling, clutching at the door frame as the dog ran past her to hop and yap at Stanton's boots.

'Edith?' The call came from a concerned-looking shoemaker opposite. 'What's the matter?' He shot Stanton a wary look.

'Fetch Katherine!' screamed Edith Dene. 'Quickly!'

The shoemaker ran off.

'Let me help you inside, mistress.' Stanton put an unsure hand to Edith's arm, ready for her to strike him in her grief. He would have preferred it if she had. Instead, she let him, huge sobs breaking from her, the dog still hopping and yelping at their feet.

He steered her into the warm steam of her home, a large cauldron simmering on the fire, to an upright wooden settle, and she sank on to it. The dog sat at her feet, staring up at Stanton in a constant, rattling growl.

And he still had to tell her that her son partly brought his fate on himself. He drew breath to do so but paused.

From outside came the sound of running feet, and a breathless small-boned young woman came in, a swaddled sleeping baby in her arms. 'What's happened, Mother?'

Stanton stepped back as Edith opened her arms to her. 'Oh, Katherine, Katherine. He's dead! Thomas is dead!'

'No.' The blood left Katherine's face. 'No.' She staggered to the older woman, lowered herself on to the seat next to her. 'No.'

'It's true, my dear.' Edith could hardly speak through her tears. 'This man here has brought the news from where Thomas was working.'

Katherine shot Stanton an anguished glance and he nodded. 'I'm sorry, but it is.'

Now she also broke into dry, gasping sobs over the head of her still-sleeping infant.

'Worse,' said Edith. 'He was murdered, Katherine.'

'Murdered?' Katherine's appalled gaze flew to Stanton again.

He steeled himself to state his dreadful message once more. But Katherine's next words stunned him.

'You're telling me my husband was murdered?'

Husband? 'Your husband is – was – Thomas Dene?' He felt foolish as he said it. He'd heard 'Mother' and assumed. Wrongly. 'A stonecutter?'

'Yes.' Tears left Katherine Dene's eyes in a steady, silent stream.

A husband who'd also promised himself to Agnes Smith. Stanton wouldn't, couldn't tell her that now. 'I'm sorry.' The useless words again. 'Has he left a son or a daughter?'

'A son,' she whispered, kissing the top of the baby's head.

'And four more at home.' Edith shook her head.

'Oh, Mother,' came Katherine's long, anguished cry. 'What's to become of us?'

'Hush, girl, hush.' Despite her own grief, Edith pulled her son's young widow into her arms. 'We'll find a way.' She looked at Stanton over the top of Katherine's head as the younger woman sobbed without cease into her shoulder. 'Have you buried him?'

'It was all in hand when I left. It happened two days ago.' Stanton didn't need to say any more. The heat of the summer day answered for him. 'The rector at Claresham also promised that Thomas would be buried properly in the churchyard.'

Edith nodded, dry-eyed now, though her face looked to have aged ten years. 'And who did it? Who killed my son?'

'An outlaw.' Stanton swallowed. 'He has also killed others in Claresham.'

Edith crossed herself as Katherine sobbed on, lost in her grief. 'Then this outlaw will hang?'

'The outlaw, a man called Nicholas Lindley, is on the run,' replied Stanton. 'He had already been captured but escaped from the village gaol.'

'Then he must be found, devil take him!'

'There's more.' Stanton held up a hand. Dropped it as he realised it was something Barling did. Barling, who'd ordered him to tell this heartbreaking truth to two women whose hearts were already broken. 'I hate to have to tell you this in your time of grief. But Thomas Dene helped the outlaw to escape.' *As did I. But I'm still alive.* 'The outlaw then killed him, we assume to cover his tracks.'

'Never!' The angry scream took him by surprise. The baby too, waking with a loud squeal, and the little dog jumped up to bark again. But it wasn't Edith who'd called out.

Katherine thrust the crying baby at Edith and stood up to face Stanton. 'Never. My husband was a good man.' She jabbed a finger at him. 'A fine man.' Again. 'An honest man. A godly man!'

Honest? thought Stanton, but 'I'm sorry' was all he said.

'Sorry?' Katherine's dark eyes flashed in her fury. 'You should be ashamed, speaking ill of the dead. Ashamed!' Her anger broke into tears again and she slumped back on to the settle.

Edith rose to her feet, yelling baby in her arms.

Stanton hesitated. *The truth is always better, no matter how painful it is.* Barling's words to him before he came here.

'I think you should leave, sir,' said Edith.

But Barling hadn't meant telling a newly bereaved widow that her dead husband had been committing adultery with another woman. And if he did, he could go to hell. Stanton wasn't going to do it. Not here, not now. It could wait for another day. 'I'll do that, mistress.'

He went to the door, Edith following with the baby. He took a last glance back.

Katherine was doubled over now, rocking and moaning.

'Mistress Dene,' he said to Edith, 'I wish that I had not had to come here today with such dreadful news. Please believe me.'

'Believe me that I wish that too, sir.'

Stanton unhooked the heavy satchel containing the stonecutter's tools and laid it down at her feet. 'There's likely a hammer missing from this bag,' he said quietly.

Edith blinked, nodded. Held the baby even tighter.

'Is his pilgrim badge in there?' called Katherine to him.

'Pilgrim badge?' replied Stanton. 'I'm sorry, I don't recall seeing one.'

'He wore it around his neck,' said Katherine. 'Silver. From the shrine at Canterbury. We got it when we went there. It was in the shape of the head casket of Saint Thomas Becket.' Her tears started again. 'It was supposed to protect him on his travels. Saint Thomas protecting my beloved Tom.'

'I'm sorry,' said Stanton again. 'But I haven't.'

Katherine's tears fell harder.

'Please leave, sir,' said Edith.

He went out, pushing his way through the knot of curious people that had gathered.

He needed to get back to Claresham as quick as he could.

And break the heart of another woman.

Chapter Twenty-Nine

'You can see what a skilled stonemason Thomas Dene was, Barling.' The rector Osmond indicated the newly laid floor of the chancel in the empty church at Claresham.

The heavy rain echoed on the roof, but unlike Edgar's hall, not a drop found its way in.

'Dene had a very good hand,' said Barling. 'I could not help but notice his work at his funeral yesterday. A cruel twist that his body lay above it.'

Osmond pursed his lips and nodded, setting his chins wobbling. 'Cruel indeed. Though I must confess I noticed little at the funeral Mass yesterday, save the grief of Agnes Smith. It quite took over.'

'It did, though I suppose it was to be expected. She has had to face so many deaths in such a short time.'

'God sends us trials, Barling.' Osmond pulled a mournful face. 'And we know not why.' He crossed himself with great extravagance. 'Now, you said you would like to speak to me in private. Shall we retire to the rectory?'

'We are alone here in your church, sir priest.'

'Yes, quite.' Osmond set off for the door anyway. 'But we will have greater comfort in my home. We will be able to eat too.'

Barling followed him with a last look at the floor. He knew that many stonemasons took pride in the fact that their work would outlast them, would exist to glorify the Lord long after their deaths. He offered up a brief prayer for Thomas Dene that it might be so for him.

He joined Osmond outside, sheltered in the porch from the pelting rain that pattered loudly on the full-leafed towering trees edging the churchyard and the rest of the rector's property.

Osmond appeared much cheered again. 'A pleasure to have you visit my home. Over there you'll see my tithe barn. Filling nicely it is.'

'A fine building, sir priest. As is your house.' Built of solid stone, the rectory had a costly slate roof.

Osmond gave a wide smile. 'Then let us go there with all haste. I have no wish to change my clothes yet again.'

They hurried along the soaked, neatly gravelled path to the rectory, where the front door stood open, awaiting them.

'Yet modest,' added Osmond. 'In keeping with my calling in life.'

Barling did not reply as they entered, shaking rainwater from his robes.

Where Edgar's hall was far larger, the lord's manor was always in a state of dirt, disorganisation and decay. Not so the rectory lived in by his nephew.

The high-roofed main hall was dry and airy. The floor rushes looked recently laid and gave off a fresh scent. The plaster on the walls was picked out in an intricate design of red and yellow squares, with painted blue flowers in the centre of each. Over the huge fireplace a number of large panels were hung, depicting the lives of the saints. Gold glimmered from within the rich colours, as did a large crucifix hung as a centrepiece. A long, carved chest shone with hours of polishing and beeswax, reflecting a large pot that held bunches of scented pink roses. The chairs arranged around the table were padded in the finest tapestry. Osmond sank into one, gesturing for Barling to take another.

'I declare this heat has my humours unbalanced.' The rector fanned himself hard. 'And no doubt that's what has laid my uncle low again.'

Barling did not respond directly. He was used to Edgar's drunken sloth by now. 'It is warm indeed, sir priest. Despite this rain.' He eyed the contents of the table.

Not only did it hold a huge selection of meats and cheeses and the best puddings and bread, every plate, dish, bowl and drinking vessel had the gleam of silver. The washing bowls had petals floating in them. Sir priest clearly liked the very finest things in life.

As both men rinsed their hands before eating, a servant hurried in, clad in neat russet tunic and braies.

Barling bowed his head to say grace, Osmond joining him in a rapid mutter and finishing first.

The servant went to fill Barling's goblet with good wine, but he refused it.

'I will have water,' said Barling with a nod to a large jug.

'You do not have wine, do you, Barling?' The rector's eyes went even smaller in his fleshy face as he took a drink.

'No, sir priest. But that is of no consequence.' Barling broke off a little bread and nodded in the direction of the servant. 'As I have said, I wish for us to speak in private.'

'Leave us,' said Osmond to the servant, who withdrew at once with a bow. He went on: 'He's a good sort. Efficient. Reliable. And a solid man for keeping his master safe.' The solemn look was back. 'Of great importance in these dangerous times. I never thought I would see the day here in Claresham. Now, why is it that you want to speak to me alone? Is there something troubling you?'

'No, sir priest. Simply that you may be able to shed some light on recent events here.'

'Not I.' Osmond's eyes rounded as much as they were able. 'I am as shocked as anybody.'

'I am sure you are,' said Barling. 'Nevertheless, I would value your esteemed opinions.'

His flattery worked.

Osmond smiled in self-satisfaction. 'Of course, Barling. Ask away.'

'Your uncle said in the court at York that murder had not happened before. Is that true?'

'By the blood of the Virgin it is.' Osmond took a deep bite of the slice of gamey pie he had in one hand, adding the sheen of grease to that of sweat on his upper lip. 'I hope you're not calling him a liar.'

'Not at all, sir priest,' said Barling. 'I merely like to remind myself of the facts. He chose his next words carefully. 'And your uncle is very fond of the grape.'

Osmond shrugged. 'My uncle does indeed like his wine.' He raised his goblet to Barling. 'As do I.'

'As do many men. For most, it causes them no bother. But for a few, it can cloud their recollections. Often quite badly.'

Osmond waved a hand dismissively. 'My uncle is advancing in years. That can be even worse.'

'Indeed. But to your knowledge, there have been no other murders here?'

'Goodness, Barling.' Osmond fixed him with a stare. 'I hope you're not asking me to reveal what is discussed in the sanctity of the confessional.'

Barling felt the colour leave his face in horror at the very idea. 'No, sir priest. Never.'

'Good,' said Osmond with an unpleasant grin. 'Sometimes I wish I could share what I hear, for it would keep folk amazed for a year. Of course I cannot.' He bit off more of his pie. 'I can say that there is nobody who has confessed to a murder.' He chewed fast, hard. 'No one in the many years since my uncle set me up here as rector. And we have had no need of confessions. The murder of Geoffrey Smith marked the onset of Nicholas Lindley's carnage. I eagerly await his capture. Then I shall be pleased to hear his confession. Right before we hang him. Which we will do with all haste. Very convenient having you here, Barling.'

'I am not sure I have ever been so described, sir priest.'

'You know what I mean.' Osmond waved a hand. 'It is of course an honour too. I am a great admirer of King Henry's approach to the administration of the law. Excellent to see justice done with such great efficiency.' He wiped the grease from his fingers. 'I shall need his Grace's law myself one day, though I pray God is good and that it will not be for a long time.'

'To which law do you refer, sir priest?' asked Barling, unsettled by Osmond's sudden appreciation for the King's law. 'Perhaps I can assist or advise you.'

'I am referring to the assize of mort d'ancestor,' replied Osmond. 'For when my uncle dies, I shall be making a claim on his estate. My uncle has never been married and has no children of his own. I am compiling a solid appeal.' His small eyes met Barling's. 'Though of course I pray that I will not need it for many, many years. My uncle, the lord of Claresham, is still hale. If God is good, Sir Reginald Edgar won't be lying in my church any day soon.' He spooned a large helping of almond pudding into his mouth.

The rain on the roof gathered yet more strength.

Barling frowned to himself. Wet journeys could mean longer journeys and much more hazardous ones. He hoped Stanton would not be further delayed. Oddly for Barling, he quite missed having the younger man by his side. Usually his own company was all he required.

'My, that's good. I shall have some more.' Osmond licked his lips, then nodded at his fireplace and sighed. 'Dene was going to carve me a new mantel, you know. Now I shall have to seek another mason.' He sighed again. 'Dreadful times, Barling. Dreadful times.'

'Dreadful,' said Barling. For it was dreadful indeed to witness the naked greed of William Osmond, rector of Claresham: greed that went far, far beyond another mound of wobbly pudding.

⌣

Riding into Claresham for this, his second time, couldn't be any more different for Stanton.

Six days ago he'd ridden in behind Edgar and Barling, half-asleep from the hot sunshine and the slow-paced ride. Folk had been out and about in the full light of day.

Now he rode in late at night to silence, other than the wind in the tall, dripping trees that lined this stretch of road and the call and answer of owls. Although it had stopped, the rain in which he'd left Claresham must have carried on and on. Everything was soaked, and deep puddles sat in the fields as well as on the muddy road.

The fast pace of the splattering hooves of his lone animal echoed into the quiet.

Six days ago he'd not yet laid eyes on the murderous liar Nicholas Lindley. Six days ago Bartholomew Theaker was alive. Thomas Dene as well. And Katherine Dene was a married woman. Just as Agnes Smith thought she was about to be.

He put a hand to his face to push the tiredness away and urged his exhausted Morel on.

Barling needed to know about Dene's wife and children. He'd tell Barling first. No doubt the clerk would come down hard on him for not telling what was left of the Dene family. He didn't care. It would have been too much. Barling hadn't been there. Too much. Stanton would tell him tomorrow. First he had to sleep. He was tired, so tired. As was his animal. But he pushed, pushed. He patted the sweating neck of the surging horse. They were nearly there.

And then Morel fell from under him.

Stanton went over her right shoulder, no time to react, the ground an agonising crack to his face, his bent arm and knee as he hit the wet, stony road.

Damn it.

His wind was gone as well. He fought to get a breath into his lungs, rolled away from paddling, iron hooves even as it felt like a huge fist pressed on his chest. He lay on his back, the rustling trees above soaring into the cloudy sky.

Damn it all to hell.

But it was his own stupid fault. He'd pushed his horse too hard for too long. The dark hid holes and furrows in the road. He should know better. He got some air in. Got a bit more. Rose to his good knee. He put a hand to his face and felt wet but no give of broken bone.

And froze.

Morel hadn't fallen from a misplaced hoof.

A thick rope stretched tight across the road. Ready to bring an animal down. And the rider with it.

Run. Now. He got to his feet. Held back a yelp of pain as he almost fell again, his knee folding under him. He couldn't. Couldn't run.

All he could do was hide. He took off into the woods, shambling, scrambling to get out of sight as thorns and branches caught on his clothing. A thick evergreen bush loomed up before him and he forced his way in, trying to be fast, be quiet, terrified he was neither. He peered out at his horse, still lying injured on the road. Her whinnies told him she was in agony. At least one of her legs must be broken.

A fierce anger flashed through him. But he could do nothing, nothing except thank God his own neck hadn't snapped. Or that his knee wasn't broken. He tested it again. Still without strength, the pain pulsing through it. He was stuck in here.

Think, Hugo, think.

Right then. Stuck maybe. But at least hidden. Hidden was safe. He forced his breathing quiet. Quiet would keep him safe too. He'd hide out in here all night, wait until dawn broke and somebody else came along the road and—

Oh, Jesu Christus.

He could see somebody else on the road all right. But a somebody who stepped from the woods. One wrapped in a long dark cloak, face behind a concealing wrap as well. Utterly silent. Looking right, left. Not looking at poor Morel, suffering on the ground.

Looking for the rider, moving at a steady, fluid pace as Stanton strained to see in the gloom.

The figure's clothing made it a shadow amongst shadows, the clouds not helping.

And then, with a gust of wind, they slipped past the small moon, bringing a poor light.

Bringing enough light for Stanton to see the figure standing over his injured horse, to see the figure raise a gloved hand.

And that hand was closed around something, something that the figure slammed into Morel's skull in a blow so hard he could swear he felt it as well as heard it.

Lindley. Stanton shoved his fist into his mouth to stop his cry. *No.*

Morel wasn't dead, not yet, the blows raining down on her again and again, until she was – after she was – in a savage, sickening slaughter.

When it was over, Stanton felt a trickle of moisture on his hand. He realised he'd punctured his flesh, biting it so hard to stop his screams of horror.

Lindley straightened up. Threw the stone away.

And now he was looking left, right again. Looking left, right, as if he sniffed the air. As if he could smell Stanton and his terror nearby.

Then he was on the move again. Taking those fast, silent strides that made him seem a ghost.

But one that was back in the bushes. Only the odd snap of a tiny twig, only the odd sway of a branch as Stanton squinted, peered, trying to track where he was.

With a stiff gust of wind, the darkness swept in again, as if the moon closed her eyes to the horror on the road below her.

A wave of sweat drenched Stanton. His hands went to the ground, searching as quickly, as quietly, as he dared for anything, anything at all, he could use as a weapon. He didn't dare drop his gaze.

Not that he could see a thing.

His hands met twigs, damp leaves. Nothing. He had nothing. Nothing to use against the man who'd caved in the skull of a horse with just a rock and his own murderous strength.

He heard a snap of a twig. Definitely. A bit closer. He could swear it.

He wanted to laugh now at his own boneheaded plan to hide in here until morning.

Lindley was searching, searching for him now. And the man knew these woods, knew how to move among them in almost complete darkness.

Think, Hugo, think.

Hiding was no good. He couldn't outrun Lindley on the road. Had he been in one piece, he might've stood a chance. He was fast, very fast, on a good surface. But not now, not with his knee like this.

Think, Hugo, think.

The day when he was out with Barling. When Barling told him to look at the layout of the lands. Of the village.

He forced himself to picture it. The road looped round a number of long fields. But if he cut through the woods, he would reach the village's houses much, much sooner.

Another snap. This one sounded a bit further away.

Or did it?

No matter. He had to do this now. *Now.*

Stanton took off, bent double, his knee a stab of agony at every step, half giving way every time he put his weight on it. But he didn't care.

Branches lashed his face, tore his hands as he ran on blindly, his breath a huffing sob in his terror and pain.

Then he heard it, through his own noise, somebody else crashing through, behind him, next to him, in front of him, he didn't know.

All he knew was that he had to get to a cottage, any cottage.

And then he saw it.

The thatched roof against the trees, the shed next to it.

It was the Webbs', thank God, the Webbs'. Three souls lived there; Lindley couldn't kill them all.

A louder crash, definitely louder.

Now Stanton was yelling, running. He didn't care; the Webbs would hear him, they had to.

And then he was stumbling across the yard, then screaming, hammering at the shut front door.

'Let me in! For the love of God, let me in!'

Chapter Thirty

'Please!' Stanton hammered again, his neck twisting back and forth as he tried to watch the woods, watch everywhere. Watch for the figure who killed men and animals with savage strength.

Then a sound sent by the saints themselves.

The sound of a key in the lock. The door opening. A crack, no more.

'Who is it?' Margaret Webb's voice. Afraid.

'It's me, Hugo Stanton. Let me in, I beg you. Lindley's out here, he's here!'

Margaret shrieked and yanked the door open, Stanton stumbling into the room.

'Thank you, mistress.' He bent over to try and get his breath as she slammed the door and locked it with shaking hands.

He couldn't stop. 'Oh, thank you. Thank you.'

She trembled from head to foot. 'You have Peter to thank, sir.'

Stanton straightened up.

To see Peter Webb standing there as sweaty and breathless as him. Unlike Margaret, who wore her underskirt and shift, with a large shawl over them for modesty, Peter wasn't dressed for bed but for a day's work outdoors. 'You have found me out, sir.' His voice shook.

'Found you out?' Stanton still couldn't get a full lungful of air. Couldn't understand either. 'What do you mean?'

'I was out in the woods just now.' Peter swallowed hard and exchanged a look with Margaret, who put a hand to her forehead. 'I'd been out awhile. Then I heard the most terrible sounds. So I ran home. Fast as I could. Like the devil was chasing me.'

'What you heard was Lindley ambushing me,' said Stanton. 'Then he killed my horse. And came after me.'

Margaret gasped. 'So the devil was abroad.'

Peter crossed himself with a look of horror, hands trembling. 'And so was I. May God help me.'

'Did you see him, Webb?' asked Stanton.

'No, sir.' Peter's hands were shaking still.

'He was on the roadway.'

'I . . . I wasn't on the roadway, sir. I was in the woods.' Another look to Margaret, who bowed her head. By contrast, Webb straightened as much as he could with his stoop. 'Where my traps are. I was out poaching.'

'Poaching?' A surprise, despite the terrors of this night. 'Does Edgar know you do this?'

'No, sir.' Webb's voice dropped. He looked at Margaret again. 'I need to tell the King's man everything.'

She nodded in a wordless reply.

Webb made his way behind his loom and emerged with a closed sack. He opened it up and removed a glossy hare skin. 'You see this, sir? I can sell it at one of the market towns. This' – his hands tightened on the small hide – 'this is the difference between us being able to pay the rent or not.'

'Between eating or not.' Margaret's voice held despair.

'There's only us two that can earn any kind of living,' said Webb. 'You've met John, sir.' He shook his head.

'Where is he?' asked Stanton. In his panic, he'd not noticed John's absence.

'Safe in our fulling shed, sir, I promise you,' said Margaret. 'I bolted the door myself.'

'He likes it best in there,' said Peter. 'He stays calm. At least for some of the time.' He shook his head. 'With how he is, having to feed him is the least of our worries. Until now. If Sir Reginald finds out I've been poaching . . .' He trailed off, unable to form the words.

Stanton could guess. The bullying lord didn't have a merciful bone in his body. 'Put your skins away, Webb. You saved my life tonight. I wouldn't dream of repaying you by making such trouble for you.'

Webb hauled in a deep breath. Let it out. Looked at his wife. 'I thank you, sir,' he said, 'from the bottom of my heart.' His own relieved smile lit up his worn, lined face. 'To your good one.'

'The kindest one,' whispered Margaret, managing a watery smile.

A shout came from outside.

Stanton knew his panicked look would be the same as those of both Webbs.

Then came a loud hullo. Followed by more calls, different voices. His own name.

Morel's carcass had been found.

Chapter Thirty-One

'Stanton! Thank God you are safe,' Barling called to him from further along the road.

The knot of people he stood with raised their voices too.

'I was lucky, Barling,' said Stanton as he hurried up to them, Peter Webb beside him. Margaret had locked herself in the cottage until her husband returned. 'That's all.'

'I would say very lucky.' Barling's pale face shone in the light of the lantern he carried, as did the faces of the many others who had come running, lights aloft. A lot of them held sticks as well as their lanterns. They grouped around Morel, exclaiming, clutching each other at what lay before them as well as Stanton's arrival.

'A miracle.' Osmond's eyes looked ready to leave his head. 'Nothing less.' The priest had obviously been summoned from his bed. Like so many others, he had flung his cloak over his linens.

'One that your horse wasn't blessed with, man.' Edgar pushed his way out from the midst of the huddle, fully dressed. His coarse visage could be the setting sun in this light.

'What happened, Stanton?' asked Barling. 'All we know is from these men here.' He raised his lamp to show two white-faced men leaning against a cart. 'They were travelling back from a market, their own horse slow from a pulled leg. They saw the rope across the road, then your animal, and so raised the alarm.'

'I wasn't riding slowly,' said Stanton. 'Morel hit the rope hard and I came off. I hid. And then I saw a hooded figure' – he swallowed – 'kill my horse.'

'Lindley!' cried Osmond. 'May God protect us.'

His cries were echoed by every one of the group, with people herding closer together on the dark road.

'He chased me. But I ran,' said Stanton. 'And Peter Webb here saved me, along with his wife. They took me in. Otherwise . . .' He couldn't finish. Shrugged.

'You have the gratitude of the King, Webb,' said Barling.

'Thank you, sir,' replied Webb. 'I am honoured.'

'Can we leave the niceties to one side?' Edgar. As usual. 'Barling, your own man has been attacked! A fine horse too.' He looked over at poor Morel.

Stanton couldn't do so.

'I am fully aware, Edgar,' said Barling. 'I wanted to hear from Stanton's lips what happened, as that will help decide the next course of action.'

'Which is?'

'What's happened?' The call came from Agnes Smith as she ran towards the group. 'Tell me you've got the swine.'

'Of course not, girl.' Edgar spat his words as she arrived, panting.

'There has been another attack,' said Barling.

'On the King's man no less.' Osmond pointed to Stanton.

'Dear God.' Her free hand went to her mouth. 'Are you all right, Hugo?'

'I'm fine.'

'You should not be abroad on your own, Agnes,' said Barling. 'It is far too dangerous.'

She held up her other hand, into the light. 'I'm not afraid of Lindley.' She held a sturdy axe.

Stanton flinched as people moved back with a cry.

'Agnes, lower that. At once,' came Barling's sharp order. 'Now give it to me.' He held out his hand.

She caught the full force of the Barling tone. Stanton knew its impact. Scowling, she placed the weapon handle first in his open palm to many sighs of relief. 'I will put it away safely.' He shook his head at Agnes. 'If you don't know how to use a weapon, it can be used against you. I will make sure that you are brought back home safely.'

'I'll take her.' Simon Caldbeck stepped from the group, a stout stick in one hand.

'No. Agnes needs to come to the hall with us, Barling,' said Stanton. He had to do this tonight, no matter what had happened. She needed to know the truth about Dene. 'Sir priest will also be needed.' To his relief, Barling didn't question him, though Edgar did. Agnes was louder, more insistent than them all.

Stanton raised his voice over them. 'It's about Thomas Dene.'

The questioning stopped. Dead.

'Thomas?' Her face went white. 'What about him, Hugo?'

Stanton ignored her question. She would soon find out, God help her.

'Then we shall make all haste, Stanton.' Barling turned to address the villagers. 'As for next steps, we need to start a search for Lindley. At first light.'

His words were met by some more cheers and quite a few anxious looks. Not Edgar.

'God's eyes!' Edgar clenched a fist in anticipation. 'And I shall be the one to lead it, Barling.'

Stanton exchanged a look with Barling and the clerk read his urgency.

'Go to your homes, good people. And pray for our success.'

That it would be so. But Stanton couldn't think about that just yet. First, Agnes.

Chapter Thirty-Two

Telling Agnes the truth about the life of Thomas Dene had cost Stanton dear, Barling knew.

Sitting at the table once again in Edgar's hall, Barling had listened to his young messenger's account carefully and without comment while in his heart he offered fervent prayers of thanks. When he'd first seen Stanton's dead horse on the road, a gut-wrenching terror that his assistant had suffered the same fate had seized him. But God had smiled.

Stanton's account of what he had discovered about Dene came as a great surprise – Barling would be the first to admit that. But one thing the law had taught him was that people, far from being in the image of God, were capable of so much wrong.

Edgar had remarked crudely and relentlessly and drank to match.

Osmond had been a flurry of exclamations.

Agnes herself had been disbelieving. *The woman who calls herself Katherine Dene is lying. Thomas had no wife. She's lying.*

Distraught. *My life is over. Over, do you hear me? Dear God, I missed his pilgrim badge when I washed him. How? How could I? But he was destroyed. Destroyed, my gorgeous Thomas.*

Disbelieving again. *That woman is lying, lying. I don't know why. A thief of some sort, she has his tools now. That's it, a low, base thief. Never his wife. Never.*

Then, as she'd had her heart shattered into even smaller pieces by Stanton's account, Osmond decided that her soul was in peril also. He'd insisted, now he had found out she had been committing adultery, that she make a full and urgent confession to him.

Agnes had fought it, but once Barling had also ordered her, she had gone to a private room with Osmond.

Edgar had continued to blabber on, Barling throwing him the odd response as he, Barling, mulled over the latest findings.

No doubt utterly spent by now, Stanton had sat in silence, barely touching any food, preferring his wine, a poultice on his injured knee.

Now the rector was back.

'The baggage will confess nothing,' he said as he walked back in. 'Nothing.'

Edgar snorted. 'Then she'll burn in hell.'

'Give her time to examine her conscience,' said Barling. 'To reflect on her actions.'

'Well, I am not going to waste any more time on her tonight,' said Osmond. 'Uncle, I'm off to my own bed. But I'm not walking there alone.' He shuddered. 'Think of what a prize a priest would be for Lindley.'

'Take a couple of my servants with you,' said Edgar.

'More than a couple, I'd say,' said Osmond. 'May God give us comfort after this dreadful night. And let us give every thanks for your merciful escape, Stanton.'

'Thank you, sir priest,' replied Stanton.

Osmond left with a wave.

'Escape.' Edgar snorted in disgust. 'Escape. Too many bloody escapes, if you ask me. Too many. Should never have happened, Barling.

Should all've been . . . been' – he waved a hand – 'dealt with.' He belched. 'Long ago.'

The lord's obnoxious drunkenness was sorely trying Barling's patience now. 'Edgar, as I have said over and over, matters are being dealt with. I am dealing with them, under the authority of his Grace's justices. As for escapes, it was Thomas Dene who helped Lindley escape.'

'And look what happened to Dene! His head caved in! For helping the swine!'

'We do not know why—'

'But I helped the bastard!'

Barling could see Stanton's stunned expression at the edge of his vision. He knew his own would not be far off.

Edgar carried on. 'Before anything happened. No one was murdered. Nothing! I found Lindley hiding in one of my stables. It was the night before the one of Smith's murder. Chap was in a piteous state. I gave him some work to do. Rewarded him for it with charity. The boots off my own feet. My own feet! Said that was what he wanted. Not money. His feet were ruined from wandering for miles.'

'Edgar, why on earth have you not told me this before?'

'Because it was something of nothing. I'd helped the man. He had his boots. Should've been gone. On his way.' He got to his feet, swaying hard. 'Instead, he won't leave us alone. Bringing us all to hell.' He staggered out, cursing loud and long.

Stanton stared after him, then looked over at Barling. 'How could he not tell you this?'

'Stanton, people keep secrets for all sorts of reasons.' The very best of reasons, as Barling knew only too well. 'This at least explains in part why Edgar is so quick to blame everybody for Lindley's escape. He had allowed it himself, and did it first, not bothering to enquire in any way about why a beggar might be roaming the land. Had he made such enquiries, who knows what he may have discovered?' He gave a sharp sigh. 'The man's approach to the law, to order, defies belief.'

'At least his outburst explains the matter of Lindley's boots,' said Stanton. 'I did wonder how such a ragged man had such good ones.'

Barling nodded. 'I had also noticed those but assumed he had stolen them from somewhere.'

'As for secrets,' said Stanton, 'some I can understand more than others. Now that we're on our own, let me tell you about the Webbs'.' He provided Barling with a brief account.

Barling sighed. 'Now we face a difficult dilemma. Edgar should really be told.'

'No, he shouldn't. The Webbs saved my life, at risk to themselves. A few hares don't matter to Edgar. They do to the Webbs.' The younger man's words were forceful. Calm. Convincing.

'Are you honestly trying to convince me that breaking the law should be rewarded, Stanton?'

'In this case, yes.'

Barling gave a small smile, which he knew surprised Stanton. 'Ah,' he said. 'You are indeed learning to think things through. Before long I believe you will be fit to hold another position with the court. Yes, you are no scribe, but I am sure we can find a better way for you to serve your King and—'

'No!' Stanton's face was a sudden mask of barely suppressed fury, shocking Barling as much as the loud interruption.

'I believe that—'

'No.' Stanton cut him off again. 'I don't want it, never want it. Do you hear me?'

Barling was rarely bewildered. He was now.

Stanton's visage, normally so easy to read, had become a closed, furious mask.

Barling did know, however, when not to respond, when not to antagonise one who was greatly aroused. He held a hand up. 'Very well. I shall not suggest it again.'

To his relief, Stanton relaxed once more, the younger man's brow clearing as he swallowed hard. 'Thank you, Barling.'

'Then we move on,' said Barling, forcing his own attention back to the matter at hand. 'I have a secret to share with you also. Another that relates to Agnes Smith. I will be brief.'

Stanton listened, his face now filled with growing horror as Barling related how Lindley had also set about Agnes on the night of her father's murder, stealing through the woods using concealing clothing in the same way.

When he'd finished, Stanton looked as though he might be sick. 'Then Agnes was almost a victim of Lindley too.' He brought a hand to his neck. 'So many. Barling, why is he doing this? You have spent years hearing the crimes of killers. You must have some idea.'

'I know this,' said Barling. 'There are many reasons why a man becomes an outlaw. An unfettered desire to kill is among them. It is rare. But Stanton, it is very, very real. Tomorrow we seek to end it.'

'We will.' Stanton nodded. Hard.

Yet Barling still wondered, wondered what could have made this quick young man into someone who would be so angry at the idea of serving his lord King.

Barling would find out. One day. He would make it his business to do so.

As for his own secrets, they were buried so deep they would never see the light of day.

Ever.

Chapter Thirty-Three

A waste of time this. *Waste.*

Stanton sat on the horse lent to him by Edgar, sweat trickling down his back. He missed his poor dead Morel, with her pace like a fast-flowing river. Being astride this animal was more like sitting in the sticky mud that remained from the heavy rain. The sluggish horse plodded up a long, featureless hill, the gradual incline covered in poor grass and a few shrubs and without a single leaf or tree to cast any shade from the searing afternoon sun. The storm clouds had long disappeared and the heat was worse than ever.

Ahead, Edgar advanced on his huge palfrey, with loud snorts coming from the horse as he drove it on.

Barling rode next to Stanton, a bit less awkwardly than usual. Perhaps the clerk was learning. As ever he wore his black robes, even on this stifling day.

Stanton's conscience nipped at him. Barling wasn't a bad fellow. The clerk had clearly thought that offering Stanton a chance to serve Henry was a wonderful gift. If only he knew the truth. But he didn't. Yet Stanton shouldn't have reacted with such anger. It wasn't fair on the man, no matter how annoying he could be.

'What do you think Edgar hopes to find up here, Barling?'

The clerk turned at Stanton's question. 'That, Stanton, I do not know. But I can certainly guess that it will be precisely the same as what we have found up to now: nothing.'

'But we shouldn't even be bothering with this stretch. Look.' Stanton gestured around, ahead, with one hand. 'There's nothing except miles of open land. Lindley would be easier to spot than a scarecrow on a ploughed field. And we've been at this since morning.'

'I suppose we should give thanks that it is a new location,' said Barling dryly. 'There was that field we rode past three times.'

'Fields that people should be working in.' Stanton glanced back at the line of villagers trudging along in the heat. 'Like Simon Caldbeck, the ploughman. And people like Peter Webb: he should be at his loom. The miller's out here as well.' He had to say it. 'You should never have allowed Edgar to lead the search, Barling.'

'Of course I should.'

'Admitting you're wrong isn't a sin, you know.'

'I shall make allowances for your rudeness in this heat, Stanton.' Barling took a careful look round to make sure no one could overhear. 'It was no accident that I allowed Edgar to be in charge of this today. Edgar has done nothing except criticise and condemn how the law proceeds since we arrived here. He is responsible for undermining our efforts at all times, such as when he dared to try to lay the blame for Lindley's escape on you. It is often the case with those who stand and carp: once they are asked to carry out a task, they are unable to.'

'Then all these hours have been to teach the lord a lesson.'

'No,' said Barling. 'A man like Edgar is incapable of learning anything about himself by failure. That would require a degree of courage. What I am doing is making sure that, after today, Edgar's voice is much less influential. Without his constant obstacles, we will be able to make much better progress. And this conversation is, as always, only for our ears.'

'Hah.' Stanton grinned at the picture of how furious Edgar would be if he knew. 'I just wish you'd told me your plan earlier.' He reached for his water bottle.

'To be honest,' said Barling, 'I did not think for one second that he would last this long. When he came into the stable yard this morning, he could hardly walk. None of us had a great deal of sleep, but he looked to me like he had been up all night with his wine jug. He had had a copious amount throughout the day as well.'

'People of Claresham!' Edgar pulled his horse up. 'Gather round. The King's men as well.'

'Now what's he doing?' said Stanton.

'Something foolish, I am sure,' murmured Barling as they arranged themselves in a group before Edgar with the sweating, exhausted folk of Claresham.

'My lands have inspired me today on our search.' The scarlet-faced Edgar swayed in the saddle as he gave a wide gesture. 'Look at them. Far as the eye can see.' He stifled a hiccup.

Stanton saw many glances exchanged.

Edgar went on. 'From here, you can see everything. Every. Thing. And that is what I want to do. Make sure I see everything.' He pointed a wavering finger at the group. 'That' – he gave a deep swallow – 'you do. Some people say that I don't apply the law correctly.' Another swallow. 'After today, after seeing everything . . .' Another. 'I do. See. I will not tolerate any wrongdoing ever again.' A gulp. 'Or from before. All the wrongdoers. Ever. I will see them. Everybody will see them. Every. One.' He grimaced. Then vomited all over his horse. And fell off it.

The thud of his big body hitting the ground was met with more groans than gasps.

'Oh, my lord.' A groom came rushing to Edgar's side to see to him.

Stanton saw Barling rise a little in his stirrups to take a look.

'Out cold,' said the clerk to him with the barest twitch of a smile.

Barling continued with his voice raised. 'Good people. You can see that your lord has been taken ill. Our first priority must be to return him to his hall.'

Set looks met that announcement.

'There will also be a new, orderly search for Nicholas Lindley tomorrow. This time I will lead it.'

If Barling had been expecting a better response, he didn't get it.

The set looks at the King's clerk didn't change.

And on the ground, Edgar threw up all over his groom.

Chapter Thirty-Four

Finally, Aelred Barling had lost his calm.

Stanton couldn't help a smile inside at the row that now raged in Edgar's hall, the lord locked in verbal combat with the King's clerk.

With a stab of his short eating knife, he brought the roasted pigeon to his mouth and took a bite. Delicious, as was all the other food laid out. He actually had an appetite on this warm evening. They hadn't had sight of Lindley, thanks to Edgar's wild search. But all had remained peaceful in Claresham today. Well, except for the hall at this moment.

Barling had had his plan to fully take over the search. Edgar had decided to take no notice, despite having fallen off his horse in a drunken collapse.

'These are my lands, Barling.' The scowling Edgar sat hunched at the head of the table, busy guzzling wine to replace what he'd spewed earlier. 'Mine. You have no right to take over as you did today.'

'I did not take over, Edgar. I did what I was entitled to do.' Barling had his water from the spring and a furious look.

'I think you invent what you are entitled to, Barling.'

Stanton reached for a piece of bread.

'How dare you, sir,' said Barling. 'You know full well I consult the law every step of the way.'

'Maybe you do. Or maybe you don't. Does he, Hugo?'

Stanton looked up, alarmed by Edgar's use of his name and, worse, by his attempt to draw him into the argument.

'You leave my assistant out of this, Edgar.'

'He can speak for himself, can't he?' Edgar grinned at Stanton. 'Or does the court not allow it?'

Barling made an impatient noise and drank from his cup.

Stanton understood what was going on now. Edgar was starting to enjoy himself hugely. He'd succeeded in making Barling annoyed and he knew that gave him the upper hand. 'I'm not a big one for speeches, my lord.'

'No.' Barling rose from the table. 'And neither should you be. I am going to retire now. I have much to see to tomorrow, and that ride of many miles has tired me out.' He went to the door. 'Unnecessary miles at that.' Then he was gone as fast as his stiff steps would allow.

'I should go to my bed also, my lord.' Stanton rose to his feet, cursing silently that Barling had stormed off. So much good food sat in front of him.

'Sit, sit.' Edgar waved a hand. 'Just because your master has gone off in a huff doesn't mean you have to as well.'

He didn't much want to stay here with Edgar. But he wanted to go to bed hungry even less. 'Thank you, my lord.'

It was a big mistake. He knew how much Edgar liked to talk. And talk he did, long past the time Stanton finished eating and the servants had cleared all the dishes of food away, leaving plentiful wine for Edgar.

Edgar drank and talked and talked and drank, pressing Stanton into goblet after goblet too.

Every time Stanton thought Edgar had finished, the man would start again, with more blather and a full cup.

Darkness had long fallen and the moon now hung in the open window.

A huge yawn broke from Stanton, causing Edgar to pause.

'You're ready to retire, are you, Hugo?'

'If that's all right, my lord.'

'Of course, of course.' Edgar waved a hand.

'Thank you for your generous hospitality, my lord.' *And thank the saints I'm going to bed.* Stanton winced as he got to his feet. The room span a bit from all he'd drunk as well.

'Something the matter?'

'It's only my knee. Hurt it when Lindley sent me off my horse. Goodnight, my lord.' He started to limp off.

'Let me have a look.' For a big man, Edgar could move very fast.

He stood in front of Stanton, bending over to put a large hand on his sore kneecap. 'Had an injury like this myself.' Squeezed it. Hard.

'Ow.'

'It'll mend.' Edgar straightened up.

Still stood close. Very close. Close enough for Stanton to see every broken vein in the man's face, in his hooded eyes.

'I'm sure it will, my lord.' He went to step past, but Edgar moved too.

'Young joints always do.' He smiled, his rows of yellowed teeth inches away. 'Beautifully.'

And then one of Edgar's big hands was on the back of his neck, the other fumbling for his crotch, the lord's wide, wet mouth closing on his.

Damn it all. Stanton shoved him off. Hard.

The lord reeled back. 'Come on, Stanton.' No more smile. 'You need to pay for all that good wine.'

'No, I don't.'

'Don't you dare test me, boy.' Edgar lunged for him again.

Stanton was ready for him. He stepped smartly out of reach, sending the lord staggering.

Edgar clutched at a chair back for balance, swearing hard.

Stanton had seen men like him plenty of times in the dark recesses of the worst bawdy houses – had had them try to corner him a few times as well. 'I'm sure your nephew has preached to you that sodomites go to hell. So stay away from me, Edgar. And you'll stay out of hell.'

His words worked like they always did.

'Hell?' Edgar's tone was vicious as he flung the chair aside with a loud clatter. 'Hell? You can talk. You're Satan coming to tempt me again. Now get out of my sight.'

Stanton didn't wait, not while he had the chance to get away.

He always made sure he did that too.

Chapter Thirty-Five

Stanton's heart soared. Rosamund, his Rosamund. Astride Morel as he rode next to her on an unknown mount. Her golden hair streaming behind her, her cheeks a delicate pink in the sunshine, her lips parting as she gasped her delight. He held out his hand to grasp her smooth fingers, to feel her touch, to share her joy. But he couldn't reach; she rode faster than him. 'Hurry, Hugo, hurry!' He tried to respond to her laughing call. But he couldn't. She was fast, too fast. He couldn't reach, couldn't—

'Sir, sir! Come, you must hurry!'

Stanton didn't recognise the voice that pulled him from his dream. He opened his eyes, squinting in the bright light of day.

A frantic servant stood by the bed.

Stanton sat bolt upright with an oath. 'I'm late. Barling's waiting for me, isn't he?'

'No, sir, no.' The servant's eyes were wild, terrified. 'It's Sir Reginald. Our lord has been murdered.'

'What?' Stanton wasn't sure if he still dreamed.

'In his solar. The King's clerk says to come at once.'

No dream. Stanton yanked on his clothes, ran through the hall past groups of sobbing servants to Edgar's solar.

He slowed as he approached the door. It would never be long enough, but this was too soon after Dene.

'I'm here, Barling,' he called out, as much to prepare himself as the clerk.

'Then come in, Stanton,' came the clerk's call in return. 'But be warned of what you are about to see.'

Stanton drew in a deep breath, as if he were to plunge into a deep pool of water. He was glad he did, as a sickly stench like that of a newly slaughtered pig met him.

'God's eyes.' He put a hand to his mouth and nose. Blood, so much blood, obscene in the harsh sunlight that streamed in through an open window.

'A scene from hell.' Barling shook his head. 'We use the words often, but I have never seen anything so close.' He blessed himself with a hand that looked to Stanton much less steady than usual. 'And I pray I never will.'

Edgar lay on his bed, on his back with his arms out, his bed linen splashed with scarlet.

'His throat has been slashed,' said Barling. 'A servant found him when they went to wake him. You can see the open shutter where Lindley must have entered and left.'

'Lindley knew it, didn't he?' said Stanton. 'Because he'd been in the manor before. Like Edgar said.'

'Indeed.' Barling gave a sombre nod. 'We need to question the household, of course. But I think we already have truth from poor Edgar's mouth.'

Edgar's mouth. Closing on his. A few short hours ago. The same mouth that had accused Stanton of being the devil. Gaping wide in a silent scream now. And forever. Too much.

'Are you all right, Stanton?'

'I'm fine, Barling.' He pushed past the clerk.

But once the petrified servants were assembled in the hall, it was like all the other murders.

Stanton could hear the answers even before Barling asked the questions.

No one saw or heard anything. The manor was secure. But Lindley, 'the devil', must have found a way to get in through the window and slay their master.

'And can you tell me,' asked Barling next of the servants, 'what work Lindley did for your lord?'

'Work, sir?'

'None.'

'No work.'

Barling pressed them as Stanton watched faces for any sign of a lie, but saw none.

'I mean,' said the clerk, 'the work for which Edgar rewarded Lindley with a pair of boots. Here in the manor.'

'Boots?'

'Lindley was here?'

'No, no, not here. Never.'

'Oh, God save us.'

'Very well,' said Barling to the servants. 'If you think of anything else, if you recall anything, you must inform me at once. In the meantime, convey the news immediately to the rector that his uncle is dead, and that he needs to come to administer the last rites. Make sure you move in pairs or more. Is that clear? I also need you to summon the men of the village with all haste, as this new outrage has made the search for Lindley all the more urgent. Also, tell the men to ensure that their womenfolk are locked away in safety.'

The servants left with a clatter, leaving Stanton alone with Barling.

'Are you now going to tell me what the matter is, Stanton?'

'There's a lot the matter this morning, Barling.'

'Stanton, you are probably the worst liar I have ever met.'

Stanton pulled in a breath. 'I may be the last person to have seen Edgar alive. Last night. Here, in this hall.' He gave Barling his account, willing the clerk to disbelieve him.

Barling let him speak.

Angry shouts came from the courtyard, but still Barling didn't interrupt Stanton.

When he'd finished, Barling nodded slowly. 'Ah. Then our outlaw did perform some work.'

'But the servants said he didn't, Barling. They told you that a few minutes ago.'

'Barling!' Osmond barrelled in, cutting off Barling's reply.

'For the love of God, what has happened to my uncle?'

Chapter Thirty-Six

'I will search the village first.' Barling's voice rose above the angry shouts and jeers of all of the men of the village assembled in the courtyard in the sun's stark light.

Stanton stood with him, mindful that the villagers might turn on them at any minute. He knew Osmond was in the solar with his uncle's body. If he had to, he'd run and get him. But summoning a priest from his administering of the sacraments was a last – a very last – choice. Neither did he want to leave Barling alone. The clerk might say the wrong thing at any second.

He kept an eye on the door, ready to haul Barling in if need be.

'We've just come from the village!'

'Our women are locked up in our homes. Should we search under their skirts?' This from a sneering Caldbeck.

Hoots, jeers greeted the ploughman's impudence.

'Unlike the late Sir Reginald Edgar, I will do this in a methodical way.'

Stanton cringed. He'd guessed right about Barling's actions. Calling shame down on the murdered lord would do Barling no favours. The clerk was correct, but this was not the time to say it.

'Our lord not good enough for you?'

'Hell's teeth, sir!'

'Have a bit of respect, man!'

'God save Sir Reginald's soul!'

Barling did not respond, or even flinch. Instead he carried on. 'And Stanton and I will look in every dwelling.'

Now the jeers became howls of protest.

'He questions our word!'

'Lindley's not in our homes!'

'While the real outlaw is still taking lives!'

Stanton got ready to pull Barling inside, put a hand on his arm.

But Barling shook him off to try to shout over the crowd again. 'Wild pursuit has not served us well up to now!'

'For the love of God, compose yourselves!'

Stanton looked around as the rector walked out to face the crowd.

'My uncle has been murdered. Lies dead in this hall. There should be prayers, not a riot.'

His words brought a simmering silence.

'Thank you, sir priest,' said Barling. 'I shall conduct my search as I read the law. Not in fits and starts, but in order. Line by line by line. A proper search may well yield vital information. I am going to start now, Stanton with me.'

'And me also,' said the rector. 'My uncle's soul is already in Paradise, I have no doubt of that.'

Stanton did.

The rector continued. 'Now I wish to find who sent him there.'

'So if you are not coming with us,' said Barling to the villagers, 'go to your homes. It is one or the other.' His gaze met Stanton's. 'Are you ready, Stanton?'

Osmond's demand for composure had worked at first but the quiet hadn't lasted long. Every stop at every home brought new calls of protest from the men outside and the women within.

Stanton also couldn't quite believe that they were wasting time like this, but he had no opportunity to try to talk Barling out of it.

The clerk had even brought one of his wax tablets with him to list names and dwellings, to more howls of derision every time he read from it or wrote on it.

Their checking of the empty home of Bartholomew Theaker brought the worst insults of all. The body of its owner had gone, but all else was the same, except the blossom tree, its petals now shed and lying on the ground like snow.

They moved on, from door to door, Osmond's insistence on blessing every home once they'd finished checking adding to their slow pace.

Stanton heard every word of barely muted insult. A few times his cheeks burned and he knew Barling must be able to hear it all too. Yet the King's clerk stayed as aloof as if he sat on the dais like the judges at York.

Then they came to one house that Stanton knew well.

'This is the Webbs', Barling,' he said.

'Peter and Margaret Webb?' Barling looked at his list.

'Correct.' Even Stanton was tempted to smack the tablet out of his hand. He knew who the Webbs were.

'Knock on, Stanton.'

Stanton did as ordered, the warm planks in the sunshine and the noise so different from the dark and the quiet of the night he'd been pounding on it.

No answer. He frowned.

'Sir!' Peter Webb's sombre face was one in the group of village men.

'What is it, Webb?' asked Barling.

'Margaret's with John in the fulling shed, sir. He was bad this morning, so we agreed she should stay in there.'

'Very well.'

Stanton crossed the yard with Barling and Osmond, Webb following them. Webb opened the door to the shed to the sharp, foul stench of the stale urine used in the fulling work. Stanton coughed hard, Barling also recoiling, as the rector clapped his linen kerchief to his own nose.

A loud report echoed out.

John, of course, treading in the dark.

'I can't see Margaret,' said Stanton to Barling.

'You can't?' Webb frowned. 'Margaret!'

No answer.

Only John's steady steps and splashes, a creature in his own dark world with no understanding of what was going on.

'Margaret!'

'Check the cottage, Stanton. Now.'

Stanton ran the few yards back to the cottage, Webb behind him, older, slower, calling for his wife.

He hauled open the door.

No jeers, no catcalls now.

For on the floor of the Webbs' cottage was the still form of Margaret Webb, lying face down on a pile of newly woven cloth, her white coif a bloodied mess of scarlet.

Chapter Thirty-Seven

A stunned-looking Peter Webb staggered past Stanton to his wife, and then John was in too, hollering and crying.

A wave of panicked yells came from outside as well, some men fleeing back to their own homes to check on their loved ones.

'Stay calm, stay calm, good people!' came Osmond's useless call.

'Margaret?' Webb stared at his wife's body, one hand clutching at his chest.

'Stanton!' Barling's order rose above the din. 'Remove that wild boy. At once.'

Stanton looked to Webb to help. No use. The man appeared about to pass out.

He grabbed for John's jerkin, hanging on as the man twisted and yelled.

'Get him out, Stanton.'

'Out, come on.' Stanton went to wrestle John out, but the man flung himself back to his mother, breaking from Stanton's grasp and sending him to the floor.

He landed hard on one hip.

'Stanton.' Barling's sharp rebuke.

Stanton went to clamber back up, grabbed for John again. Got him.

Then he saw it. The tiniest twitch of one of Margaret's fingers.

'Barling, she's still alive!' Stanton thrust John from him, pushed the suffocating wool down to give Margaret the best chance for air.

'Oh, Margaret, Margaret!' Webb was on his knees next to him, still clutching his chest, his breathing ragged.

John had retreated to the corner, slapping his own head hard, and carrying on his sudden shouts.

As Stanton did what he could, Barling's crisp orders came echoing in while Osmond loudly proclaimed a miracle.

'Fetch somebody who can dress her wound. Then I want her taken back to the lord's manor under constant guard. I do not want her to be vulnerable to any further attack from Lindley.'

Stanton had done his best in freeing Margaret's mouth and nose. Doubt bit at him now. She hadn't moved since that one – that only – tiny twitch. Her eyes were still closed.

'If you'll excuse me, sir.' He looked up to see the midwife, Hilda Folkes. 'I shall see to Margaret now.'

'Of course.' He went outside, his legs like he'd been running far and fast.

Barling gave him a firm nod as Webb came out behind him, the weaver's grip firm on a quieter but still moaning John.

'What happens now, Barling?'

A rude shout from the crowd. Caldbeck.

'We carry on our search of every home,' Barling replied.

Something niggled at Stanton when he said that; he didn't know why.

'Then may God protect us.' Osmond quailed and blessed himself.

A storm of protest met his answer, with shouts that it was a waste of time, that it was useless.

Barling wasn't having it. 'Do I really have to point out that Margaret Webb would be dead by now if we had not searched the village first? The search goes on.'

'A lot of folk would still be alive if Nicholas Lindley had hanged!' Another rude shout from Caldbeck.

'Sir, if I may.' Webb had got a little colour back in his lined face, much to Stanton's relief.

'What is it?' asked Barling.

'I, for one, want to continue to help hunt for the man who did this to my wife. Can my boy go with her, with Margaret, to the manor?'

'Of course.' Barling signalled to a reluctant pair of the late Edgar's servants to escort John.

'Thank you, sir.'

'As I say, the search goes on,' said Barling.

'If God wills it.' Osmond looked petrified.

Barling started to list whose home would be next as the calls of protest went on.

'Are the dead ones still on your list?' Caldbeck. Again.

And then Stanton understood the niggle. Smoke. Homes with no one living in them, like Theaker's, had no smoke rising from the thatch. But the living did. Except one. No smoke rose from the roof of the Smith family's cottage. Dear God, Agnes could be at death's door too.

'Barling!' He grabbed at the clerk's arm. 'Forget the list. There's one that's more urgent. I fear Agnes Smith has been set upon.'

'What! Why?'

'Come on.' He gabbled out his reasoning as they ran, Osmond huffing along with them as the crowd of village men surged behind in a shouting mass.

'Agnes!' Stanton hammered on the door.

Silence.

He tried to open it. 'It's locked!'

Barling clicked his fingers at one of Edgar's men. 'Break it down. Now.'

A couple of swift axe blows had it open.

'Agnes!' Stanton forced his way in through the damaged planks. 'Agnes!'

Silence. The hearth was dead. The floor mercifully empty. No Agnes lying there as Margaret had been.

'She's not here, Barling.'

Barling stepped in behind him, Osmond too, gasping from his run. 'We always need order.'

'I'm sorry,' said Stanton. 'I should have followed your plan.'

The first angry shouts broke out.

'What the devil is going on?'

Barling sighed. 'Stanton, go out there and placate them, or at least as much as you can. Let Osmond and I continue.'

Stanton did as he was ordered, though he had no idea what he was supposed to say. He held up a hand to get silence. 'We are searching Agnes's cottage,' he began.

'No, you're standing outside of it!'

A roar of unpleasant laughter met the call from the ploughman.

'You know what I mean, Caldbeck.' Stanton tried to be heard over the din. 'You all do.'

His words had no effect, with the mocking chorus continuing.

But then the laughs stopped dead. Turned to gasps of horror.

Stanton looked around to see Barling walk out with an ashen-faced Osmond.

The clerk held a long-bladed knife high in one hand, the metal dulled with the stain of dried blood. 'I found this hidden in the log basket.'

Stanton didn't follow. Nothing was making sense.

But Barling went straight up to one of Edgar's men. 'Do you recognise this?'

'God save us.' The man nodded, his lips white. 'That's one of the knives from Sir Reginald's hall. His lordship always had Geoffrey Smith put a special stamp in the metal. Said it would stop people thieving.'

The weapon used to slay Edgar. Stanton closed his eyes as realisation began to dawn. *Agnes. No.* Opened them again.

'I believe we have found our monster,' said Barling. 'But we were too late. Far too late. She has slipped away.'

Osmond's mouth set in a thin line. 'Slipped away with her murdered father's hard-earned money. I know where Smith kept it from collecting the tithes and it is gone.' He shook his head. 'Such wickedness.'

'Agnes Smith is an outlaw now,' said Barling. 'The King's reach extends over the whole of the land. She will be brought to justice and she will hang.'

A huge roar met his words, every voice and face eager to witness justice at last.

'And may God have mercy on her,' said Osmond. 'For no one else will.'

Stanton's gaze fell on a stunned-looking Caldbeck. For once, the loud-mouthed ploughman had nothing to say.

Chapter Thirty-Eight

'I trusted I would be lord of Claresham one day,' said Osmond. 'If God was good enough to spare me.'

Stanton sat to his right at the long table in Edgar's hall, Barling opposite, a lit candle holder on the table bringing light to their faces but leaving the rest of the hall in shadow.

From outside came the clatter of hooves dying away in the distance, the last of the pairs of messengers dispatched by Barling with hastily scrawled letters to alert people for miles around.

Stanton wished he'd gone too. Anything was better than sitting here looking at what rested on the tabletop in front of them: a bundle of cloth containing the knife Barling had found in Agnes's cottage.

'As I knew, it would take the sad death of my uncle for it to be so.' Osmond put his head in his hands. 'But I never thought it would be in such heinous circumstances.' His gaze went to the bundle and his mouth turned down in revulsion. 'For the love of God, take that thing out of my sight.'

'Stanton, perhaps you could dispose of it.' Barling reached out and pushed it over to Stanton.

Stanton took it from him, the hairs on his neck rising from having in his hands the object that had taken the life of a man. As to what he should do with it, he had no idea. 'How best should I do that?'

Barling glared at him. 'Not now,' he mouthed.

'If the world had not gone mad,' said Osmond, 'you could ask Geoffrey Smith to melt it down. It was his hands that would have fashioned it, that had fashioned so much else. But you can't.' He gave a snort of disgust, for all the world like the late Edgar. 'Because he's dead.'

Stanton placed the bundle in his satchel, hoping Barling would tell him as soon as possible about what he should do with it. He hoped he could leave it wrapped when he did and not have to look at the sickeningly stained blade.

'Murdered just like your unfortunate uncle, God rest him,' said Barling. 'And it was Geoffrey's own daughter who killed him.'

Osmond shook his head. 'The she-devil. What drove her to such evil?'

'Agnes Smith was something which is of more advantage to a killer,' said Barling. 'She was clever.'

'Bold too.' Stanton had thought that desirable. Knowing what it truly meant now sickened him.

'Indeed.' Barling nodded. 'Agnes claimed to me that she was attacked in the woods before she found her father's body. No one else saw either of those events, neither the attack nor her father's murder. Worse, she used those lies to put the blame on another. It was late at night. She had plenty of time and opportunity to kill her father with the branding iron.'

'But why?' asked the rector. 'I mean, Geoffrey Smith was hardly a saint. Why, he confessed to me once that he—'

'Sir priest, you cannot be referring to what you have heard in the sanctity of the confessional.' Barling looked at him askance.

Osmond raised a hand. 'Forgive me, I'm not thinking clearly in my shock.'

'As to why Agnes would want to kill her father,' said Barling, 'her father had promised her in marriage to Bartholomew Theaker, a man who physically repulsed her. Agnes was the stonecutter Thomas Dene's devoted lover, and by killing Theaker she thought she was then free to marry Dene.'

Stanton nodded. 'Little did she know that he was already married, with a flock of children.'

'Dene was merely taking advantage of her,' said Barling. 'He was happy to spin her any story to satisfy his lust. But for Agnes, it was more than lust. She had given her dark heart utterly to him. She told me how they were planning a life together. She was utterly consumed with passion for him. Dene, realising that with Theaker's death Agnes was now free to marry him, had to come clean about his existing marriage. Her murderous rage was now unleashed at the lover who had let her down.'

'God's eyes,' said Osmond.

'Ambushing and trying to kill Stanton was a futile attempt to keep the truth from coming out,' said Barling.

The rope. The road. His horse. Stanton stared into the moving light of the candle, trying to banish the images, the sounds from his head.

'And,' Barling continued, 'I believe she had another purpose in attacking you, Stanton. It made her lie to me about being attacked by a hooded figure in the woods that much more credible.'

'But could a woman have done what was done to my animal?' asked Stanton. 'The strength of . . .' He swallowed, didn't want to say the words. 'It all.'

'From my experience in such matters over the years,' said Barling, 'pure rage, that most dangerous of emotions, gives a person, man or woman, strength way beyond what one might expect. It also makes a soul blind to the implications of committing a mortal sin.'

'Surely Agnes did not love my uncle, Barling,' said Osmond. 'Why should she be driven to kill him of all people?'

'As lord, Edgar had to agree to all marriages of villeins,' he replied. 'Geoffrey Smith was a freeman, so he could have given Agnes in marriage to another freeman. But Theaker, though comfortably off, was a villein and so needed the lord's permission to marry. Edgar clearly had given it, as Theaker and Agnes were betrothed.'

This explanation puzzled Stanton. 'But she had already found out that Thomas Dene was married, had killed him. Why would she have bothered to murder Edgar?'

'A question well worth asking, Stanton,' said Barling. 'Remember, when I questioned Agnes, she said that Dene would use her betrothal to Theaker as a barrier to their being together. Dene even said to her one day how much happier our lives could have been without the hand of Sir Reginald Edgar. She acted upon that. I suspect she had already decided to do so. In her lust-fevered mind, he'd been a barrier to her happiness. Even if Dene was dead, in her twisted mind, Edgar still had to be punished for daring to deny her her desires.'

'I suppose so.' Stanton could still hear the uncertainty in his own voice.

'The throes of youth bring not only unstoppable passions,' said Barling, 'but passions which defy all logic. Again, I have seen it many times. It can make one blind to anything except the object of one's desire and its pursuit.'

Stanton fixed his gaze on the candle again. Barling could be looking into his own grieving heart.

Fortunately, the clerk was in full flow and seemed not to notice.

'Thwarted,' he continued, 'it can lead to all kinds of madness. And Agnes was by this time thwarted beyond all reason and not in her senses. She had killed her father, her betrothed, her lover. Tried to kill you, Stanton.'

Stanton pulled his gaze from the candle, his horse's dying moments echoing in his head again. 'She did,' he said quietly.

'She was possessed by Satan more like.' Osmond shuddered.

'And she was in this manor,' said Barling. 'Knew its layout from the day she killed Theaker. She was here in the care of the servants. She was also here the night after she murdered Dene. When she confessed to you, Osmond.'

'Yet she would confess nothing, the baggage.'

'And as for Margaret Webb.' Barling gave a deep sigh. 'Had you not intervened, Stanton, she would have been another life lost at the hands of Agnes Smith.'

'Peter's life would've been destroyed too.' Stanton shook his head. 'His grief when he thought his wife was dead will stay with me for a long time.'

'Yet as Peter Webb himself pointed out, Margaret called Agnes a whore over and over,' said Osmond.

'Yes,' said Stanton. 'Agnes said that to me the day we found Theaker's . . .' He stopped, shook his head as her actions all fell into place. 'The day she met me on the path. Her hair all wet. Said about having been bathing. And then she brought me to the reed pond. Where we found Theaker's body. He'd struggled with whoever held him down in the water.'

Barling looked at him. 'Bold, remember?'

'Wicked more like,' said Osmond.

'But what of Lindley?' asked Stanton.

Barling brought a hand across his face. Exhaustion was etched there now.

Stanton knew how he felt.

'I have concluded only this,' said Barling. 'That Lindley was most likely a man wrongly accused all along. But Agnes helped him to escape, knowing in her cunning that he would take the blame for her.'

Stanton's spirits rose, despite his exhaustion, despite the awful happenings at every turn. *Lindley. A man wrongly accused all along.* 'So I was right? About Lindley?'

'I said "most likely",' said Barling. 'Nothing more.'

Stanton didn't care that Barling found the energy to glare at him. He, Hugo Stanton, had seen the truth. When all others doubted him.

'A terrible business this,' said Osmond. 'All of it. What is to happen now, Barling?'

'As I said, Agnes Smith might have given us the slip, at least for now.' He got to his feet. 'The warnings about her have gone out. I shall go to my solar and start all the extra necessary work now, as well as updating my records.'

'Then I shall leave you as I go to my bed.' Osmond rose to his feet with a wide yawn. 'I have to prepare for my uncle's funeral on the morrow. A sad task. I shall sleep here in the manor.' He shook his head. 'A sad task for a sad day.' He went out, muttering to himself.

'You also look ready for rest, Stanton,' said Barling.

'I am, but I think I'll sit with Margaret awhile. Had we seen this sooner, she would still be hale.'

They went to the door, where Barling paused. 'Had you not seen her moving, she would have simply perished on the floor. A life saved, Stanton.' He nodded and set off for his solar.

'Goodnight, Barling.' Could that possibly have been a bit of acknowledgement from Barling? Who cared if it was. A middle-aged woman lay in a room nearby with the most terrible of injuries.

He picked up a large piece of gingerbread from the untouched selection of food on a side table and bit into it without tasting it. He wasn't hungry, but he needed a bit of nourishment to keep him going. He set off for Margaret's room.

He could sit with her awhile. It wasn't much.

But it was something.

Chapter Thirty-Nine

Stanton went to the door of the solar, where he knew Margaret had been taken, shoving his half-eaten gingerbread in his belt pouch.

Outside, two plainly dressed women sat on a settle, one dozing with her cheek on her hand.

The other was Hilda Folkes, who got to her feet as soon as she saw Stanton.

'God keep you, sir,' she whispered. 'And your keen eye in saving Margaret's life.'

'God keep you also.' He spoke quietly too. 'How is Mistress Webb?'

Hilda crossed herself. 'Very, very poorly, sir. Her wound has been bandaged, and I did what I could with my knowledge of herbs.' She grimaced. 'Margaret Webb is very lucky to be still alive. But she has not regained her senses. Who knows if she will survive such a savage attack? It will still be many hours before a physician can get here.' Her lips pursed. 'But I can tell you this much: hell is not hot enough for Agnes Smith.'

'May I see Mistress Webb?' asked Stanton.

'I would say certainly.' Hilda darted a nervous glance at the door. 'But her son, John, is still in there. He's like a restless bear. A smelly bear at that. He doesn't like anybody near her.' She nodded to where her friend slept on. 'That's why there's two of us. In case he leaps on us.'

'I'll be on my guard,' said Stanton. 'Thank you.'

He stepped inside, closed the door behind him.

'Huh.'

As the midwife had described, John paced the floor, wide awake, his lopsided sight on Stanton, his heavy brows drawn in a deep scowl.

Trouble was, John's path was up and down between Stanton and the bed on which the wounded Margaret lay.

With a small candle lit next to her, she was utterly still, eyes closed. Her lifeless hands had been placed on her stomach. She could be a corpse.

Next to the bed sat a low stool.

Stanton eyed it longingly. His weariness threatened to have him off his feet soon. He took a step towards it.

John blocked him, stopping in front of Stanton.

'Look, I've got something for you.' Stanton opened his hand to reveal a piece of the gingerbread, which had interested the wild man before.

And did again. John's hand darted out, grabbed it. As before, he brought it right up to his good eye. Then sniffed hard at it. But this time he didn't shove it in his clothing. Instead, he went to Margaret's side and tried to put it in one of her hands, closing her fingers round it. They fell open again as if they were a soft, empty glove. He tried again, with the same result.

Stanton crossed himself, a deep sadness gripping him. He should go. He'd no business in here.

Then his breath almost stopped.

Margaret opened her eyes. A little. Looked right at him. One of her fingers moved, by the smallest movement. But it was there. Like he'd seen earlier in the cottage.

He went quickly to her side, keeping a wary watch on John.

'Mistress Webb.' Stanton kept his voice low lest he cause her head to hurt even more. 'You're awake, praise God.'

She opened her mouth to speak. No sound came out.

Stanton could see from the tremor in her lip, from the panic in her eyes, that she was straining to form speech. But she couldn't.

'Mistress, don't tire yourself out trying to talk,' he said. 'Rest as much as you can.'

Her gaze moved to John instead.

Her son bent towards her and she made a few movements with her hand, weak but definite.

To Stanton's shock, John responded with a nod. He reached a filthy, square hand out and grabbed Stanton by the arm.

Stanton flinched, jerked back, expecting a blow or similar.

But all he got was John's insistent pull towards the door.

From the bed, Margaret let out a long, long ragged breath. Then her eyes slid half-closed again, the whites still showing. Damn it all, he hadn't saved her at all. The life was slipping from her even as he watched. Hilda. He had to get Hilda.

Stanton allowed John to drag him out so he could summon her.

She looked up in alarm at John as they emerged.

'Come quick. Margaret's fading fast,' began Stanton.

But John let out a loud bellow, slapped at the wall.

'God protect us.' Hilda ducked away, while her friend woke in a frightened shriek.

John was already moving down the corridor, Stanton still in his grasp.

'See to Margaret, Hilda. Please! Don't let her die alone.'

Stanton didn't catch her reply. John had quickened his pace.

And they were headed for the front door.

Chapter Forty

The Webb family home loomed ahead in the darkness.

Sweat covered Stanton the second he saw it. Nothing to do with the warm night. The sight of it brought back every panicked step he'd taken when Lindley had murdered his horse on the road and would have done the same to him.

Not Lindley. Agnes.

Stanton tried to change their path to alert Peter Webb that he was there, but John would have none of it.

He dragged Stanton past the house and to the door of the fulling shed. Still with his grip firm, John opened the door with his free hand and stepped inside, bringing Stanton with him.

'God above.' Stanton brought a hand over his mouth and nose.

The sharp stench made the air thick, made it hard to breathe.

John didn't seem bothered. He let go of Stanton to go and light a grey tallow candle with clumsy movements of his stubby fingers. The tiny flame made little difference in the darkness of the high-beamed shed.

Stanton's mouth had filled with spittle in protest at the stink and he swallowed it down. Why on earth had Margaret sent him here with her son? The answer was, she hadn't. The twitching of her fingers would've been the same as the useless twitching of her mouth.

Most likely John wanted to come back to where he spent his days and nights, unable to understand why his mother lay speechless in a bed at the lord's hall.

Bed. That was what Stanton wanted more than anything else right now. Bed and sleep for a week if he could.

John peered over at Stanton, his big tongue moving and glistening in the poor light like an oversized slug.

'It's too late for work, John.' He had no idea why he said it. He might as well have sung a bawdy tune to the witless John.

John ignored him, which came as no surprise. But he didn't go to the fulling pit. Instead, he went to the far corner, piled with barrels, and gestured to Stanton.

Stanton drew in a deep breath to sigh in frustration, then coughed it right back out again. A deep breath in this place was a bad idea.

But John repeated his gesture.

'I can't help you, John.' Stanton went over to him, his exhaustion almost complete now. 'I don't know your work.'

John stood next to a large basket of what looked like dirty wool scraps; Stanton could hardly tell in the dim light.

'Huh.' John bent to rummage in the basket and pulled something out.

Not wool scraps. A boot. Stanton could only stare, stunned. Followed by another.

Stanton's heart felt like it was about to leave his chest.

Boots of the same type as the ones Edgar wore. That Lindley had got from the lord. That Stanton had seen on Lindley's feet. Dirty boots. Not clean like Edgar's.

A fresh wave of sweat broke over him.

But if the boots were here, then Lindley must still be here. Not fled. Hiding out in here. Stanton's question to Barling just an hour or so ago repeated in his head: *But could a woman have done what was done to my animal? The strength of it all.*

Agnes had no need for such strength. She had a man. She had Lindley. Lindley hadn't run off; he was working with her, seduced by her too.

Stanton whipped round, peering into the darkness of the shed.

Lindley could be watching him from the shadows even now, waiting to pounce. Or Agnes.

A flicker of movement caught the corner of his eye and he staggered back into the stack of barrels with a yell. 'No!'

A huge sleek rat skittered across the floor, a flick of fur in the light before the dark swallowed it again.

He had to get out of here. Now. He made for the door.

But John was there before him, still clutching the boots, blocking the door with his powerful body and muscular arms.

'Get out of my way, John.'

John's answer was a hard shove to Stanton's chest, sending him sprawling to the floor.

Stanton struggled to his feet, gasping for breath. He didn't care about the stink any more. He was alone with this madman.

The madman who had the boots, crouching by the door, refusing to let Stanton past.

A man of huge strength, the mind of a savage.

Could John have been the killer all along?

Have sense, man. That's what Barling would tell him. Stanton forced himself to steady.

John had brought him here at a signal from Margaret. John had shown him the boots. There must be something else.

'All right, John.' Stanton raised a hand in what he thought was a gesture of calm.

John flinched. Yet he still didn't move from the door, still held the boots.

'Sorry, fellow.' Stanton turned to go further back into the shed again, forcing himself to start to search in the shadows.

Barrels mostly, all with loose lids. He lifted one and recoiled. Stale urine, stored there for use in the fulling. As was another. And another.

His foot met a soft, unknown pile. He squatted down to see what it could be, put a hand to it. His finger went through a rotting sheepskin, and another couple of rats shot past him in a sharp, shrill squeak. Stanton stifled a yell.

Still at the door, John watched, boots in hand. The rats ran close to his feet, but he didn't move an inch.

Baskets full of good wool were next. Still nothing.

His heart began to race less. A bit.

More barrels, many of these empty now.

Then he came to the last one, right at the back. It looked just like the others. But he couldn't open the lid. He tugged, pulled. It wouldn't budge.

Stanton went over and grabbed the candle. He held it up over the stuck barrel and saw why it was so. It was nailed shut.

John was still at his post, but his gaze was locked on Stanton and he breathed in a series of long, low moans.

A quick look around showed Stanton a small, rusty pair of shears. Not great, but they'd do. Just about. By the time he'd levered out the nails, his hands were a mess of splinters and nicked skin. He prised the lid open. And a worse stench leaked out.

He wrenched the lid off and his stomach heaved. Not only because the stink engulfed him.

But because, crammed in the barrel, was a bloated, rotting body.

The body of the outlaw Nicholas Lindley.

Chapter Forty-One

Stanton fought his bile.

The thing in the barrel didn't look like Lindley. It didn't look like any man.

Part of the skull was missing, caved in from a hard blow.

The face – what he could see of it – was swollen beyond recognition, greyish, mottled. The eyes . . .

No, he wouldn't look too closely at them. He wouldn't look at all. He didn't need to.

His bile rose again and he fought to contain it.

He knew it was Lindley. The ragged tunic on the shoulder. The straggly beard.

And the hair. The dark chestnut hair, an unusual colour, striking when the man was alive, if it had been clean. And now? He straightened up, refused to look at the barrel's obscene contents any more.

Over at the door, John's moans had increased and he rocked on his heels in rhythm to them.

Yet John knew about the boots. Had known where to find them. As had Margaret, as far as Stanton could tell: it was her actions that had sent her son to show them to Stanton. But what of Lindley's rotting corpse, hidden away in here as well?

John hadn't come near. The wild fellow was getting more and more agitated, arms flailing.

Was Lindley yet another victim of the deadly handiwork of Agnes Smith or somebody else helping her? But Margaret would never help Agnes. The two women despised each other.

Nothing made sense. Stanton needed to fetch Barling. Now.

But first Stanton had to get past John.

John, who eyed him with the wary stare of a dog that was wondering whether to bite at an arm or a leg.

Stanton sickened further, not from the stink this time but from how John Webb had been pulled into all of this. John would have no idea why he'd been put to tasks like hiding a dead man's boots. Maybe even hiding a body. Guarding the door, to keep Stanton in.

Stanton knew he couldn't take John on in a fight. But all he needed to do was get him clear of the door.

His hands went to his belt pouch. This mightn't work. He had to try.

Stanton drew out another piece of gingerbread, made a great show of sniffing it.

John's one-sided gaze was on it too.

The scent of ginger and honey mixed with the other foul reeks in the shed made him want to spew his guts. But he couldn't. With a careful eye on John, Stanton broke off a piece, made a great show of eating it.

John's full attention was on it now. He even took a step away from the door.

Now or not at all.

Stanton flung the rest of the sweetmeat at John's feet. The man bent to pick it up.

Then Stanton was past him, out the door, slamming it shut on a roar from John.

Stanton thrust his left shoulder to the panels as John shoved hard against them, scrabbling for the iron bolt with his free hand. Got it.

A harder shove from John, sending Stanton's hand slipping from the bolt.

The door opened a crack. John's power was winning.

Stanton locked his knees, forced his whole weight on to the wood. Shut again.

He had the bolt, had the metal. But it wouldn't slide shut. The door was open a crack.

Summoning the strength in every muscle he had, he gave a last heave, shot the bolt home.

The panels still shook against Stanton's body as John tried to open the door. But it held firm.

Stanton let out a long breath, went to step back.

And a heavy hand grabbed his shoulder.

Chapter Forty-Two

'Get off!' Stanton turned and struck out hard at the hand that gripped him.

But it was Aelred Barling he'd broken from and sent staggering.

'God's eyes, Barling. I'm sorry. Are you all right?'

Barling nodded, breathless and holding the limb Stanton had struck. 'I came as fast as I could, but I am not the youngest, nor the swiftest. I came down from my solar to enquire after Margaret, and Hilda was praying over the unfortunate woman.' He loosed his hand to cross himself.

Stanton matched him, relief surging through him that Barling was here and he could tell him of his hideous discovery.

Barling continued. 'She is slipping fast from life, God keep her. Hilda told me that you had gone with John and that the wild man had hold of you.' Barling nodded at the door. The rattling had stopped, but a constant low moaning carried on. 'I see you have secured him there now. A wise move, given his shocking behaviour.'

'It wasn't shocking. What I found was. A new murder victim, Barling. It's Lindley. Lindley's dead.'

'What? Open that door at once.' Barling went to match his words with his actions, but Stanton halted him.

'No. Don't. We can't go in, at least not now.' He told Barling of the night's events: Margaret's seeming to send John to bring Stanton. The discovery of Lindley's boots. Lindley. The barrel.

Barling frowned. 'If Lindley's corpse is as you describe, then he is not a new victim but a hidden victim. Until now.' His frown deepened and he pointed over at the cottage. 'We urgently need to speak to Peter Webb. First his wife, now his son, his fulling shed – all have become part of this.'

'Do you think the whole Webb family are somehow in league with Agnes?' Stanton asked as they hurried over.

'As things stand, it is certainly looking that way,' replied Barling. 'Though why they would form such an unholy pact is beyond my comprehension.' He raised a hand as they arrived at the cottage door. Knocked. 'Webb. Open up. It is Aelred Barling.'

Silence.

Knocked again. 'Peter. Peter Webb.'

Still nothing.

A terrible thought occurred to Stanton. 'Barling, Margaret was attacked in this very cottage yesterday. What if Peter is lying there like she was?'

'May God be good that it is not so. We must enter.' Barling nodded curtly. 'The window, Stanton.'

Stanton ran round to the side, Barling following after.

He forced the shutter of the small windows, hauled himself up on to the sill and climbed in, braced for whatever fresh horror he might find.

He let out a long, long breath of relief.

The cottage was empty. All was cosy and orderly, with a fire cover on and the smell of a tasty meal in the air, waiting for the owner to return.

From outside came Barling's sharp order. 'The door, Stanton. The door.'

Stanton made his way over and opened up to let him in. 'Webb's not injured or dead. In fact, he's not here. He'll be out poaching in the woods, I'll wager.'

'As is his habit as he disclosed to you.' Barling walked inside. 'Despite the hour, we will wait until he comes back here to his home. It is imperative that I question him.' The clerk settled himself on the low stool next to the fire, his back as straight as a rod. 'You may as well sit also.'

'I'm not keen to sit. I'm keen to hear the answers.' Stanton paced the beaten-earth floor. 'Just not the ones about the barrel. When I searched that shed, I'd never have imagined that's what I would find.' He shuddered. 'A nightmare. I'm not sure . . . Barling, are you all right?

The clerk had gone even paler than usual. 'Yes.' He stood up. 'Yes, I am. But I have not been.'

The clerk spoke in riddles. 'In what way?'

'The search.' Barling flung out an arm. 'I said I would search every home. Every single one. And I was doing so. In the most methodical order. But I have not searched this one.'

More nonsense now than riddles. 'We did search it. We found Margaret. Lying right there on the floor.'

'Found Margaret, but in the shock and confusion saw to her and nothing else.'

'Agreed. But surely we found what was most important.'

'We only know what is important if and when we find it. And to find, we must seek. Fully. I missed a search. This cottage. We search it. Now.'

⌣

Barling bent to a large pile of Webb's newly woven cloth. 'We need to search everywhere, Stanton. The knife in Agnes's cottage was hidden right in the bottom of the log basket. She had concealed it well.'

'Then I'll start in there.' Stanton matched his words to his actions, lifting out each piece of wood. 'What if Webb walks in on us? He won't be pleased.'

'He can be as pleased or displeased as he likes. Everyone else has had their homes searched.'

Stanton held up the poker. 'I'll keep this handy. Just in case.'

Barling worked his way swiftly through the smooth cloth. 'Nothing in there.' He straightened up.

'Same with the log basket.' Stanton stepped over to the shadows behind the loom.

The baskets beside it were Barling's next task. Margaret's spinning. Nothing more.

A murmur of disgust came from Stanton.

'What is it?' asked Barling.

'I knew Webb kept his hare skins in a sack behind here. But there's another two sacks as well. One has his ropes and snare handles. But the other has a couple of fresh kills in it. There's a lot of blood.'

'Regardless, make sure you search it.' Barling turned next for the neat and tidy bed behind the half screen.

He pulled off the covers, shook them out.

'Nothing.' Stanton stepped from behind the loom.

'Nothing here, either.' Barling threw the wool blanket back on the flattened straw of the bed.

'What's that?' Stanton pointed to the corner, where the mattress met the wall.

'What?' Barling squinted hard. 'I cannot see anything.'

'The straw on one side. Near the top.'

Barling shook his head. 'I cannot make it out. Not in this light.'

'I can. It looks newer.' Stanton got on the bed, thrust a hand into the area he meant. 'And it's looser.' He rummaged around. Stopped. 'I've found something. Something wooden.'

'Get it out, man.'

Stanton burrowed at the straw, then hauled up a stout wooden box with a grunt of effort. The unmistakable rattle of coins came from it.

'Webb's own money, no doubt.' Barling could hear the disappointment in his own voice. 'As every hard-working man should have if he is prudent.'

'But how much money?' said Stanton. 'It's really heavy. And locked, of course.' He shoved it across to Barling, who tested its weight.

'By the name of the Virgin. I can scarcely lift it.' He looked at Stanton. 'This concerns me. I need to open it up. At once.'

'Of course.' Stanton clambered from the straw and grabbed a small-headed kindling hatchet from beside the fire. 'Stand clear, Barling.'

In three sharp blows, he hacked off the lock.

Barling opened up the lid and sucked in a long breath. 'No wonder it is so heavy. This is not the store of wealth I would ever expect to see saved by a weaver struggling to support a wife and a witless son. This is a hoard. A large hoard.'

'And not only money.' Stanton shook his head.

'No.' Barling took them out and placed them on the straw. A small silver cup. A carved ivory of the Virgin. Then a shiny object – shinier than the coins – caught Barling's eye. 'And what have we here?' He lifted it out.

'Dear God,' said Stanton. 'I know whose that is.'

'As do I,' said Barling. *Oh, Agnes, I am so sorry.*

For in the light, in the palm of his hand, sat a small silver pilgrim badge of the head shrine of Saint Thomas Becket. At the very top was a little hole where it would have hung from the neck of its dead owner.

And that owner was a murdered stonecutter: the late Thomas Dene.

Chapter Forty-Three

Agnes Smith came to consciousness again, wondering why her bed was so hard, why she was so cold. Why she couldn't move her arms, her legs. Why breathing was so hard, swallowing was so hard. But the answers falling on her one by one in seconds almost crushed her.

She wasn't in her bed. She was still in this place of horror, where she'd been for so many hours – hours which she could no longer count.

Last time in her bed, she'd woken to a figure from her nightmares over her, on her. The figure who had cut the air from her, sending her into oblivion. The figure who must have brought her here. Who had bound her arms and hands to her sides, her legs together, in tight bands. Who had fastened something on her neck that was still there, that meant she could hardly take a breath or swallow her own meagre spit. Her ears whined, her heart banged from lack of air, air that was cut off further by coarse sacking tied over her face and head.

Half smothered like this, she had sunk again and again into dreams, a few glorious, many hideous. But each one ended in terror, a terror that sharpened with every passing minute.

She tried to call out yet again, a useless, smothered noise that she knew couldn't be heard three yards away. Tried to move, but she could only wriggle, turn over. Cold, wet, gritty stone scraped against her hands. The figure had put her in a place where she wouldn't be found. Ever.

Then she'd die here. Alone. Thirst would take her. But not for a couple of days. Days in which she'd lie helpless in her torment, her filth . . .

No. She would not die this way. Even if she choked herself trying to get free, try she would. She kicked out as best she could. There was stone in this place; she'd find a sharp edge, work at her bonds until—

Footsteps?

She froze.

Then came a male voice. But not the relieved calls of a rescuer. Instead, a quiet hiss of evil.

'Look at you, wriggling like a dying fish.'

It was muffled through the coarse material, but she knew it, dear God help her, she knew it. Whether that was worse, better, than a stranger's she didn't know.

'I'm going to take the sack off your head now.' Hands at her neck. 'But if you make a sound, I'll throttle you again. Do you hear me, girl?'

She risked a nod, and the sack was gone, even the dim candlelight making her squint as she used her sight for the first time in hours to see that it was a cave she was in. And that Peter Webb was in here with her.

He dragged her to a sitting position against a damp boulder and hunkered down in front of her. 'Make no mistake, I'd love to rape you, whore.' He raised his calloused hands to each side of her face, then slid them down her throat to her breasts, his hard, filthy grasp bringing a stifled cry from her as she strained at her ties to break free. 'Shush now. I'd love to, but that wouldn't fit with what I'm going to do with you.' Now his hands had moved to her thighs, his thumbs sliding down between them.

She'd rather die. She wrenched her body to one side. 'Go to hell, Webb.' It was as much of a scream as she could get out.

One of his hands clamped over her mouth. 'Shut up.' The other back on her neck. 'Shut up. Shut up.' Tightening.

Her air was gone. Webb's furious face in front of hers blurred.

'Have you shut up, Agnes?'

She tried to nod. Breathe, she had to breathe.

Then his hand was off her and she pulled in ragged, painful gasps.

'Good.' He slid over to sit beside her. 'Listening is always better in a woman than talking, I find. Women might learn a thing or two if they only listened. Especially if they listened to a clever man like me. To be honest, all folk would. It's a shame they can't know of my cleverness, a shame. They'd be lost in admiration. Lost. But that's the beauty of where you and I are now, Agnes: I can tell you how clever I am, for you'll never breathe a word.'

She didn't dare respond. His big hand was idly stroking at her neck again.

'Now, poaching, that's easy, see? Easy. I could even tell my stupid wife about that. But thieving? Now, that's another matter. It's one thing to take a small animal from the woods and kill it and skin it, another to take a good candlestick. People keep their valuables in much safer places – behind bolted doors, in locked chests. It takes such great skill. Cleverness. It's quite something.'

Her teeth clenched. 'It's low.'

He tightened his hand more, making her gasp.

'Not the way I do it, see?' He shook her by the throat. 'See?'

A croak. 'Yes.'

'They let me into their homes, me with my fine woven cloth in my hands, watching as they find their coins to pay me far less than my hard labour is worth. Same as you did in your home. But I spy a good pair of tongs, a fine pot. All the time they're asking after my health, my imbecile of a boy, smiling at me with pity, feeling sorry for me, I'm looking for what I will take later. Bits here, a couple of coins there: never a big haul. Folk tear their houses asunder looking for lost things, things that are in my fulling shed, safely hidden away. Ready for me to sell on whenever I go to a market town to sell my cloth.' He gave her a broad wink. 'Clever, see?'

His hand wandered down to her breast again. Though her stomach clenched, she didn't dare react.

'But in the worst of luck for me,' said Webb, 'I got caught stealing. Just the once, see? Because I was clever.'

Still caught. Agnes kept her contempt silent.

'Bad luck, Agnes. That was all. Nothing more.' Webb wheezed a low laugh. 'It was actually that drunken dolt Edgar who caught me. Edgar. Of all people. Usually couldn't find his drunken cock in the dark, that one.' His look darkened in a deep, sudden anger.

Her heart, already thudding in her chest, raced faster. His hard face could be another's now.

'About three years ago I'm at his hall, urine barrel on my cart in his stable yard. I pick up a nice pair of shears I see lying around, put them under my cloak. Right at the second Edgar comes around a corner, heading to his horse to go out for a ride. He sees me, catches me. Right in the act. Of all people to catch me. But not through cleverness, mind. Only luck. You understand that, Agnes?'

She nodded, praying to God that He would send luck her way. She had nothing else to hold on to.

'I knew you would. You're quite clever too. But I think fast.' He tapped the side of his head. 'Fast, fast, fast, that's me. I beg for mercy from Edgar, say I need the shears to cut my cloth as my own had broken. I bring a stream of quick tears from my eyes, cry over my useless son, say my poor, dear wife would be on the street, would starve if Edgar locks me up. And the old drunken fool gives in—' Webb stopped, as if he heard a noise.

Her heart pounded harder as she also listened out. But nothing.

Webb went on. 'Says he'll let it pass. This time. But he threatens me. Me! He tells me that if it ever happens again, I'll be punished and lose my right hand. With my craft as a weaver, that would mean destitution and starvation for me. Think of that. Not only would I no longer be able to make honest money, my thieving and poaching would be over too. Also, my hidden money would become obvious if I couldn't work. My carefully built false life would fall to pieces. It couldn't be allowed to happen, Agnes. It just couldn't. And I think you can guess who almost brought me to ruin, can't you, Agnes?'

She could. But she wouldn't say it. Wouldn't give Webb the satisfaction.

'I asked you a question.' His hand tight at her throat again. 'Answer me.' Squeezing.

'My father,' she rasped out.

'Good girl.' The pressure lessened. 'He was working in the forge. You were out whoring in the woods with Dene. A nice empty home with a good store of coin. I'm helping myself when your precious Pa walks in. Oh, he's angry at first. But I wheedle on at him about my son like I did to Edgar. But no, Geoffrey bloody Smith says no matter, it isn't for him to decide. He'll report my crime to Edgar, and I can plead for mercy to the lord. No matter what I say, Smith will have none of it. Says to me that he's sure the lord will be lenient with me, a law-abiding man otherwise. Tells me to go home, locks the cottage and goes back to the forge to carry on with his work. And then . . .' Webb sighed, shook his head, pulled his sleeve up to reveal a stained bandage. Unpeeled it layer by layer, releasing the foulest stink.

Her bile rose at the sight that now wavered before her.

A long, deep burn. A wound that had turned rotten, seeping, stinking.

'Then your cursed father did this to me.'

Agnes knew what was coming. She dug her fingernails deep into her palms to hold in the screams, the tears of grief, of rage that surged within her.

'Did it in his precious forge. Him working at his anvil, the noise from his hammer nice and loud. Up I come behind him, grab for the branding iron leaning against the wall. Swing. Your pa turns, parries my blow with the hot metal he has in his tongs. It sears into my arm.' He smiled. 'It's the one strike he lands. The next is mine, straight at his head. Cracks it right open. He falls on to his side, down like a tree.' The smile dropped. 'Then I roll him over on to his back with my boot. He's still alive. Just. Looking up at me. I take the branding iron in both hands. Smash it into his open mouth again and again, the same gob that he was going to use to betray me to Edgar.'

Her heart might stop now and she wouldn't care. Every word from Webb was a new wound in it, making her relive the horror she'd found that night in the forge, telling her exactly how he'd savaged her lovely, loving pa.

'Food for thought, eh, Agnes?' Webb nodded. 'And I almost had you, when I spotted the fatty, Bartholomew Theaker, wheezing his way along to the forge to talk to your father.' He gasped a laugh. 'I'm surprised he couldn't smell Dene on you.'

She dug her nails deeper.

'But I dodge home, wait a few minutes, until I hear the hue and cry. And then come running back out to help. I wanted to shake Nicholas Lindley by the hand when we caught him. Poor sap. Still, rather his head in the noose than mine. But there was no gallows. Instead, we get the King's men. That little shit of a fellow, that Stanton, comes into my house. Asking all sorts. Goes away with nothing except the solemn lies I tell him, swallowed whole.'

Oh, Hugo, why didn't you see more, ask more? screamed Agnes in her own head. *Why?*

'And that was where your betrothed, the thatcher, gets in my way again. I needed my roof mending, went to the reed pond to find Theaker. Margaret didn't know; she'd been called away by that harridan

Folkes to help some woman birthing. So there I come. Theaker's having trouble bending down to cut a tough bunch of reeds. His own huge belly's getting in the way. He makes a jest of it, his face all red, smiles at me, asks me to help. I roll up my sleeves without thinking.'

Agnes let out a moan. *Oh no, no, no.*

Webb gave a broad wink. 'You know what's coming, don't you, flower? You're not so daft, are you? Your Theaker notices my bandage, the one covering this cursed burn I got from your precious father. Theaker asks me about it, doesn't seem very convinced by my vague answer. I can tell by looking at him that the lardy oaf will say something to Stanton the second he sees him. So I shove your betrothed's head under the water, drown him in the reed pond to shut him up. He bubbles, flails, but with my hand on his neck and his own huge weight, he can't get free.'

Agnes thought she might be sick with horror. Then Webb made it worse.

'And it felt so very, very good to make sure he'd never rise again. I'd been itching to do it anyway. Theaker had stopped me getting hold of you the night I killed your father.' The darkness moved across his face again. 'See, this one was your fault, really. Trouble was, your dead fat thatcher gave me yet another problem.'

Chapter Forty-Four

Stanton looked at Barling, the younger man's face drained of all colour. 'Agnes swore to us she would never be parted from her lover's pendant if she'd found it on his body. Yet it's here. Hidden in the Webbs' house.'

'While Webb is out. Out.' Barling said the words aloud to confirm his dreadful realisation. 'Out in the woods. In the dead of night.'

'Like the night I was ambushed,' said Stanton. 'By a hooded figure. That killed my horse.'

'Who we thought was Agnes.'

'But not Agnes. Peter Webb. Not poaching. But trying to kill me.'

'Just as Agnes said to me: that a hooded figure had attacked her on the night her father was murdered. And would surely have killed her too.' Barling pulled in a sharp breath. 'Yet the girl has been blamed for everything. By me. There is no pact between Agnes and the Webbs. It is all Peter Webb.'

'Because Webb has made it so, damn him.' Stanton shot to his feet. 'Barling, you have to send out new orders. Straight away. Agnes is being hunted down as a murderess. If folk find her before we do, she'll be torn apart.' He shot to his feet.

'We can do our best. But I fear we are too late.' Barling also stood, though more slowly, the weight of guilt pressing down on him.

'Stanton, she is probably dead already. Buried where we will never find her. Webb has used her to cover his tracks all along. Covered them so very, very well.'

'But what if she's still alive, Barling? We have to try. We must!'

'Alive where, Stanton? We have searched the entire village and she is not here.'

Stanton swore long and hard. 'I don't know.'

'Precisely. Rather than rushing off in what will in all likelihood be the wrong direction, our best hope is with Peter Webb himself.'

'Webb?'

'Yes, Webb. The order of his home shows he fully intends to return here. Given that we are almost at daybreak, I am sure it will be soon.' Barling picked up the poker. 'I do not want to risk raising the alarm, for it might warn him and he would slip away.' He pointed to the kindling hatchet. 'You take that. We will be ready for him when he does appear. Get that rope you found ready to secure him.'

Stanton went back over behind the loom to get it. Stopped. 'Barling.'

'What is it?' Barling dropped his voice. 'Have you heard something?'

'No. But I've seen it.' He gestured to the sacks, the ropes, the snare handles. 'This is what Webb uses for poaching.'

And Barling did see. 'And he does not have them with him. That means his business out there in the woods tonight is for another matter.'

'God's eyes. It could be Agnes.' Stanton's anguished gaze met Barling's. 'Yet we have no idea where.'

'But I think we do.' Barling pulled in a sharp breath. 'She told me about it. The glade. By the waterfall. Where she met her lover. And where Webb first attacked her.'

'We could be wrong.' Stanton bent down and grabbed the axe. 'But I'm going, Barling.'

'I'll come with you.' Barling gripped the poker tighter. 'But I don't have your youth, your speed. So you run, Stanton. Run. Fast as you can.'

———

'I suppose you could call it a very large problem, eh, Agnes?' Webb sniggered.

She couldn't answer, her stomach still churning at the hideous end of poor Bartholomew. She hadn't loved him. But she should have been kinder to him.

'I knew I had to do something about it, and quick. Clever, see? So I run back home, no one around. Luck's on my side; Margaret's still at that birth. I take my handcart with its empty barrel, get to the gaol fast. No one around still. Oh, and did I mention that I'd grabbed one of my good hammers and put it under my tunic?'

'Oh, dear God.' The gaol. She knew what was coming now. The real fate of Nicholas Lindley, the man she'd held responsible for Pa's death. The man she'd wanted hanged, that she'd screamed to the world to do so.

'God had nothing to do with it.' He grinned. 'Just me. I get to the window, call inside to Lindley. Offer him the hammer to break his way out through the bars. Didn't want to break them for him, mind. Otherwise, it'd be obvious they were done from the outside.' He tapped the side of his head, grin wider than ever. 'Always thinking, me.' His grin dropped again in an eye-blink. The darkness was back. 'But the bugger doesn't bite. At least not at first. Keeps whining on about the King's man, that Stanton, that Stanton has seen the truth and all would be well, saying he has faith in him. Faith in Stanton?' Webb spat hard in disgust. 'So I use Stanton's name. My one chance to get Lindley out. Tell him that Stanton has been to question me only a short while ago. That Stanton has said to me that Lindley's guilty. That he'll hang. No question.'

'But he wasn't,' she croaked. 'He wasn't guilty.'

'Nah. But Lindley, he starts to weep. Goes on and on about how he's innocent, but that there's no hope for him now. I'm looking around, still no one, but that can't last long. I have to get him out before Theaker's found. I tell him there is hope, that he can use my hammer to break out. He's still crying but not so hard, asks me why on earth I would help him. I tell him I don't care if he's telling the truth, that all I want is paying for getting him out, as I need the money. He's crying again, says he has no money. By now I'm sweating it. Then I see his good boots. Tell him "I'll take those." All of a sudden he's happier, he's doing it. The hammer's in his hand, the bars are loosened and out, then he's out. I take the hammer from him, tell him "Climb in the barrel." "Wait," the bugger says, "my boots." He slips them off, and I thank him. So in he gets. "Crouch down," I say, "so I can get the lid on." He looks up at me with those dopey dark eyes. "Thank you," he says, and ducks his head. I bring the hammer down in one almighty strike.' Webb punched his fist into his open palm.

His broad, wet smile was worse than the darkness. For it was pure joy. A man's skull. Opened. That was his joy.

'And next, of course, my cleverness again,' said Webb. 'Dene, the stonecutter, a man who worked with hammers all day every day. Do you see, Agnes, do you?'

'Not Thomas as well.' Betray her, Thomas might have done. 'Not my Thomas.' But she'd loved him, loved him, loved him with all her heart.

'Yes, I'm afraid so. He fitted my story too well. And he was your fault too. If you'd not been out whoring with him in the woods, if you'd stayed home in your cottage, then I wouldn't have come robbing. See? If you'd stayed home, your Thomas would still be alive, still have his handsome face in one piece.'

'Stop it. Stop.' She shook her head, her heart shattering at the depraved logic that Webb spewed forth.

'Thing is, Agnes, I really couldn't stop,' said Webb. 'Not by then and not now. Like I loved thieving more than poaching, now I love hunting more than thieving. Now I know why the wolf hunts the lambs. The fawns. Not only for food but for sport.'

'Killing people is no sport.'

Webb actually squeezed her like a lover.

'Oh, but it is.' He planted a kiss on her cheek with his slack, wet lips.

That her hands, her fists were free. Not just to shove him from her, to land blows on him for his assault. But to wipe away the damp, revolting spittle that sat on her cheek, then block her ears so she wouldn't hear another word.

'Dene's death should have satisfied everyone that Lindley had performed his last foul deed and was gone. Yet the King's men carried on poking their noses in. I'd had enough of them, especially that Stanton. All smiles at my wife, all swagger. Has the luck of the devil and all. He should have snapped his neck coming off that horse. That would have sent that whiny clerk scuttling back to where he came from; he'd never dare put a toe out alone. And then the fool Stanton sets off running to my door. I barely got there before him. But thanks to my quick thinking, I tell him a great story. The best, because it was partly true. That I'm a poacher. And the soft, soft ninny believes it all. Believes it because he's so grateful to me for saving his yellow hide.' He grinned again. 'Didn't save his horse, though, did he, Agnes?'

She wouldn't respond. He didn't seem to notice or care. Simply carried on.

'Then I'm in another search party, being the loyal man that I am, near wetting myself laughing inside as that drunk Edgar leads us all in circles. But when Edgar makes that rambling speech about not tolerating any wrongdoing ever and naming all the wrongdoers he has on his lands, I'm not laughing any more. I know I'll be named for theft. I'd promised Edgar three years ago that I'd never do it again, on pain of losing a hand. And with Stanton now knowing about my poaching, they'd all start talking. I'd lose my hand; Edgar wouldn't think twice. And in carrying out the sentence, they'd see the filthy burn on my arm that I got from your father. Sir Reginald Edgar had to go.'

'You've killed Edgar as well?' The question came out as a horrified whisper.

'Course. I know the layout of the lord's hall very well from collecting urine for my fulling shed. From my thieving, I have a way of slipping in through a damaged wall out of sight at the back of the stables. Then inside I go through a broken kitchen shutter. I pick up a knife from the kitchen, slit Edgar's throat, then leave the solar window open as a false clue. Or should I say, you did, Agnes.'

'What?' Maybe her mind was slipping.

He stood up abruptly and walked behind her. She couldn't see what he was doing.

'I was in a bit of a tight spot by now.'

Still she couldn't make out what he was doing.

'After I killed Edgar, I ran to your cottage. Where you were sleeping so soundly. To be honest, I thought you'd be a better fighter. I got you here easy.'

The sound of his footsteps, and he was back before her once more, saying words that were taking her reason.

'I needed to remove any doubt about who the killer is once and for all. I figured out that you had many reasons for carrying out the murders. The whole village knows about your temper too.' He sighed again. 'Yes, I'd love to rape you, whore.'

And now her mind did start to slip, and a voice that could be hers but sounded more like an animal in pain ripped from her.

'But I have to deny myself the pleasure. Because it should appear to all, Agnes Smith, the vicious murderess, that you have gone to hell from your own guilt.' He held up a perfectly knotted noose. 'Gone there by your own fair hand.'

Chapter Forty-Five

'How do you like being the hooded figure in the woods, Agnes?' Peter's voice was close to the sack tight on her head.

She tried to get a curse out, but he'd silenced her with a cloth tight round her mouth.

Unable to see, she stumbled as he forced her along, her legs free but her arms still tight by her sides.

She'd tried to be a dead weight, but his grip could be made from iron, each step bringing her closer to her own end, yet she could do nothing to stop him.

A plea to God, a plea to the saints, a plea to her dead pa – she'd started them all. But she could finish none, as her terror scattered her wits and all she could think of was the life being throttled from her. A sob bubbled up in her constricted throat. She'd done nothing, nothing to deserve this end, save go and lie with the man she'd loved. She shouldn't leave this world hanged by the neck like the worst criminal.

Like she'd screamed for Nicholas Lindley to be hanged by his. Her legs sagged again and Webb wrenched her forward.

'Keep going.'

But her legs weren't weak from fear but from a wave of self-loathing, which threatened to crush her. She could see herself now, a harridan in the street, attacking the cowering Lindley, tearing at his face and screaming for him to die.

And he'd done nothing to deserve it. Nothing. He'd spent days and nights waiting for his end, knowing that he was innocent of Pa's murder and no one would be coming to save him. Sobs racked through her now, stemmed by Webb's cruel bindings cloying her throat. All she could do was beg for Lindley's forgiveness over and over.

Webb jerked her to a stop. 'We're here, Agnes.'

She knew they were. She could hear the constant splash of the little waterfall. A sound that had always been the music to her lovemaking with Thomas. At this dawn it signalled her death.

He tore the sack from her head with a smirk. 'In your special glade.' He looked at her and grinned. 'Tears, eh? Well, if you can't cry over your own death, then what can you cry over?' He held up the noose to her again. 'I'm going to put this up now.' He shoved her to her knees on the ground. 'Stay there. And don't move.'

He walked a few steps away, threw the noose up over a tree branch. He swore. It had tangled in a thick bunch of leaves.

Agnes watched him, her pulse beating so fast it made her shake.

The dark leaves were turning pale green as the first light of dawn reached them. Birds were in full song.

She didn't want to die. And she wasn't going to.

Her arms were bound by her side, her mouth was gagged, a tight band at her throat closed off most of her air. But her legs were free. She could run, outrun Webb as she had that night in the woods. She knew she could. She had to. It was her last chance. She raised one knee, swaying a bit, as she couldn't use her arms for balance.

Webb was still busy with his rope, still cursing.

She was up, she was off, she was running. She was gone.

Long, unsteady strides, branches whipping her face, but she was doing this, she was—

Her hair. Her chin snapped up, her head back as she was jerked to a painful halt by a hand behind her.

'You stupid whore.' Webb slapped her face so hard she would have fallen had he not still had hold of her hair. 'Stupid. Stupid.' He yanked her back the few steps she'd gone, quickly securing her to a tree with another piece of knotted rope that he pulled from his bag.

She tried to draw in air through her nose, fill her lungs to get out a cry for help. But all she did was make muffled noises that were easily drowned out by the waking woods.

Webb cleared the noose in a few deft twists.

It now hung free, just above a large tree trunk.

'And now we're ready.' He lifted her up, sat her hard on the trunk. His face was level with hers. 'If you could see yourself, Agnes. You look exactly like the despairing sinner that I need you to be. All tear-stained and sorrowful. And definitely a woman who despaired enough to hang herself.'

His hand reached for her neck, and he freed the thin strap that had been round it for so many hours, keeping her short of breath and voice.

She pulled in deep, deep breaths through her nose, her last, she knew, her very last before the final tight embrace of the noose.

He held the strap up in front of her. 'Won't be needing this no more. It did its work in sending you senseless so I could take you from your bed. No one will notice its mark once you have the noose on top.' He tapped the side of his head. 'See? Always thinking, me.'

Then he lifted the noose. Placed it over her head. The thick rope sat heavy on her shoulders. He closed it up, closed it so it was a light hold.

He ripped off the gag.

She opened her mouth, let out a scream.

The noose tightened. Choked it off. She could still breathe, barely. Kept her mouth open. But she could hear her pulse in her head.

'I'll cut your arms free when you're dead,' he said. 'You won't have any marks on you from those linen bands. I made sure of that.' Webb walked over to where he had secured the rope. 'Best of all, when they find your swinging body, your face purple, your bowels and bladder voided, they won't even put you in the hallowed ground. You'll wander for all eternity, your name damned and a curse for all who say it. Thinking again, see?' He grinned at her with every one of his foul teeth. 'Now, my dear. Up you go.'

He gave a vicious yank on the rope.

The noose closed tighter. But the rope was so thick, she had a little air. Then he pulled and pulled and she was being lifted by her throat; her neck was taking all her weight. She couldn't breathe. And the pain. Dear God, the pain. The pain.

Webb secured the rope in a solid knot, then came to stand before her.

She couldn't breathe, couldn't. But she had to, she had to. Her feet and legs kicked out. She wasn't moving them; they were moving themselves as if they tried to kick the rope away to get her some air.

'A lovely dance, Agnes. Lovely.'

Her sight was going. Black dots sprinkled over her vision. She couldn't breathe. One pointed toe glanced against the top of the tree trunk. She tried with the other. She could reach. Reach the trunk. With the tips, the very tips of her toes. Enough to give her the tiniest relief on her neck, give her the slightest of breaths.

Webb swore hard. 'You're nothing but trouble.' He marched over to free the rope and haul it up further. But he'd tied it so tight, he couldn't get the knot undone. He set about it, swearing again.

Mad with pain, with terror, with death hovering near, she wanted to laugh and laugh. Her legs, her long, strong legs. Her legs had given her a few more precious moments of life. And had made Peter Webb furious.

Then a noise came from the woods. Loud enough to be heard over the waterfall. The definite rustle and crack of somebody making their way through the undergrowth.

She glanced over at Webb, praying he'd been too busy with the rope to hear.

But hear he had. He was staring at the source of the noise, the darkness from within him stealing across his face.

A call. 'Agnes!'

Praise God, it was Hugo Stanton.

Again. 'Agnes!'

And he was looking for her.

She tried to choke out a scream to warn him. Couldn't.

Webb stepped back into the bushes. Hidden.

Another call. This one filled with horror. 'God's eyes! Agnes!'

Stanton had seen her.

Chapter Forty-Six

'Agnes! Hold on!'

He'd been right, thank God, he'd been right. But he was almost too late.

Stanton tore through the last of the clawing branches, slashing them from him with the hatchet.

Agnes. Bound. Choking. Only her straining toes on a fallen tree trunk keeping her alive.

Down, he had to get her down.

He ran into the clearing. 'Hold on!'

A strangled sound came out through her blue, swollen lips.

'Save your breath!' He ran for the trunk. He'd make it in one leap, like he did on to horseback—

A slam to his side had him crashing to the ground, hatchet flying from his hand.

Peter Webb stood over him. 'You're no fighter, boy.' A boot drove into his guts, once, twice.

Stanton tried to roll out of reach. *No.* No air, no strength.

A third.

No.

'Let me see to the Smith whore first,' said Webb. 'She's already a pretty sight, but her last moments will be the best. You can watch from down there.'

Another kick.

'Then it's your turn.' Webb turned and walked back to the trunk. 'First you, Agnes.'

Stanton dragged air into his searing chest. *Get up, get up, get up. You have to do this.* He forced himself to his feet, feet that staggered under him.

Agnes kicked out against a dead branch on the trunk, snapping it off to leave a long, sharp point.

He met her gaze. He had one last chance.

Webb had seen it too. 'Is that your plan, girl? You and him? Him?' He glanced back at Stanton, then looked to Agnes again. 'My death with a sharpened stick.' He spat hard and snapped the branch off in his big hands. 'And now.' He went to grab her ankles, pull her feet off the trunk.

And then Stanton was running at Webb's back, running, his hand pulling out what he had in his satchel.

Gripping it hard, then plunging, plunging it deep into Webb's back, just like wood – no, harder, different – but it was in, in, and there was so much blood, but he yanked it out, and he was up on the trunk and the rope, blood on the rope, but it was cut and she was down.

And he had her. Had Agnes safe in his hold as she pulled in breath after hacking breath, unable to form words as Peter Webb lay dead beside them.

And her eyes went to what he held in his hand and back to his, and he nodded: *Yes.*

A blade. A good blade. With its special stamp in the middle. Forged by a skilled craftsman's hands.

Stanton tipped his head back.

Above him trees, the sky.

Life.

The bed of heaven to you, Geoffrey Smith.

Chapter Forty-Seven

One week later

'It is by the law of his Grace, King Henry, that this court assembles today.'

Aelred Barling addressed the packed crowd of villagers in front of him that had assembled in Edgar's hall. 'I arrived here sixteen days ago to investigate the murder of Geoffrey Smith, sent by the King's itinerant justices. The justices charged me with this great and proper responsibility because the late Sir Reginald Edgar, of this estate, had not provided the court with a detailed and supported accusation of the outlaw Nicholas Lindley. In short, Edgar had not established guilt.' His gaze roved over the room, resting for a moment on those who had been caught up in this dreadful onslaught of evil.

He nodded to where Stanton stood by the door, shoulders straight, cloak neat, hair combed. For once.

Barling went on. 'We now know that it was not Nicholas Lindley who murdered Geoffrey Smith but Peter Webb, freeman and weaver of Claresham. Webb also tried to take the life of Agnes Smith, Geoffrey's daughter.' He gave a nod of sombre acknowledgement to where Agnes sat to one side.

'He did, sir.' A hoarseness from the assault to her neck by Peter Webb still clogged her voice. Yet she sat straight, her long hair uncovered, not loose this time but scraped up into a neat bun.

Barling knew why she had arranged it so.

It left the skin on her neck exposed, the deep welt from the rope Webb had tried to hang her with still an angry red on her smooth, white flesh. It told as much of her story as words could.

'Webb even tried to kill my assistant, Hugo Stanton,' said Barling. 'Fortunately, Stanton was able to kill Webb first.' He folded his hands and looked around the room again. 'Mark my words, if Webb were still alive, he would be going to the gallows, and I would be sending him there without hesitation. I would be doing so according to the law of his Grace, according to the King's justice. But Webb is dead.' He observed more than a few nods, heard a number of whispers praising God. 'We have been fortunate in that God has spared Agnes Smith, whom Webb would otherwise have murdered. She owes her life not only to the quick thinking of Stanton, but also to his courageous actions. She is also a witness before God of what Webb did, as he told her in anticipation of trying to hang her. I will now give a summary.' Barling read steadily from his notes, keeping each account as brief as possible.

He was aware of shocked faces, hands to mouths and cheeks, murmured oaths and prayers.

'In summary, then,' concluded Barling, 'Webb took the life of thatcher Bartholomew Theaker, Geoffrey Smith, stonecutter Thomas Dene and your lord, Sir Reginald Edgar. He took the life of Nicholas Lindley, a man who was in fact no outlaw but a friendless beggar, to whom he showed no mercy.' He allowed a few moments of quiet for all to remember the many lives taken, with hands raised to make the sign of the cross.

'Yes, Webb is dead,' continued Barling. 'Many would say that is justice enough. However, justice also requires that we get at the truth. In order to understand that truth, we must have all the relevant facts, of which I now have a full record. But today I want to share an important part of that truth with you. I will address why Webb killed each of his victims, the reason he did so being of fundamental importance.'

He looked down at his notes. *Line by line by line.* 'And there is another witness, another whom Webb sought to slay.'

Muted murmurs of conjecture and craned necks met his words.

He met Stanton's eye. 'All is ready?'

'It is.' Stanton turned and opened the door.

Gasps and prayers broke out.

Hilda Folkes entered, an unsteady Margaret Webb leaning against her, Margaret's head still heavily bandaged.

Stanton stepped to take her weight on the other side, and he and Hilda helped Margaret into a high-backed chair to the right of Barling.

She was clearly very weak, her arms and hands resting on the carved chair handles for support. Stanton and Hilda remained next to her as agreed.

'We offer thanks to God for your presence here, Mistress Webb,' said Barling.

His words were echoed through the whole room, though the open-mouthed stares told Barling that everyone believed she had perished.

'Thank you, sir.' Her voice was not strong, a little slurred. But her words were clear.

The murmurs of astonishment came louder.

He addressed the court once more. 'Now, I mentioned having a record of all the facts. In order to achieve that, we need to understand who the murderous Peter Webb, a man who appeared to all the world to be a law-abiding freeman and hard-working weaver, really was.' He looked again to Margaret. 'Mistress Webb, I know that you are still grievously wounded, so I will try to be concise. Now, is it true that your husband was a skilled, prolific poacher for many years?'

'Yes, sir. He was. I . . . I knew about the poaching.'

A ripple of surprise went through the room.

'May I ask, as I am sure many here are wondering, why you, a woman known for her high morals, went along with such dishonest behaviour?'

'Sir, Peter always told me that we lived one step away from destitution.'

Now the surprised whispers became ones of derisory disbelief.

'Charged enough for his cloth, he did,' came an audible mutter from Caldbeck.

Barling's gaze swept the room again. 'I would remind all present to listen and to listen without comment. Rushing to judgement has played a major part in getting us to this sorry day.' He could tell from the sceptical expressions that thoughts remained the same. Well, they would soon change. 'So, Mistress Webb, your husband claimed that your household was at risk of penury at all times.'

'Yes, sir. He said he poached to help our income. That he had to.'

'Because?'

'Because we'd no one to help us, keep us as we got older or if we got sick.' Her voice tightened. 'Because I'd never been able to produce any healthy children, sir.'

'But you had produced one healthy child.'

'Yes, sir.'

'And that child's name?'

'John, sir. My son, John.'

Barling looked out at the court. At perplexed expressions. 'Then tell us, Mistress Webb, about John.'

Even in a life that was hell there could be heaven.

Sat on a low stool before the fire, Margaret Webb looked down at the little head against her full breast, her tiny boy drinking his fill for the fourth time that day. She put her work-roughened hand over his little smooth one, marvelling that anything could feel so soft. So perfect. She kissed the top of his downy skull, the life pulsing fast and strong in the small dip in the top.

With John steady in one hand, she stretched out with the other to poke the fire, over which the pot of pottage steamed, wincing as she did so.

Peter had kicked her so hard in the ribs yesterday that she thought he'd broken them. Again. But she could breathe without pain, at least most of the time, so she was probably bruised and nothing worse.

It had been her own fault. She'd been slow to rise at cockcrow; John had had her up three times in the night.

Peter was tired too, from all his disturbed sleep, so if he used his boot to rouse her, then so be it.

And right at this moment he wasn't here. He was out trapping hares, an act that gave him pleasure, as much from taking something out from under Sir Reginald's nose as from strangling the creatures with sharp wire.

Peter wasn't here and she was alone with her precious boy. Bliss. The one, the only baby she'd ever carried without loss, without Peter's punches and kicks pounding the child from within her. She put those thoughts away.

Bliss.

John paused in his eager suckling. She lifted him from her breast, held him to her shoulder, where he belched like a proud old man.

'Listen to you.' She slipped him from her shoulder, held him up before her, his dark pools of eyes gazing into hers as he gave a sleepy smile. A hiccup. As she kissed his tiny round nose, she froze.

The latch.

She gathered John in one arm, got to her feet, grabbing for the bowl. Too late.

Peter was in, a full sack in one hand.

'Good evening, Peter.'

His scowl said everything. 'Where's my supper?' He threw his sack on the ground.

'It's ready,' she said. 'I'm just putting it in the bowl right now. I didn't want it to get cold—'

He was on her in two steps, his fingers digging into her face on either side of her mouth, forcing her to look at him. 'It's not ready for me, is it?'

Her baby in one arm, bowl in the hand of the other, the fire at her feet, her sore ribs. She didn't dare move. 'I'm sorry.'

'You always are.' He didn't even raise his voice. He never did.

But his fist met the underside of her jaw – so hard, so fast – and her arms flew out with the blow, the pain, the bowl going one way, shattering, the baby – her baby, John – going the other as she landed on her back.

Peter stood over her. 'Now you've broken a bowl.' His boot again.

She didn't care, didn't care. All she cared was that she couldn't see John, couldn't hear him.

'You clumsy whore.' Peter took up another bowl, sat before the fire and started to help himself to the pottage.

Don't sob, no noise. Peter doesn't like it. *Margaret got to her hands and knees, crawled across to the little bundle that was John. Still, so still. No cry. He lay on the floor next to the sack, the head and glassy eyes of a dead hare lolling from it.*

Please, God, oh please, sweet Jesus, oh please, please, please. *Her hand reached him, touched him, then she could see his little face.*

And he blinked. Then hiccupped.

Oh, praise God, praise His holy name. *She sat up on one hip, picked John up, holding in her agony. Held him to her.*

He hiccupped again. Vomited all over her, once, twice. His eyes rolled.

She didn't scream, she couldn't. She didn't dare. All she could do was stare as the soft dip on the top of his head swelled red and angry and wrong.

From behind her, Peter: 'I said you were a clumsy whore.'

It would be wrong to say that a silence followed as Margaret paused to gather her strength.

It was a quiet broken by weeping, by many stifled sobs. More than a few deep-voiced oaths.

Margaret herself remained dry-eyed, though the knuckles of her fists gripping her chair had turned pure white as she began to speak again. 'John had that swelling on his head for days and days. And from that day on, he was never the same. His tongue. His right eye.' Her voice caught. 'He . . . he stopped turning his head to me when I talked to him.'

'And how old was John when Peter did this?' Barling allowed no emotion in his words, his face. He could not. His calling was to bring out the truth.

'Six weeks, sir.'

'Did Peter ever express any remorse for what he did to John?'

'No, sir.'

'And did you ever bear any other children?'

'No, sir. Though it wasn't for want of Peter . . . trying.'

Angry hisses filled the room now, a louder rumble of curses.

Barling waited for the reactions to settle as he consulted one of the pipe rolls before him, then addressed her once more. 'Mistress Webb, the King's court protects the life and limb of married women against the savagery of husbands, against such men who would maim or kill them. Moreover, if a woman is in fear of violence exceeding a reasonable chastisement, then such a husband could be bound with sureties to keep the peace. Did you approach your lord, Sir Reginald Edgar, about your rights under the law?'

'Sir, I did consider it, but only consider it. Peter had always been sure not to damage my hands or my face very often, that his worst work would be hidden under my clothes or my coif.' The shadows below her eyes had deepened in her exhaustion. She paused for a long breath and pressed on. 'I hid everything from the world, the same as I did my distress over John. But like with everything, Peter could tell what I was thinking. So he warned me. He told me, with his hand to my throat, that if I ever, ever said a word to anybody about what had happened, he wouldn't kill me. But he would kill John. I was terrified for my son, sir. So I kept my silence. Did everything Peter said. I kept John safe.'

'Mistress Webb, I can see you are growing very weary,' said Barling. 'I shall not press you for too much longer. But I need to ask you this: did you know that Peter had murdered Geoffrey Smith?'

'No, sir. Nor anybody else.' She clutched the arms of her chair. 'I swear to you on my son's life.'

Under normal circumstances, Barling would correct her, remind her that her oath was to God. But he did not need to, nor even want to. The life of her son was everything to her.

'Thank you, mistress,' he said. 'I commend your honesty and your great strength in coming here.' Barling looked at the assembled court. 'We now see Peter Webb for who he really was: a savage brute within his own home.' He let that sink in before he addressed Margaret again. 'I would next ask that you take up from the hours when your husband was out, as we now know, murdering Sir Reginald and abducting Agnes Smith.'

'I swear to you that I did not know,' said Margaret. 'I assumed he was off poaching.'

'Of course,' said Barling. 'Now, if you can give us your account.'

Margaret's hands worked her spinning in her lap as she sat before the fire, sending the bobbin up, down, as the loose wool became a strong thread. Always a little bit of magic this, she often thought, one object changing its form to become another.

Not that she ever said. Peter did not approve of magic.

Her bobbin was almost empty, and she reached down to her basket to feed in another handful. Empty. She clicked to herself in impatience. She needed to get more done tonight and be ready to start at first light. Peter would have something to say if she didn't.

She got up, went outside and crossed the yard to the fulling shed, candle in hand, owls calling in the night air.

Margaret opened the door to the shed, her patient, hard-working boy labouring away, left foot, right foot in the stinking fulling pit as always. His anxious face looked over as the door opened, relaxed into his heart-rending beam as he saw it was her and not Peter. He stepped from the pit and threw his arms around her in their special greeting, which was secret from Peter.

She returned John's hug, then crossed over to the baskets where the raw, sheared wool was stored.

Her stomach lurched. Hardly any in there. It would be the same as her not filling her basket for spinning. Peter's work was up and down at the minute, with all the terrible events that had been happening too. But he wouldn't think that. He'd use his fist on her; her fault that work had stalled.

John was beside her now, looking to where she looked; his way of helping, bless him.

She checked every basket again. Still not enough. Now she felt sick.

Straightening up, she scanned the shed. Barrels. More barrels. One basket shoved in at the back of one, not in the usual place.

God be praised. Peter hadn't forgotten to refill, only misplaced one.

She hurried over to it, John with her. Pulling it from behind the barrel, she peered in. Her stomach lurched again. It was full of filthy scraps and ends of wool. But maybe, just maybe she could find usable bits in here. She dug a hand to search through.

John stood next to her, idly chewing his tongue, no doubt enjoying his break from treading.

To her surprise, her fingers found leather. Good leather. She pulled out whatever the thing was.

A boot. A good boot.

She dug in the basket again.

Another one. What on earth?

Well, whatever they were, they were no concern of hers. Or John's. If Peter knew they'd been at them, they'd both receive a beating.

But something wasn't right: you couldn't really poach boots.

John sighed loud and long, and she made her decision.

Never mind. Boots weren't worth getting a beating for. She thrust them back into their hiding place.

'So I left the boots,' said Margaret to an utterly silent court. 'Got as many scraps of wool as I could, kissed goodnight to my John. I did a bit more spinning and went to bed. When it was first light, I woke as always, and Peter was asleep beside me. I did all my jobs as usual. I was out sweeping the yard when the news about Sir Reginald came out.'

'Such terrible news this morning, Mistress Webb.' A couple of Edgar's servants, pausing at the gate. 'Have you heard?'

Margaret listened in revulsion at their breathless account of their lord's murder.

Her hand went to her mouth. 'When will it all end? When will Lindley be caught?'

The taller of the servants shook his head. 'Not while that King's clerk, that Barling, is in charge.'

'More of his daft questions from him just now,' said the other. 'Wanted to know about Sir Reginald, God rest him, giving Lindley a pair of boots or some such nonsense.'

Her mouth dried. 'Boots. Are you sure?'

'Course. Asked us hisself.' He spat in contempt. 'Silly bugger.'

His friend tugged at his sleeve. 'We'd best be off. A sad day, Mistress Webb.'

'A sad day indeed.' She watched as they set off, both hands locked on her broom, unable to move.

Boots. Hidden in her shed. That she knew nothing about. That the King's man enquired about, enquired about as he asked questions about the murdered Sir Reginald.

She had to get those boots to Barling. And she had to be quick, before Peter woke.

Heart pounding, Margaret hurried over to the fulling shed, left her broom outside against the wall and went inside.

John had already started his treading for the day and returned her quick hug.

She went past him to the basket behind the barrels, her hands trembling as she plunged them into the wool. Praise God, the boots were still in there. She shoved them under her apron; she could be back in no time at all.

Then a voice from behind her.

'Margaret, what are you doing?'

'It was Peter, of course,' said Margaret. 'He ordered me to put the boots back and come with him to the cottage. He told me that if I didn't, he would drown John in the fulling pit. I went with him. What else could I do? I walked in. He was still behind me. And that's all I remember.'

'It could well have been your last thought, Mistress Webb.' Barling gave a sober nod. 'That was certainly your husband's intent, striking you on the head with savagery and leaving you, as he believed, dead on the floor.' He addressed the court once more. 'Webb then calmly left his home and brazenly joined the search for Lindley. What was the next thing you remember?'

'Lying in the room at Sir Reginald's hall. I didn't know how long I'd been there, but I saw John and my heart soared, for he was safe with me, at least for the time being. But it was the briefest of wakings. Then I heard Hugo Stanton enter.' She paused to give a grateful glance at Stanton. 'I managed to open my eyes, tried to tell him about the boots, about Peter. But I couldn't speak. I had the words in my mind but I could not get them out.'

'A blow to the head often does such a thing, sometimes until the end of a person's days. Thank God you were spared that torment. But in torment you were, lying there with the vital information you had. And only one person could help you, is that not correct?'

'It is, sir.'

'And who was that person?'

'My son, John.'

Barling saw the looks of disbelief on the faces before him. 'Perhaps you could tell us how he did so.'

'That I can. You see, the whole world has always seen my John as a witless fool.'

'But you found out differently.'

'By chance, one could say, when he was four years old,' said Margaret. 'But I always say God's hand guided me.'

The package of cloth was heavy on Margaret's shoulder. The walk to the monastery had taken longer than she thought, but she had to hurry. Peter was alone with John, and that always made her sick with fear.

If her little boy went near the fire, unable to see properly with his poor, turned right eye, Peter might not notice. Or care. Or would get John away from it with his usual slap or punch instead of a tap on the shoulder. The same would happen to John if Peter grew tired of his noises, his honks that to her could be a baby goose, his strange cackle, his half hiss, half spit with his tongue wagging out.

Yet they weren't merely noises. Margaret knew in her heart that John wanted to tell her things. She'd thought for a long while that Peter's assault had made her son a fool who knew nothing. Until John started to point at the pail of milk. And made a sound to her. Pointed at a cat. And made another sound to her. She'd tried so hard, so hard. Always when Peter was out poaching.

'Milk, John. Fire, John.'

Nothing. Just wet kisses on her cheeks, arms around her neck with his little heh-heh laugh.

No laugh for Peter. Ever. Only cowering and wet britches.

She quickened her pace.

The fat, cheery monk at the gate let her in, pointed to where she had to deliver the cloth.

The scent of the most delicious roasted meat wafted from open shutters as she walked past. The monks' midday meal, no doubt. Her stomach growled as she glanced in. Such full tables. And—

She stopped dead. Stared. Couldn't help herself.

For the room full of eating monks was alive with silent movement. Hands fluttered fast, fingers would make a shape for a second and then would make another and another.

A monk caught her eye and she hurried away, dropping her cloth.

On her way out, she saw the red-cheeked monk was still there. Though this delayed her further, she had to know.

'Good brother,' she said, 'if you'll pardon my rudeness, I saw some of the other monks a little while ago, in the refectory, behaving in a . . . strange way.'

The monk chuckled. 'Not strange at all, mistress. We follow the Rule of Saint Benedict, which insists on silence during our daily activities outside the Divine Office. Silence is indeed a virtue, but it is most impractical. So we, as so many monks have, devised a way of communicating without words.'

Margaret looked at him, not daring to hope. 'Then you do not need your ears?'

'Nor our tongues.' The monk gave a beaming smile. 'Yet we can ask for the soap in the bathhouse.' He moved his fingers. 'Or the butter at table.' Again, but differently. 'You see?'

'I do, brother.' Her heart soared. She had hope now.

He chuckled again. 'And Saint Benedict is still satisfied.'

'Then,' said Margaret, 'I went home. Tried out with John what the monk had described. It took a while. A long while. But we did it. We did it. I could understand John, and he me. It was our secret, our precious, precious secret. So, lying in Edgar's hall, I could not speak, but my fingers were able to tell John to take Stanton to our shed and show him the boots.'

Barling saw different expressions in the court now as Margaret spoke on.

'My son never had the devil in him. But my husband did. I hope he hears my words today from hell. And knows that my boy, John, my precious boy, helped to send him there.'

Barling allowed a long silence before he spoke again. Her words demanded nothing less.

'We have reached the conclusion of my record. Almost.' He held up a hand, careful to keep it completely steady. 'Agnes, I said at the beginning of this hearing that it would be about truth.' His mouth dried at what he was about to say. But he had to, no matter how much it cost him. 'In truth, I made a wrong accusation against you. I did not do so out of any malice, for my only interest is in serving the King and his rule of law. As one of the King's men, I made a mistake in the course of doing so and offer my apologies for it.' His voice sounded steady in his own ears, praise God. 'And now that is the end. I dismiss you all.'

Barling rose to his feet, spent.

And then came a call.

'God save the King's justice!'

Others joined in, joined in until the hall echoed.

Barling looked to Stanton, expecting to see pride in the young man's face.

But no. Merely a brief, unsmiling nod.

And he wouldn't meet Barling's eye.

255

Chapter Forty-Eight

Hugo Stanton had finally got his wish.

Today, on this perfect summer morning, with white, fluffy clouds in a blue sky and birdsong on a fresh, cool breeze that had sprung up overnight, he would leave the King's service forever.

He would return to the monastic posts, bringing letters from monastery to monastery. Ride far. Ride fast.

And nothing else.

Osmond had agreed to support this decision, delighted with Stanton's request to serve the church once more.

'An excellent path to follow, my boy,' the rector had said. 'Perhaps one that will eventually lead you to take your holy vows, in complete service to the Almighty.' As Osmond was no longer only the rector but about to become the lord of Claresham on the death of his uncle, his word would carry great weight.

Barling had known that too when Stanton presented him yesterday evening with Osmond's letter, laying out his case for leaving. It hadn't taken long. Barling had tried to change his mind, trying to persuade him that he should continue in the service of the law. To his credit, the clerk kept good on his word not to pry into why Stanton did not wish to serve the King directly.

'You have a sharp eye, Stanton.'

'Not sharp enough, Barling.'

'You have great courage, Stanton.'

'Fear more than courage, Barling.'

'You speak up for the truth, Stanton.'

He had no argument against that, so he'd said nothing.

'Very well.' Barling had reached for his own parchment. 'I will write to the justices and advise that you will be serving the church instead in a noble and worthwhile undertaking. The hour is late, but I will have it ready for you by the morning.'

Now the morning was here.

Barling's letter – a thin, neat roll closed with its red wax seal – had been brought to him by a servant.

Stanton had placed it in his satchel with Osmond's, then picked up his bundle. Went to the stables, mounted the fine horse given to him by Osmond.

And ridden out of the courtyard without a backward glance.

The road lay before him. But he had one stop he wanted to make.

He pulled up outside the rectory, secured his horse and entered the graveyard next to the church.

Nothing more than the song of the birds and the breeze in the trees and bushes broke the silence as Stanton walked through slowly, stopping at every fresh mound to say a silent prayer.

Geoffrey Smith.

Bartholomew Theaker.

Thomas Dene.

Stanton shook his head. He'd made the right choice to go. He could easily be lying under a mound of brown, drying soil as well.

And last, Nicholas Lindley. Tucked away in a quiet corner. Utterly alone.

Stanton drew his hand across his face when he heard a voice behind him.

'Without your intervention, there would be two more graves, you know.'

Barling.

Stanton turned as the clerk walked up, clad in his neat black robes as ever.

'With better intervention there'd be none.' Stanton looked over to where Peter Webb's mound was by a wall, at the farthest edge it could possibly be. 'Well, one would be good.'

'Indeed.' Barling crossed himself as he stood next to Stanton at Lindley's grave.

'But four is too many. Five, if you count Edgar.' He nodded to the church. 'He's in there, of course. In his great stone casket.' His gaze met the clerk's. 'Is that why you missed out a line in your account, Barling? Is Edgar too grand to have the whole truth told about him? Is it that you didn't want the whole of Claresham to hear that Sir Reginald Edgar liked to lie with men?'

'Ah.' Barling gave the hint of a smile. 'You noticed.'

'Yes, I noticed, Barling. So when you were there last night, going on at me about the truth, you might as well have been talking to one of these headstones. The truth didn't matter when it came to protecting Edgar. Line by line by line, Barling. Unless you don't approve of one of the lines.'

'I did not miss a line to protect Edgar. I missed a line to protect somebody else.'

'You mean me.' Stanton shook his head. 'Barling, I couldn't have cared less if the whole village heard Edgar wanted to lie with me. It was the truth.'

'Not you.'

Stanton frowned. 'Then who?'

'I missed a line to protect this man.' Barling's gaze went to the mound before them. 'Nicholas Lindley.'

'Lindley? I don't understand.'

'Do you remember what Edgar told us the night Webb ambushed you, about finding Lindley in his stables?'

'Yes.' *I found Lindley hiding in one of my stables. It was the night before the one of Smith's murder. Chap was in a piteous state. I gave him some work to do. Rewarded him for it with charity. The boots off my own feet. My own feet! Said that was what he wanted. Not money. His feet were ruined from wandering for miles.* 'I thought it was a bit odd that Edgar hadn't mentioned it before. But Edgar was always fuddled from drink.'

'Edgar may have been a drunk. But he knew perfectly well what he had done with Nicholas Lindley. The same as he wanted to do with you, Stanton.'

'Oh.' *Edgar's wet mouth on his. The lord's tongue strong, pushing past his teeth, hand at his groin before he shoved him off.*

'Oh indeed.' Barling shook his head. 'You were the King's man, of a status where you could repel Edgar's unwanted advance. But Nicholas Lindley was a penniless beggar. Alone and desperate. Found hiding by the lord on his property. He did whatever it was that Edgar wanted him to do. I sincerely doubt it was the first time for Edgar, given his behaviour with you. Edgar justified what he did by making a payment in the form of a pair of his boots, like he said Lindley had asked for. I am sure it salved Edgar's conscience. If he had one.'

'And Lindley was about to move on from Claresham,' said Stanton. 'He told me that.'

'I am sure he was,' said Barling. 'I cannot say definitely, but I would imagine that Edgar had told him to once he had finished with him. But before Lindley could leave Claresham . . .' He held up his hands, dropped them.

'Webb murdered Geoffrey Smith.' Stanton tipped his head back with a long breath. 'And Lindley, the beggar, was blamed. Put in gaol, awaiting execution.'

'Yes.' Barling gave a sober nod. 'Edgar might have been a drunk. But he was also a ruthless man who would not hesitate to act in a way that was best for him. As far as he was concerned, a murder had taken place. The villagers were convinced that Lindley was guilty. After all, he was an outsider. Not one of them. Edgar was also very possibly terrified that he'd forced a murderer into giving him his pleasure. That aside, he was happy to go ahead and hang Lindley. Not only would the villagers' demand for justice be satisfied, but more importantly for Edgar, Lindley, the man who knew that the lord was a predatory sodomite, would be silenced for good.'

'Then why didn't Lindley tell me?' asked Stanton. 'I can understand why he didn't when you and Edgar were present. But I was alone with him.'

'Oh, Stanton, Stanton. The sin of sodomy is among the gravest there is, with the worst acts the gravest of all. Had you had the opportunity to read the great writings of Saint Peter Damian, such as I have, you would know that.' Barling bent his head, spoke almost to himself. 'The devil's artful fraud devises these degrees of falling into ruin. The higher the level the unfortunate soul reaches in them, the deeper it sinks in the depths of hell's pit.' He raised his gaze to Stanton. 'The depths.'

Stanton frowned. He'd never seen Barling look like this before. The man appeared very troubled. No, haunted. But, wait – he had. Once. At Theaker's wake, when Barling said something about dwelling on mistakes. Then, as now, the clerk's strange, distracted appearance disappeared in a heartbeat.

Barling snapped back to his usual self. 'Lindley would not have dared to tell you, a complete stranger, Stanton. The one confessor available was Osmond, Edgar's own nephew. So Lindley had to keep his silence, though he must have been in great torment, with the terrible injustices that had been done to him. It is no wonder that Webb was able to persuade him to break out of the gaol.'

'Out, only to be slain and left to rot in a barrel.' Stanton shook his head. 'While we all blamed him, feared him. Hunted him.'

'Except Edgar's hunting of him was always ineffectual,' said Barling. 'He dragged his heels over and over about searching for Lindley. I had assumed it was his drunkenness, his usual chaos. But Edgar, as I have said, was ruthless rather than evil, which Webb was. Once Lindley was gone, Edgar was happy. What Edgar really wanted all along, what he really needed, was Lindley's silence about what he had done.'

'Which Webb had provided.' Stanton looked at the mound again. 'Poor Nicholas Lindley.'

'Or whatever the man's name really was,' said Barling. 'Edgar referred to him as Timothy to me on the day you found Theaker's body. Edgar said it was merely a slip of his tongue. That may or not have been true.'

'Who knows with Edgar?'

'Indeed. But I am sure Lindley had a different life before he became a beggar,' said Barling. 'He was well spoken. His hair and beard were not overlong, suggesting he had not always been so unkempt.'

'But he has no life now.' Heartsick, Stanton glanced over at his horse. He needed to leave this place.

'No,' said Barling. 'For which I am partly responsible.'

'You?' Stanton stared at him, stunned by his response. 'How?'

'The very first day, I was preoccupied with the correct following of the law. With making sure that the crime was properly dealt with in a uniform manner. I was adamant that nobody could look into the case more effectively than me. I should have listened more carefully to you, Hugo Stanton. You were so very clear that you believed Lindley was speaking the truth. I did not take heed of what you were saying, of the doubts you presented. And so I failed Lindley.'

Stanton had no words.

'I can help him in the next life,' said Barling. 'I have paid Osmond for indulgences for his soul and will be praying for him every day. And yes, you are right. By leaving out this line, Edgar's reputation, such as it is, survives. But Edgar's willingness to send an innocent man to the gallows cost him his life, so he has paid the highest price. Nicholas Lindley, a totally innocent man, a victim of Edgar as much as Webb, paid it too.' He shook his head. 'The least I can do is keep his tragic story from the ears and tongues of those who would condemn him for eternity.'

'Perhaps they wouldn't condemn him if they knew the whole story.'

'But a story with no living witnesses, Stanton, save what Edgar did to you. A story about a lord and a beggar. The beggar lies dead, with nobody to speak for him. The lord leaves a nephew with a powerful voice, not merely the rector but the new lord of this place as well. Believe me, the condemnation of Lindley would fast drown out any of Edgar.'

'I suppose you're right.'

'Not always, remember?' Barling gave him a fleeting smile. 'But in this matter, rest assured that I am.' He gestured to Stanton's horse. 'I shall keep you no longer. Godspeed.'

'Are you going back to the hall?' said Stanton. 'I can ride alongside you for a while if so.'

'No, I shall stay here with Nicholas for a little longer.' He raised a hand.

'Godspeed, Hugo Stanton,' he said again.

Chapter Forty-Nine

Stanton rode slowly away from the graveyard through the village of Claresham.

The sun climbed high now and the whole place had come to life.

Women at the well, full buckets of water in their hands, stopping to chatter and gossip, while a small boy chased a cat around their skirts. A peasant drove a plodding cow along the roadway, neither of them in any hurry. The warm smell of baked bread wafted on the air, along with that of brewing ale. Two girls stretched a newly washed linen sheet over a rosemary bush, giggling and blushing as Stanton nodded to them as he rode past.

Then he was approaching the Webb cottage.

Margaret sat outside on a low stool, her back leaning against the wall of the cottage, head still bandaged but with her spinning in her busy fingers. To his surprise, she wasn't alone.

Agnes sat with her, winding wool from another basket as John swept the yard, dust puffing up from his wild, hard sweeps. At the top of a tall ladder, Caldbeck was laying fresh thatch on the damaged roof.

Margaret raised a hand to stop him, saying a few quiet words to Agnes, who helped her to her feet.

Caldbeck looked around and nodded. 'Stanton.'

Stanton nodded back. 'Good day to you.'

Caldbeck returned to his task as both women made their way to the gate, where Stanton waited, Margaret leaning on Agnes's arm for support.

'Thank you for stopping, sir,' said Margaret. 'I wanted to thank you with all my heart. You saved my life. And you saved my boy's. My precious boy's.'

John swept on, lost in his own world, his heh-heh laugh telling how funny he thought this whole broom business was.

Stanton flushed. 'I did what I could, Mistress Webb. That's all.'

'But if I had been gone,' said Margaret, 'Peter would have either worked John to the grave or beaten him there. You saw what no one else did. And your compassion, your good heart, brought you to my bedside. Thank you again, sir. From the bottom of my heart.'

Stanton shifted in his saddle. 'I would do it all again, mistress.' But he wouldn't. Because he couldn't. Because he was leaving it all behind.

'You saved my life too, Hugo,' said Agnes. 'And brought justice for my father.' She swallowed hard. 'For my Thomas.'

'I wish I could have saved him as well,' said Stanton. *I wish I could have saved them all.* 'I'm sorry I couldn't. It must all be so hard to bear.'

'It is.' Agnes lifted her chin to him. 'But you brought us truth, you and the King's clerk. And while it may be hard, we are nothing without it. Nothing.'

'Nothing,' echoed Margaret.

The noise of the broom stopped.

John had spotted him. He gave Stanton a huge wave and an even bigger grin, then set about sweeping again.

'Where to next for you, Hugo Stanton?' asked Agnes.

Stanton had made his decision. The letters were in his bag. He took a last look over his shoulder at the churchyard.

Historical Note

My story of Hugo Stanton and Aelred Barling is of course fictional. But as with all historical fiction, much of what takes place has been inspired by or is based on real history.

King Henry II is undoubtedly best known in the popular imagination for the murder of Archbishop Thomas Becket, a murder for which the King was blamed. Four knights broke into Canterbury Cathedral on 29 December 1170 and slew Becket in the most brutal manner. My fictional Fifth Knight thriller series had its origins in that event.

But less well known is Henry's influence on law and order, which continues to this day. He is credited with having laid the foundation of the Common Law. When he came to the throne in 1154, he set about reforming the English legal system. Henry's realm was in deep disarray following civil war and he needed to impose order. He introduced major changes to land law, with efficient systems for dealing with cases of dispossession and inheritance. His reform of criminal law was also hugely effective. He issued new legislation at Clarendon in 1166 and Northampton in 1176 to deal with serious felonies, such as murder, robbery and theft. Juries of presentment were established, consisting of twelve lawful men in each hundred (a subdivision of a county) and four in each vill (village). These juries were not there to decide on guilt or innocence but to support an accusation. Juries of presentment are the ancestors of the Grand Jury, which is still part of the legal system in the United States.

The royal justices, who travelled the country hearing cases, were another innovation of Henry's reforms. He first introduced them at Clarendon but refined the system at Northampton. The country was divided into six circuits, with three justices, the justices of the general eyre, allocated to each. Twelfth-century chronicler Roger of Howden lists the eighteen justices itinerant and their circuits for 1176. Ranulf de Glanville, Robert de Vaux and Robert Pikenot went on circuit in Yorkshire, Richmond, Lancashire, Copland, Westmorland, Northumberland and Cumberland. These are the justices who appear briefly in the novel.

Ranulf de Glanville was also one of Henry's staunchest allies, securing key victories for the King in the rebellion of 1173–74 and rising to the position of Justiciar of England. The *Treatise on the Laws and Customs of the Kingdom of England*, produced in the late twelfth century, is the earliest treatise on English law and is commonly referred to as Glanvill, though it is unlikely that de Glanville was its author.

For the travelling justices, proof of guilt or innocence of those accused of a crime could be established in a number of ways, such as witness testimony, documents or the swearing of oaths. The justices also used the ordeal, especially in cases that were not clear-cut or in those of secret homicide, where there were no witnesses. Ordeal could be by cold water or by hot iron, both of which are explored in the novel. The blessing of the water and the iron served to bring the notion of God's judgement into the proceedings. In 1215, the church forbade priests to take part in the ordeal, bringing an end to its use.

Wherever there is law there is always bureaucracy. Henry's government was no exception. The *curia regis*, the court of the King, which consisted of the Treasury, Exchequer and Bench and which provided the justices itinerant, had a scriptorium (writing office) serving it.

Acknowledgments

The brief thanks that I give in this section can't even begin to cover the debt of gratitude that I owe to so many people. My agent, Josh Getzler, continues with his winning combination of savvy, sage and fun. The team at Thomas & Mercer are as ace as always. Special thanks this time go to Jane Snelgrove and Emilie Marneur for helping me to cast my gaze wider at the medieval world. Jack Butler's editorial wisdom brought my story to a new level, with Katie Green yet again getting what I do and showing me how to be much better than I ought to be. Their professionalism is matched by their kind patience. Hatty Stiles, as ever, does a wonderful, tireless job in making sure that the world gets to hear about my books. There are many historians whose excellent work I have consulted and who are mentioned in the bibliography. But I would like to give sincere thanks to Professor John Hudson for his answers to my specific queries and for his generosity in sharing his peerless knowledge. My top beta reader, Paul Fogarty, still hasn't run away, which makes him even more remarkable than I thought. Manchester Irish Writers members also provided much valuable insight. And my Jon and my Angela are, as always, my everything.

List of Characters

Hugo Stanton, a messenger in the service of Henry II's itinerant justices

Aelred Barling, a senior clerk to the justices

The Itinerant Justices of Henry II in the City of York
   Ranulf de Glanville
   Robert Pikenot
   Robert de Vaux

The Dwellers of Claresham Village in the County of Yorkshire
   Simon Caldbeck, a ploughman
   Thomas Dene, a stonecutter
   Sir Reginald Edgar, lord of the manor
   Hilda Folkes, a midwife
   Nicholas Lindley, an outlaw
   William Osmond, rector and Edgar's nephew
   Geoffrey Smith, a blacksmith

Agnes Smith, his daughter
Bartholomew Theaker, a thatcher
Peter Webb, a weaver
Margaret Webb, his wife
John Webb, their son

Bibliography

Without the sterling work of historians, historical novelists could not do what they do, and I am no exception. Though I try to ground my fiction firmly in fact, any errors are down to me.

For anyone who wants to know more about the real, fascinating history underpinning my novel, I recommend the following books.

Barrow, Julia, The Clergy in the Medieval World: Secular Clerics, Their Families and Careers in North-Western Europe, c. 800–c. 1200 (Cambridge: Cambridge University Press, 2015).

Bartlett, Robert, Trial by Fire and Water: The Medieval Judicial Ordeal (Oxford: Oxford University Press Academic Monograph Reprints, 1986; facs. edn, Brattleboro, VT: Echo Point Books & Media, 2014).

Bartlett, Robert, The New Oxford History of England: England Under the Norman and Angevin Kings, 1075–1225 (Oxford: Oxford University Press, 2000).

Hudson, John, The Formation of the English Common Law (London: Routeledge, 1996).

Metzler, Irina, Fools and Idiots? Intellectual Disability in the Middle Ages (Manchester: Manchester University Press, 2016).

Pollock, Frederick, and Maitland, Frederic William, The History of English Law Before the Time of Edward I (Cambridge: Cambridge University Press, 1898).

Warren, W. L., Henry II (London: Yale University Press, 1973).